I0602886

WITCH SLAP

The Hollowbeck Paranormal Cozy Mysteries

Book 1

AMELIA ASH

KIM M. WATT

STERLING & STONE

ONE

Enter the Ruiner

My car was making the sort of noises that suggest phrases like *death rattle*, and I resolutely refused to make eye contact with the temperature gauge as we laboured up the steep road, squeezed between mossy stone walls that held back old, twisted trees, the tarmac uncoiling slick and damp ahead of us.

"We should've taken my car," my brother said.

"Your car was repossessed," I pointed out, shifting down a gear. The engine whined like a two-year-old passing a sweet shop.

"It wouldn't have been if you'd stopped them. You were *right there!*"

"*Me?* What did you want me to do, throw myself in front of the tow truck?" I shot him a glare. "Why didn't you do it?"

"Yes, Morgan," Ruiner said. "I'm sure that would've worked really well."

"And whose fault is that?" I went back to glaring at the road, in the hope that might make it level off a bit, but we kept climbing. We weren't in the fancy, lake-riddled, tourist-crammed Wordsworth-y bit of Cumbria, but the landscape still wasn't exactly tame, and everything was drystone walls and tumbling slopes and pockets of slumbering old forest, all flushed with rare, late-August sunshine. None of which made the route any easier on the car. My ears popped with the changing pressure, and I yawned.

My brother bristled. "Great. That's just what this day needs. You crashing us into a tree."

I clutched the steering wheel so tightly my knuckles creaked. Or it might've been the wheel itself. My doddery old Volvo estate had accompanied me through college, a marriage, and a very recent separation. All I hoped was that I was aging better than the car. It was currently loaded up with what worldly belongings we had between us, which wasn't exactly impressive, given that most of Ruiner's had been repossessed along with his fancy apartment and fancy car, and my ex had kept most of mine. Not that I had wanted it — I was fairly sure he'd been shagging his girlfriend on various bits of my furniture for months.

"Can you just shut up for five minutes?" I glared at him. "Two days ago I had my life together, and then—"

"You did not," he said. "You were working at some dump of a bookshop and renting an apartment over the worst adult store I've ever seen. And that's saying something."

"It was *my* space," I complained. "I finally had *my* space, and I was doing what *I* wanted, then you had to come along and ruin everything! Just like always."

"It's not like I asked for this," he snapped, proper anger spiking in his voice.

I regarded him, not answering, and he glared at me for a moment, then looked back out the side window. He was only at eye level with it because I'd put both the pillows off my bed on the seat, and he was perched on top of them, fluffy-tailed and sharp-eared, and a rather elegant shade of grey.

My brother was a cat. Currently, I mean, not usually. And I don't know the exact details, but he definitely asked for it. He always does.

~

HE MIGHT'VE HAD a point about me not really having my life together, though. My job was terrible. I might have been a bookkeeper for a handful of small, barely-getting-by businesses until a couple of months ago, but I've always really wanted to work with actual books. It was much more appealing than spending all my time chasing people for receipts and doing all the hard work before the accountant would swoop in and take over, charging four times as much as me for the privilege. So when I split up with Jason, that's what I did.

I don't think I chose the best bookshop for a career change, though. There were spreading patches of mould on the walls, the shelves were propped up with bits of two-by-four and bricks, the pay was derisory, and I'm pretty sure the owner only hired me so he could get me to climb the stepladders in a short skirt. Luckily, I rarely wear short skirts, and definitely not for work, so he was out of luck, but that just made him so spectacularly grumpy that he scared off the few customers who dared to venture past the grimy windows. So there wasn't much for me to do but stick covers back on the tattier paperbacks and spend most of my time re-shelving the witchcraft texts that always ended up in the science section.

My rented apartment had cockroaches *and* rats. The windows were single-glazed and leaked when it rained.

The fridge groaned like a wounded bull. Plus the neon from the adult store leached through even the heaviest curtains I could find. It was as terrible as the job, but it was cheap, and furnished (if you can call a mattress on a couple of pallets and a rickety table with one chair furnished). But it was mine. I didn't have to clean up after anyone else. I didn't have to solve anyone else's problems. For the first time in my thirty-six years, I did not have to be the grown-up.

For the entire first week I bought frothy, whipped-cream-topped, syrup-laden coffees and hefty wedges of cake for breakfast every day, until I discovered that just because you can doesn't mean you should, and that my stomach wasn't as keen on reclaiming my lost youth as the rest of me. Also, it was really expensive, and I'd blown half my food budget for the month.

I was enjoying it, though, in a weird way. I even enjoyed the lumpy mattress and the sirens going past the windows at 3 a.m. It wasn't forever, anyway. It was just what I needed for now, a break and a re-start and time to heal, and somewhere to stay until I could scrape some money back from Jason, who was claiming he was as broke as Ruiner.

Speaking of, the first I knew about his interesting new development was when a stray cat turned up on my windowsill two nights ago. I was in my PJs, making a cup of camomile tea to take to bed with me, and there he was, pressed against the glass, heavy grey coat looking a bit bedraggled in the rain. I yelped as he scrabbled around for grip on the ledge, then slipped and vanished again. I opened the window and peered out, and he reappeared with his ears back. This time he kept his footing and shot past me into the room.

"Hey!" I yelled. "Get out!" My landlord had a strict no

pets policy, which was a bit of a joke. A cat might've shifted some of the rats.

"Morgan!" the cat yowled. "You have to help me!"

I looked at the camomile tea, but I hadn't even touched it yet. And I was pretty sure there was quality control on things like that. It was a supermarket-own-brand one, after all.

"I'm a *cat!*" the cat said.

"I can see that," I said, wondering how much sleep I'd been getting. Not enough, evidently.

"It's me," the cat said. "Morgan? You know it's me, right?"

And the thing was, I did. My brother had run to me for help enough times over the years that I knew his pleading voice very well. It was the one that always ended up with me running to police stations to get him out of custody, picking him up from random locations when he had no money to get home, paying off large scary men outside clubs, and, on one memorable occasion, hauling him out of a huge country house just before the police turned up to bust a drug ring. His name was actually Rainier, because our mum had a thing for European royalty, but he'd been Ruiner to me ever since I'd given up my seventh birthday party so that he could go and drive in some rally race for five-year-olds. He'd lost, too.

"Nope," I said, grabbed the cat, and turfed him out the window. Then I closed the curtains and went to bed.

THE CAT WAS STILL THERE when I got up in the morning, crouched miserably on the windowsill with rain dripping from his whiskers. I'd have felt a lot worse if I'd been sure it wasn't my brother. But I opened the window and we looked at each other. He had wide blue eyes that were most definitely the same colour as my brother's, but that was impossible. Humans don't turn into cats.

"I've probably got pneumonia," he said.

"And I'm evidently in the throes of a mental break-down," I said, as he jumped onto the stained, cracked worktop and shook himself off.

"You're not," he said. "It's really me."

"But *how?*" I demanded. "This is … this doesn't happen. It can't happen! There are laws and stuff."

"There are? Could I sue? I should be able to sue. People can't just go around turning me into a *cat.*"

"No, I mean physics. Laws of nature or whatever."

"That doesn't help me," he said. "Do you have anything to eat? I'm starving."

I pressed my hands to my forehead. My stomach was doing a weird rolling, flip-flop thing, and there were spots floating in my vision. "Is it a brain tumour? What sort of brain tumour has me imagining *you* here? As a *cat?* This … is it paranoia? Brought *on* by the brain tumour?" I could hear my voice getting louder, but I couldn't seem to stop. "Early onset dementia? Meningitis? Some sort of toxic mould from the bookshop? Am I hallucinating? Am — *ow!*" I jumped away from the worktop, clutching my arm, which had just sprouted four thin, bloody lines. "You brat!"

"You were freaking out."

"*You're a cat.*"

"Yes! So *I* should be the one freaking out!" He glared at me with those weirdly familiar blue eyes. "What've you got to panic about?"

I looked at him for a moment, then at the scratches on my arm, and poked them. "Ow." We were both silent for a moment, then I added, "Really?"

"Really," he said.

NOW, two days later, he still hadn't given me the full details of what was going on. What he had told me was that he'd been dabbling in magic. Proper magic, not card tricks and scarves up your nose and all that. Actual magic, which is apparently a thing that exists, and now I keep wondering about those witchcraft books in the science section, and who else might've been hanging out in the bookshop to re-shelve them like that. I'd have gone back to find out, but Ruiner insisted we didn't have time. He knew a place we could get help, but of course cats can't exactly get an Uber, and the logistics of driving aren't great.

So I called in sick to work, and we went around to Ruiner's apartment to get his car, only to find it being repossessed, along with the apartment itself and all the contents. He had a proper yowling tantrum over that, and tried to bite the bailiffs, but luckily they had hefty boots on, and he was so incoherent with rage they just thought he was making cat noises. I managed to save a rucksack full of clothes, for all the good that might do him right now, his shaving kit, and, for some reason, his fancy-pants cologne, but the rest was carted out by big, expressionless men who looked like they were all called Gaz. We went back to my apartment to pick up my car, only to find my landlord stacking all my belongings on the side of the street. He'd seen Ruiner go in, and I was evicted with zero notice for breach of contract.

See why I call him Ruiner?

My landlord wouldn't be reasoned with — apparently I wasn't his preferred sort of clientele. I managed not to point out that he might be aiming a bit high for a place that required a steel nerve and anti-fungal cream just to step into the shower (I was still hoping to get my deposit back, after all), so I just loaded up my old car while Ruiner, in a fit of brotherly loyalty, vomited up a hairball on the doorstep. And now we were on the road to a town called Hollowbeck, him burping every five minutes because he'd insisted I buy him a sausage roll and a latte at the coffeeshop, even though I'd pointed out he now had a cat stomach and it was unlikely to end well. Unfortunately, I was the one suffering the consequences.

I wound my window down a bit further, and he wrinkled his snout. "The wind's getting in my ears."

"That sounds like a you problem."

"I could bite you."

"I could dump you by the side of the road and leave you to be picked up by a rescue. Or eaten by something."

"Then what would you tell Mum?"

I swallowed a sigh. That was it. That was the trump card. I resisted the urge to flick his ears and pointed at a moss-encrusted sign half-obscured by the heavy shadows of the trees. "Look. We're almost there."

We both stared at the sign as the poor old car crawled on up the hill. Age and weather had rendered what were presumably two happily skipping children into screaming ghouls, and the magician in the top hat lurking in the background looked to be launching a ravenous, big-toothed rabbit at them. *Welcome to Hollowbeck!* the sign proclaimed in barely legible gold lettering. *The most magical place on earth!*

"That seems like trademark infringement," I said, trying not to look too closely at the magician. He seemed to be staring right at us.

"Hollowbeck's not easy to find," Ruiner said. He was sitting up very straight, his ears pricked and his tail curled over his toes. "I wasn't sure we'd be able to. I had a guide when I came here before. People get lost in the forest when they don't know the way."

"How?" I asked. "There's only one road."

"It doesn't always go to the same place," he said.

"That's not possible, Ruiner."

He looked down at himself, then back at me, arching his whiskers rather effectively for a newly minted cat.

I managed not to bang my head on the steering wheel, but it was a near thing. I decided to disregard the bit about the road not going to the same place. That belonged in the *my brother's a cat* box and needed more thinking space than the car was currently giving me. But that didn't mean I could let the whole thing go. "So you took us out here, and it could have got us *lost?*"

"But it didn't," he said. "We've seen the sign now, so we're in. You'll see. It'll be just over that rise." He lifted a paw, growled, and used his snout to point ahead of us, where the trees really did look to be thinning into a ridge.

"And then what?" I asked him.

"And then we get this whole cat thing reversed, go home, and I get all my damn stuff back." He glanced at me. "And I'll help you find somewhere better to live. Your place really sucked."

I wondered if I should point out to him how many times he'd said things would work out just as he wanted, and how many times I'd had to bail him out when they didn't. And that I was in no position to bail anyone out right now, even if I'd known where to start with cats and curses.

But I didn't. I just aimed the labouring car's nose at the top of the hill, and hoped he was right. Just this once, I really, really wanted my brother to be right.

I wasn't betting on it, though.

TWO

Twee, with teeth

WHETHER HE WAS right about anything else remained to be seen, but he was right about the hill. We crested it not long after passing the sign, then coasted down the slope on the other side as the heavy, crowded trees with their twisted trunks and greedy foliage that stole the sky gave way to pretty copses and fields of glossy green, all divided by the rambling lines of drystone walls. Cows ambled through them, and wildflowers were scattered like confetti on both the fields and along the tiny verges the walls allowed. As the car settled into an exhausted rumble, I could hear birdsong through the open window. I took a deep breath, forgetting about both the ever-present engine fumes and Ruiner's intestinal distress, and coughed.

"Who are we looking for, then?" I asked him.

"Her name's Norma," he said.

"And she's a ... a specialist in these things?" I couldn't quite bring myself to say *witch*, but if she was going to be able to turn my brother back into human form, she was hardly a maths tutor.

"Don't know about this specifically, but she knows her stuff." He didn't look at me, his tail twitching.

"You don't know for sure?"

"Small issue with making phone calls," he said, raising a paw pointedly. "But I've dealt with her before. She runs the Cosy Cauldron, and she's the person to go to if you want a protective spell, or an abundance charm, stuff like that."

I thought about it for a moment, then said, "So did you not buy a protective spell from her, or is she just really bad at them?"

He snorted. "I didn't think I needed one. I hardly expected some crazy witch would—"

"*Ha!* I *knew* it was going to be a woman. What did you do? Insult her familiar?"

"*No.* I didn't do *anything*, she just—"

"That's what you said that time the twins imprisoned you in their basement and I had to threaten to call the police on them to get you out," I pointed out.

"How was I to know they'd be so sensitive about me getting them mixed up? They were identical!"

"You probably shouldn't have tried dating them both at once. What about that time I had to break into a restaurant at 2 a.m. and get you out of the walk-in freezer when you insulted that chef's tart au citron?"

"I didn't insult it. I just said it was lemon meringue pie with a French accent, and that I didn't see what all the fuss was about."

I shook my head and peered at a farmhouse mired in the fields to our left. Ivy coiled up its grey stone walls and framed the deep windows, and graceful trees leaned over the lawn to offer shade from the late summer sun. A dog frolicked among an abundance of flowerbeds with a small boy, who waved enthusiastically at the car. I waved back uncertainly. "So you haven't insulted Norma, then?"

"No. And I've done business with her before. We just go in, show her what the issue is, and *bam*. Back to humanness."

A thought struck me. "How much is this going to cost?"

"I don't know," he admitted.

"And you've got no money?"

He looked down at his fluffy chest, then up at me, eyes narrowed.

"Of course you don't." I sighed, wondering at what point a bank account could collapse into a black hole under the weight of its overdraft.

We were silent for a moment, then Ruiner added, "It's not always exactly a monetary transaction, either."

I scowled at him. "I'm sorry?"

"Sometimes it's more like a favour, you know? Barter system."

"What sort of favours, Ruiner?"

He hesitated, then said, "Last time I just had to deliver a letter for her."

"A letter?"

"Yeah." He stared resolutely out of the windscreen. "Look. Town. We're almost there."

And as much as I wanted to shove him off his pillows onto the floor and demand more details, that was all I was getting from him. He'd been evasive even before he was a cat. Things were hardly going to improve now.

THE TOWN WAS as picturesque as the countryside surrounding it, all tree-lined streets and houses set back from the road amid gardens riotous with colourful growth. Lawns were tidy yet not overly manicured, roses clambered over arches and walls, and I didn't spot a single house without at least one bird bath. Mailboxes were individually designed and painted, often to look like the houses themselves, wind chimes hung from eaves, stained glass ornaments caught the light and scattered it over the greenery, and hammocks were suspended on porches. *Porches.*

So, yeah, that was the first weird thing. Sure, there were plenty of beautiful, thick-walled cottages, and big-windowed rows of terraces in grey Lakeland stone, and semi-detached houses painted white, their window frames giving a pop of darker colour. There were even a couple of newer red brick houses, looking a bit square and prim. But there were also rambling wooden structures with generous verandas and low roofs that looked like they'd been transplanted from some farm in America, terracotta-toned buildings with Provençal-blue shutters, and domed white buildings with bright doors buried deep amid blossoming bougainvillea. I even saw a bright red barn-type thing that made me think of high latitudes and deep fjords.

Planning permission evidently did not apply around here, yet somehow the jumble of styles all worked. Everything looked comfortably lived-in and deeply friendly, like the sort of place you really would pop over to the neighbour's to borrow a cup of sugar. Dogs trotted across the lawns, cats slept on windowsills, and there were a surprising amount of people tending veggie patches and sitting at outdoor tables sharing a pot of tea for a weekday.

"What *is* this place?" I asked.

Ruiner looked at a couple of older women peering into a little free library and said, "It's Hollowbeck," as if that should explain everything.

The women straightened up to watch us pass, and a

raven flew down from the nearest tree to perch on the taller one's shoulder. The other adjusted her hat, tucking what looked like a couple of snakes back underneath it. I blinked at them. "What—"

"Don't stare." Ruiner hunkered down on his cushions, ears twitching. "And don't talk to me. We don't want anyone knowing I'm not really a cat."

"Why not?"

He hesitated, then said, "It might get the person who did it in trouble."

"Absolute bollocks."

"*Fine.* It might get me in trouble, okay? Just pretend I'm a regular cat."

"It might get you in more trouble than being turned into a cat?"

"Just trust me, alright? This place looks all cute and nice, but it's dangerous. Let's just get the counter-curse and get out again." He fell silent, his tail twitching.

"I still want to know how you even found out about..." I couldn't think of what to say other than *magic*, which just sounded ridiculous, so I waved vaguely at the street. "This."

"I'll tell you later."

I found myself rolling my eyes, which was the sort of thing only Ruiner could force me to do, but there was no arguing with him. Stubbornness was a trait we'd both inherited in equal measure, and the whole immoveable object and irresistible force was a real issue. I went back to examining Hollowbeck, looking for signs that it might be as dangerous as Ruiner seemed to think.

Dangerous still wasn't the word that sprang to mind as we drove through the narrow streets, but things got stranger the more I looked, like one of those paintings where more and more details appear the longer you stare at it. An older gentleman across the road, who I'd thought was pruning a small bush, was actually battling with rogue branches that kept trying to snatch his hat off. Where I'd been quite sure a dog was loping across the lawn, I now saw a lean, shirtless man with a dark shaggy beard, watching us pass from behind a strategically placed rose bush. A cluster of crows, standing in a circle around a carved wooden statue, all turned to look at the car, tracking us with shiny black eyes, and I had a feeling that the statue was watching too, although I couldn't see it move. A tentacle slopped out of a birdbath, grabbed a rose, and vanished again.

I opened my mouth, looked at Ruiner, then shut it again and kept driving. After a moment, I muttered, "Weird." My brother didn't reply.

THE HEART of the town was small, just a little crosshatching of streets with well-kept, mostly two-story buildings, all of which had fallen victim to the same hodge-podge of architecture as the rest of town. It lent the street an endearingly confused air, like a toddler who's decided to dress themselves.

There were a few cafes (including an enticing-looking coffeeshop called *Bewitching Brews* that I intended to visit as soon as possible), a grocery store, actual food shops like a bakery, a delicatessen, a fruit and veggie shop, a bookshop, and a collection of the sort of random shops every pretty little town seems to collect, more in the hope of snatching a few tourist dollars than to provide for the locals. I spotted three clothing shops, one of which was leaning hard into the magical aesthetic with lots of voluminous dresses in velvet and lace and tie-dye, a second that had bolted in the opposite direction and seemed to be all black leather and buckles, and a third looking a little lost with a lavender twin-set in the window and a rack of T-shirts outside, all proclaiming *Hollowbeck is Magic!*

I have never used the word *twee*, and I'm not even sure I know exactly what it means, but Hollowbeck was twee. I couldn't shake the thought. There were no shops with *for lease* signs, no cash converters or pound shops, not even any litter on the streets. Just clean pavements, plants hanging from the lampposts and packed into planters outside the shops, and people wandering between them, all smiling and nodding at each other in apparently genuine pleasure. Even over the reek of the engine, I could smell freshly brewed coffee and the scent of sun on warm earth, and the faintest touch of fudge.

"*Weird*," I said again, with more feeling this time.

"It's there," Ruiner said, pointing with his snout. At the end of the row of shops was a two-storey grey stone building, its upstairs windows deep-set and dark. Downstairs, it had big display windows with a green canopy fixed above them to offer shade, and a purple banner was tethered to a pole outside, fluttering softly in the breeze. Next to the flag was a wooden wheelbarrow full of old books and a stand offering a selection of dried herbs. Across the big display windows was painted, *The Cosy Cauldron: everything you ask for.*

I pulled into a parking spot directly in front of the shop, and we stared at the cluttered display windows. Neti pots and oil diffusers were packed in around skulls (hopefully fake), crystals, books with titles like *Charms for Minor Ailments* and *Cursing for Beginners*, curious wooden boxes, and a taxidermy fox.

"Are you sure about this?" I asked my brother.

"Yes. Come on." He pawed his door impatiently, and I got out, holding my door while he jumped across my seat and down to the ground. He stared up at me. "Ugh. I can't get used to this angle. Pick me up?"

"Not a chance." I slammed the door and locked it, more from habit that any real worry that there would be anyone desperate enough to steal my car around here. I turned for the shop and Ruiner leaped at me, scrambling up to my shoulder with his claws tearing through my T-shirt. "*Ow!* I said no!"

"You only said you wouldn't pick me up," he pointed out, so close to my ear his whiskers tickled my cheek. "Anyway, it's a safety issue. This way I can whisper."

"Whisper, then," I said, rubbing my ear. "Or better yet, shut up."

Surprisingly, he did, and I stepped onto the pavement and into the shade of the Cosy Cauldron's canopy. I could smell incense and candles and a tangled mix of herbs drifting from the door, as well as a faint cooking smell, like someone had put lunch on. My stomach rumbled and I checked my phone. It was well past noon.

I gave Bewitching Brews a longing look, then pushed through the door of the Cosy Cauldron, setting a string of bells jingling cheerily, then into heavily scented silence. The place was crowded with shelves, not just on the walls but also with waist-heigh ones that divided the shop. They were crowded with books and little statuettes, candelabras, and jumbled trays of tarnished jewellery. A rack of clothing was shoved into one corner, and baskets of unsettling straw dolls with blank faces slouched next to it. Dreamcatchers and wind chimes and freaky mobiles made from taxidermy birds and bones hung from the exposed rafters of the ceiling.

There was no one behind the counter, and I waited in the doorway for a moment, then crossed to it tentatively.

"Hello?" I called, the word falling flat in the crowded

confines of the shop. It was stuffy in here, the air close and tight with scent, and sweat was gathering on my back. Ruiner wasn't helping that, still perched on my shoulder like a misplaced hot water bottle.

We waited, but no one answered, and there was no sound of movement in the backrooms. Ruiner jumped from my shoulder and batted a little bell sitting on the counter. It chimed, oddly deep and sonorous, and I could have sworn I could feel it in my chest. The heat was making me lightheaded, and I suddenly wanted to be out of here, desperately so. There was more taxidermy on the walls, glass-eyed owls and snarling stoats, and the assault of scents turned my stomach. I coughed, too much saliva collecting in my mouth, and Ruiner hit the bell again.

"Leave it," I managed. "She's probably gone to lunch. We'll come back later."

"The door was open. She must be here."

He was right, but I still wanted to leave. "Then she's busy, with a client or something. Come on. It's too hot in here. I need to get outside."

"Just check out the back," he said, ears twitching. "I can hear someone."

"I'm not walking into someone's private property," I said, aiming for indignant. The words came out small and scared, and I swallowed hard. "Let's go, Ruiner."

Ruiner ignored me, because he was Ruiner, and jumped off the counter on the other side, trotting through a beaded curtain into the back room with his fluffy tail high. "I definitely heard *something*."

"*Ruiner!*" He didn't answer me, and I resisted the urge to shout that this was the sort of thing that would get him downgraded from cat to snail or something. "I'm leaving."

"Morgs?" His voice floated back to me, uncharacteristically uncertain.

"I'm *leaving*."

"Morgan, please come here." There was definitely a wobble in his tone, and I looked at the ceiling. A rat hissed down at me from its perch in the rafters, making me jump, and Ruiner called, "*Morgan.*"

"I hate my brother," I told the rat, which tipped its head at me curiously. Then I rounded the counter and pushed through the curtain, the beads clattering off my hands like anxious knuckles. I was straight into a short, dark hallway studded with three closed doors, and one resting slightly ajar at the end. The smell of cooking was stronger back here, and my stomach growled again. "Where are you?"

"Here."

I followed the sound of his voice to the door at the end of the hall, pushing it wide. It gave onto a room that ran the length of the building, with a cluttered, varnished kitchen at one end, a chopping board still out on the counter with a few bunches of herbs stacked next to it. The other end was given over to a living room furnished with two chubby sofas and a surprisingly large flatscreen TV, and between the two, directly ahead of me, was an enormous stone fireplace. It looked like something an old-school lord would roast a whole heifer in, all huge stone flags scorched with old fires, and ancient-looking iron tools hanging from hooks around it. It was as wide as one of the sofas and high enough that I'd barely have to bend to walk right into it. Which was unusual enough in such a plain-looking house, but there was also an actual, real, eye-of-newt-and-toe-of-frog cauldron sitting on four sturdy legs in the centre of it, the charred remains of a fire underneath.

Ruiner was standing just inside the door, his eyes fixed on the cauldron. Or probably not the cauldron. What was *in* the cauldron.

"Is that…?" I couldn't find the words.

"It's her," he said, and retched suddenly, his ears going back hard.

Horrifyingly, my stomach gave a rumble, and I turned and bolted back into the shop, one hand over my mouth. We'd found both Norma and the source of the cooking scent, and whatever my brother had got himself into this time, I was *out*. Witches were one thing. Dead witches were quite another.

THREE

The pot quickens

BEING OUTSIDE FELT like it offered no relief at all, the very un-British afternoon heat collecting under the canopy and pressing down on my shoulders and already-spinning head. What was *wrong* with this place? Why was it so hot? I made it to the edge of the pavement before my legs folded like a cheap stepladder, and I bumped onto the concrete, jarring my tailbone. Which at least gave me something to think about other than the peacefully composed face of the witch in the cauldron.

The *witch* in the *cauldron*. Perhaps it was some sort of witchy self-care thing. Perhaps witches regularly boiled themselves alive. Her arms had been hung on the rim as if she were sitting in a hot tub, so maybe that was all it was. Maybe she was just dozing and would wake up and shout at us for trespassing. I'd even seen hot tubs that looked like cauldrons. On Instagram, admittedly, but presumably they existed outside the app, too.

I swallowed hard, trying not to think about the cooking smell, and looked at the car. My water bottle was in there, but it seemed an immeasurably long way away right now.

A magpie landed on the bonnet and peered at me, cocking its head one way then the other, and a moment later a tall, broad-shouldered man with shaggy blond hair and an impressive beard emerged from somewhere to my left and hurried across the road. The crow turned its attention to him, then a moment later flew off, leaving me alone again. I concentrated on not throwing up.

"Morgan?"

"Go away," I said, not looking at my brother. "Go away unless you can tell me I didn't see what I thought I saw."

"Well, if you thought you saw Norma doing the ironing, it wasn't that." His voice still sounded a little uneven, and I finally looked at him. "I think I got rid of the last of the sausage roll."

"Great. So now we can add contaminating a crime scene to your list of misdemeanours." I couldn't get much heat into the words.

"We don't know it's a crime scene."

"She is dead, isn't she?"

"I think so. I didn't go any closer."

Both of us were silent for a moment, then I said, "We should check. In case she's just unconscious or something."

"That would be the right thing to do," Ruiner agreed. "But, then again, if it *is* a crime scene, we don't really want to be around it, do we? Don't want anyone asking questions or anything."

"Why? I thought you were innocently turned into a cat through no fault of your own. What've you got to worry about?"

He glared at me with those cat-yet-not eyes. "It may have escaped your notice, Morgs, but I am evidently not in favour with some magical sorts, and, more to the point, you, as a non-magical incomer, would be perfect to pin this on. We might be being set up."

"By who?" I glanced around instinctively. "Who even knew we were coming here?"

He shrugged, a smooth motion under his heavy coat. "People know stuff. Magically, like."

I wiped my mouth, swallowing against that extra saliva again, then said, "Well, either way. We can't just walk away. We'll check if she's alive, then call the cops."

"What? *No.* No cops. Check if you have to, but then let's just go. I'll have to think of who else to try for the counter-curse."

"Yes cops. Dead body means cops."

"Cops means we get thrown in jail, or at least have to hang around doing the *don't leave town* thing, while I am a cat. I'm a *cat*, Morgan."

"That has been noted." I got up, brushing off the seat of my cropped jeans and wishing I was wearing full-length ones, and a long-sleeved shirt, and a mask, and gloves, and preferably one of those orange, pressurised suits scientists always wear in disaster movies. "Come on. We can't exactly walk away, anyhow. Have you seen this place? Half a dozen people will have seen us go in, and it's probably all been written down in the neighbourhood watch book or something."

Ruiner looked down the street, his eyes narrowed, then sighed. "Alright. But if we're going back in there, we're having a look for curse reversals while we're at it. She must've had a book on them or something."

"We're not touching anything," I told him, and led the way back inside.

～

I WASN'T sure if it was worse walking in when I knew what was waiting for us, or better in that I was prepared. It was still horrible either way, the room suffocating with heat and the fumes from the cauldron, and I tried not to look at the witch directly as I sidled up to the hearth. There was an overpowering reek of aniseed drifting about the place, and the liquid in the pot was a murky brown, like cheap chicken stock.

I risked a glance at Norma's face, but she hadn't moved. Her eyes were closed, thankfully, and there was a faint smile touching the corners of her mouth. She was a bit older than me, and heavy blonde hair hung in curls over her shoulders and spilled down the side of the cauldron. Some small part of my mind noted that the fire can't have been very high when she got in, otherwise her hair would have burned.

I touched her hand gingerly where it rested on the rim of the pot, her skin smooth and cool under mine. She didn't so much as twitch, so I carefully slid my fingers around her wrist, as I'd learned in some half-forgotten first aid course, looking for a pulse. For a horrible moment it felt as though she were resisting me, and that logical sliver of my brain pointed out that she must've been dead long enough for rigor mortis to set in, and wondered how much the heat of the cauldron would have sped the process up.

The illogical part of my brain squawked and made me drop the witch's hand, where it rested stiffly in the same position. I swallowed and had a second try, but I couldn't find any pulse. I was pretty sure there wasn't one to find, not with that frozen resistance, but I checked her neck anyway, then stepped back, wiping my hands on my jeans and wishing I had some hand sanitiser.

"She's definitely dead," I announced.

"That sucks," Ruiner said. He was prowling around the fire. "I really thought she'd be able to help."

"Sucks more for her."

"Yeah, of course." He pawed at a tea towel that had fallen by the edge of the hearth, and a glass vial rolled into view. "What's this?"

I crouched down, happy to abandon my examination of the corpse. "Dunno." I started to reach for it, and Ruiner batted my hand. "Hey!"

"Well, fine, just grab the mysterious bottle lying next to the dead witch. That seems like a great idea."

I wrinkled my nose. "Good point." I picked up the poker instead and nudged the vial. It was empty save for a tiny bit of clear liquid still lingering in the bottom. There was a label on its curved side, and I rolled it over a little further, so that I could see the writing. There were just a series of runes, nothing I recognised or could make any sense of, and on some weird impulse I took my phone out and took a photo. Then I straightened up and said, "Right. Police."

"Did you not hear me before? Calling the police is going to get you arrested." Ruiner had lost interest in the hearth and was investigating the kitchen counters. "Anything here that looks like it could break a curse?"

"There's a broom. I could hit you with it and we could see what happens."

He bared his teeth at me. "Look in the fridge, would you?"

I sighed and opened the fridge, a big rattling old thing that made my car look positively juvenile. "Milk, goat's cheese, half a cauliflower, and some mustard. Any of those work?"

"No. And wipe off the handle. Don't want to leave fingerprints."

I closed the fridge again, ignoring him. There were magnets on the door, holding in place a shopping list (toilet paper, chicken breasts, and fenugreek, none of which sounded very witchy), a postcard from Cancun, and—

"Ruiner," I said.

"Hey, recipe books. Maybe there's a spell book."

"*Ruiner.*"

He stopped pawing at the shelves and looked at me. "What?"

I pointed at an envelope that was stuck to the fridge door. "What's this?"

"A letter?"

"Yeah." I tugged it free, the magnet tumbling to the floor, and turned the envelope to face him. "With my name on it."

Ruiner said something that would've had our mum clutching her pearls, if she wore them, then added, "Open it."

"I don't think I want to." And I didn't. My hands were shaking, and I knew that I really needed food, and that I was still in shock over the *dead body*, but also what was this? How would *anyone* here have known my name? "Did you tell her about me? What have you been saying to people?"

"I didn't tell anyone anything," he said. "I swear."

Neither of us spoke for a moment. I wanted to believe him, but at the same time, how could I? He was the one that knew this place, who had been meddling in magic and insulting witches and was now a damn cat. He was the one messing in things that were so far outside what I thought reality to be that it was definitely contributing to my queasiness, and now here was my name, on a letter in a dead witch's house. It made it pretty hard to think he was telling the truth about anything.

I folded the envelope and shoved it into my back pocket. "We're done here. I'm going to the police, and you can come or not."

"Morgan—"

"*No.* Whatever the hell you've got us both into, I'm not playing. That is a *corpse.*" I jabbed a finger at the cauldron. "I'm not cleaning this up for you."

"I'm not asking you to, I just—"

"I'm going." I turned on my heel and walked out, ignoring him yowling my name. This was too much. This was way, way too much.

~

RUINER STILL HADN'T EMERGED when I swung into the car and slammed the door with a satisfying clunk. I started the engine, giving it a little rev just in case he thought I was bluffing, then pulled out into the street. Fine, then. Let him stay with his dead witch.

I sat there with the engine idling for a moment, realising I had no idea where the police station was, then drove down the street to where a collection of signs crowned an intersection, directing me helpfully to the riverside walk, the botanical gardens, the garden centre, the medical centre, the library, and the town hall. I stared at them, then turned in the direction of the town hall and the library. What sort of town marked the garden centre and not the police station?

It didn't take me long to find the town hall, just a little further down a tree-lined street that boasted well-maintained Georgian-style terraced houses with steps up to their front doors and high, graceful windows. Some of them even had topiary in pots lining the stairs.

The town hall itself was a little more modern, although I couldn't have picked its era. It was a tall, two-storey brick building with colonnades that managed to look elegant rather than pretentious, accessorised with a peacock strutting across the lawn and shrieking encouragingly at a group of unimpressed pigeons. The hall was surrounded by gardens, and a smaller building made of the same brick sprouted out of them. *Hollowbeck Library,* the sign on the front of that one said, and as much as I wanted to head that way instead of toward the town hall, for no reason other than the comfort of a building full of books, I left the car and marched up the broad steps between the columns to the huge double doors of the hall. They were easily twice my height, and there was a note pinned to them. *At the library.*

I looked at it for a moment, then shrugged and turned away. Things were different in small towns, I supposed.

The glass-paneled library door let me into a cool oasis, smelling of books and citrus and quiet inward thoughts. The building had looked small next to the hall, but the ground floor was sunk down into the earth, and a mezzanine above me encircled the central lobby area, groaning with books. There was the faintest murmur of voices rising from the stacks that I could see retreating into the depths of the building, and in the middle of the lobby was a circular desk. Two people leaned toward each other over it, talking earnestly.

I looked around, hoping there would be someone else to help, but I couldn't even see anyone browsing the shelves, so I padded down the old wood steps, painfully aware of them creaking under my sneakers, and stopped at the bottom. The pair, a tall woman with a long skirt and slightly old-fashioned, low-cut blouse that she filled out generously, and a slightly shorter, neatly dressed man of about my age, had stopped talking to watch me. The man pushed his glasses onto his close-cropped dark hair and gave me a dimpled smile.

"Can I help you?" he asked.

"I'm looking for the police," I said, and was surprised to hear a wobble in my voice. "I went to the town hall, but there was no one there, and there's no sign for the station, and there should be, you know? There should be a sign for the police. Most places have a sign for the police." I stopped talking, gave them the brightest smile I could manage, and added, "Is there? Police, I mean?"

The tall woman swatted at the man, and said, "Benji, get the poor woman some tea and a seat. Can't you see she needs it?"

"Benjamin," he said, in the automatic tones of someone who's said it a hundred times before and expects to say it a hundred times again. "And yes, you look a bit … *do* you want a tea? A seat?"

He hurried out from behind the desk as he spoke, and suddenly I *did* want a seat, and I *did* want a cup of tea, or preferably coffee, or even more preferably whisky, but instead I just sat down carefully on the steps and said, "I really do need to find the police."

Benji — Benjamin — stopped just short of me, looking like he didn't know whether to help me up or rush off to find a kettle. He sneaked a look at the woman and waved one hand a little vaguely. "They're, um, not available right now."

"What?" I couldn't even manage to be outraged. "How can the police not be available?"

"It's a very quiet town," the woman said, and I jumped. I hadn't even realised she'd left the desk, and now she was leaning over me, her cleavage threatening to make a break for freedom. "Theodore only works nights. But we can look after you!" She petted my shoulder, and I shivered, even though it didn't feel like she'd actually touched me. "I'm the mayor. But you can call me Isabella. Or the hostess with the mostess!" She threw back her head and laughed, a dancing, delightful sound, and I rubbed my forehead. I really needed some food. I'd half thought she'd said *ghostess* with the mostess.

"What do you need help with?" Benjamin asked, crouching down in front of me with his hands dangling between his knees. He had ink smudges on his fingers, and his forearms were dark and muscular under his T-shirt sleeves. I wondered vaguely if that was from lugging books. "Lost bag, lost pet, pixies in the car, can't find the town on maps?" He smiled, as if the pixie bit was a joke, but it was a cautious effort.

"Dead body," I said, and they both stared at me, smiles vanishing. "Sorry, do you have any biscuits or anything? Only I've not eaten in forever, and I'm feeling really weird."

Benjamin and Isabella looked at each other, then she said, "Well. You heard the woman. Get her some biscuits, Benji."

"Benjamin," he said, but got up and headed deeper into the library.

Isabella turned back to me, long dark curls falling over her shoulders. "Now," she said. "Tell me everything."

I really wished I could.

FOUR

(Re)disturbing a crime scene

I DIDN'T KNOW what sort of tea Ben had found for me — or Benjamin or whatever he wanted to call himself. Not Benji, anyway. The mug was full of leafy, floating things and pretty little yellow flowers, and smelled of long summer evenings in some way I couldn't quite put my finger on, but it tasted alright. He also presented me with half a pack of bourbon creams, which Isabella looked at and said in shock, "How can you eat that rubbish, Benji? You'll be joining me before your time!" I didn't understand what that meant, but I didn't understand the last two days or this town, so it was barely worth thinking about.

And as far as I was concerned, the biscuits tasted like heaven. They tasted like my before-Hollowbeck life. They tasted like maybe my brother wasn't a cat, and there wasn't a dead body waiting back at the Cosy Cauldron, and that I didn't have a mysterious letter with my name on it still in my pocket, which I was too scared to open. I wasn't sure if I didn't want to know what was in it, or if I simply wanted it to not exist. Probably that. In fact, definitely. But I couldn't make that happen, so for the moment I resolutely avoided thinking about it, while the world started to feel a little like it was coming back into focus, aided by a hefty hit of highly processed sugar and mysterious herbs.

Unfortunately, while tea and bourbons can fix a lot, they can't fix everything. Once I'd polished off the biscuits and drunk most of my tea I said to Isabella, who was sitting next to me on the library steps, "I've left the shop open. Anyone could go in there. Is there no way that we can get the police now? It's sort of an emergency, isn't it?"

"No," Ben and Isabella said together. And then Isabella added with a quite beautiful smile, "Poor Theo has a condition. He has to sleep during the day."

I frowned. "Like what? Some sort of narcolepsy set off by sunlight?"

"More like extreme sun sensitivity," Ben said.

Isabella nodded. "Yes," she said. "That's it. *Extreme* sun sensitivity." She touched her own face, which was flawlessly smooth, and grimaced. "The poor dear. He has a very violent reaction to even the smallest bit of sunlight."

Which sounded pretty nasty, to be fair, but also really impractical for a police officer. "We need to at least make sure no one goes in there," I said. "Don't we? I mean, there's … she's…" I stopped and drained the last of my tea. "Is there someone else we can call? Another police officer? Fire station? Ambulance?"

"We shall go ourselves," Isabella said, brushing her hands off. She stood up. "Come along, Benji."

"Benjamin," he said.

BACK AT THE COSY CAULDRON, nothing looked different. The door was still ajar, and as no one was standing outside shouting or screaming, and no crowd had gathered, it seemed no one else had gone in. I tried to check the street without being too obvious about it, but I couldn't see my brother anywhere. Who knew what he'd been up to while I was gone. Nothing good, I imagined.

Ben opened the door for Isabella, and she inclined her head gracefully as she swept past him, her long skirts caught up in both hands. He looked at me. "Coming?" he asked.

I opened my mouth to say I'd rather not, but there was Ruiner to consider. Finding a strange cat in the middle of the crime scene seemed like it might not be the greatest idea in this town. They'd probably perform a citizen's arrest on him. "I suppose," I said, and he gave me a sympathetic look as I padded past him into the shop.

Isabella had gone straight through to the back, and Ben followed. I trailed after him, stopping in the doorway and trying not to look at the cauldron. Isabella was leaning over it, obscuring my view of the corpse, but I wasn't taking any risks. I had no wish for another viewing, and I was also starting to think the mayor was either a sociopath or ex-police herself. She seemed very unbothered by the body.

"How very unfortunate," Isabella said, as if Norma had dropped a bottle of milk rather than boiled herself alive. Ben made a noncommittal sound that seemed to suggest that maybe the death was less terrible than Isabella seemed to think. She shot him a disapproving look. "Benjamin," she said, making the use of his full name sound much worse than the nickname had. "She is still a person."

"She's not anymore," he pointed out. And added, when Isabella frowned at him, "I mean, she's dead."

"Yes. It's most tragic. And what must our new arrival think, to be faced with a dead body on her first day in town?" Isabella was suddenly standing next to me, one hand hovering over my shoulder, stooping so she could look me earnestly in the eyes. I almost jumped away from her, despite the warmth in her gaze. It was as if she'd just *appeared* next to me, without bothering with any sort of moving across the room, and my head couldn't make sense of it. "This very ... this *never* happens," she said. "Please don't be concerned. It's a very safe town."

"I'm sure it is," I said. "But I'm just passing through, anyway." Movement caught my eye, and I spotted Ruiner. He was peering in the open window, trying to keep himself hidden, but also examining Isabella's cleavage with great interest. He really is such a brat.

"Just passing through?" Isabella said. "That's unusual. It's not tourist season."

"No," I said. "I mean, I'm not a tourist exactly. I'm between jobs and thought a road trip might be a good reset."

"And you came here?" Isabella asked. She was still examining me from very close quarters, which was a little unnerving,

"Yes. I saw the road and just thought, *interesting*, then the sign, you know? It's pretty amazing." I tried to look like the sort of person who was easily tempted by narrow, spookily shadowed roads and signs featuring freaky, child-eating rabbits. "Nothing like exploring a new place, right?"

Isabella patted my arm, or the air above it, and I shivered as an odd chill passed over me. "You're obviously meant to come here," she said. "Only people who are *meant* to come to Hollowbeck ever find Hollowbeck, unless they're tourists, of course."

"Well, I am a tourist, though," I pointed out. "I just came to see the town, after all."

She hesitated for a moment, her eyes still on me, then said, "No, Morgan. I don't think you did."

I couldn't quite work out why that set the hairs on my arms shivering. It wasn't a threat. How could it be?

Ruiner, meanwhile, had been twitching his ears furiously at me from the window, and Ben spotted him. "There's a cat," he said. "Norma didn't have a cat, did she?"

"No," said Isabella. "I don't recognise that cat at all." They both stared at him. Ruiner gave a very unconvincing meow, which sounded exactly like a person trying to sound like a cat. Isabella and Ben looked at each other, and Isabella said, "I think we'd better take him with us. I'd rather not have a stray just wandering around town."

Ruiner leaned back and I said quickly, "No, it's mine. He, I mean. He's mine."

"Is he?" Isabella said. She gave me that interested look again.

"Yes?"

"And you just left him behind here?" She sounded curious rather than concerned.

"He got away on me," I said. "And I needed to find the police. I knew he'd turn up."

"Do you often take him on road trips?"

"Yes." I couldn't think of anything else to say for a moment, then added, "He seems to really like them. And they help him sleep. I drive him around the block if he's being particularly troublesome. With … with a bottle of milk and some soothing music."

Ruiner gave me a disgusted look and I realised I'd just described a baby. But if the fur coat fits, and all that.

"Well, I think it's very nice," Isabella said, as if using a car to put a cat to sleep was something everyone did. Who knew — around here, maybe they did. "Lovely to have company on a road trip."

"It's certainly something," I said.

Isabella twiddled her fingers in greeting at Ruiner, then clapped her hands. "Now, then. We shall lock the doors and put the closed sign up. Then as soon as Theodore is on duty, he can pop straight over here to look at the ... ah, to tell us what he thinks of the scene."

"Alright," I said. "So can we ... can I go? Since you have it all in hand?" I looked at Ruiner. He twitched his ears at me again, but I had no idea what that meant. I don't speak cat. And to be honest, I hadn't thought Ruiner spoke cat either. But apparently he was getting quite good at the whole communication-through-ear-wiggles thing. Or he thought he was, anyway.

"Well, you know, I hate to say it, but *don't leave town*." Isabella threw her hands up and gave a delighted little laugh.

Ben looked at her, eyebrows raised, and I stared from him to Isabella.

Isabella dropped her hands again and said, "I'm dreadfully sorry. That was incredibly tasteless. I've always wanted to say it, though."

I was starting to lean toward the sociopath theory.

"Not the best way to put it," Ben said, looking at me. "But she's right. Theodore will want to speak to you."

"Right," I said, ignoring Ruiner, who was doing the very best he could to roll his eyes. I'm pretty sure cats aren't actually equipped to be able to do that, and I could almost feel his frustration. It was oddly satisfying. "Okay, I guess that makes sense. We can wait at a cafe or something."

"Nonsense," Isabella said. "We can't have you sitting about in cafes waiting on us. We need to make you comfortable, and I know just the place." She pointed at Ben. "Give Petunia a call, would you?"

Ben made an agreeable noise, and I said, "Petunia? Who's Petunia?"

Isabella waved her arms in flourish, as if to embrace the whole idea of Petunia. "She owns the *dearest* little B&B. Very atmospheric and *so* characteristic of the town. You will absolutely love it. She's a sweetheart."

"I don't think that's going to work," I said. "I don't have the money for a B&B. Is there a campsite or something?" I was thinking that, if we had to stay over, our best option was going to be sleeping in the back of the Volvo, probably in a car park somewhere. If we wanted to have enough money for food, it was the best option, anyway.

"Oh, no. It'll be at the expense of the town, of course, since we — or I — am requesting you stay. Don't worry about money. It's all in hand."

Going by Isabella's odd way of speaking, I had a sneaking suspicion that money wasn't something she'd *ever* worried about. Only the very rich got to talk like extras from a period drama without worrying about someone beating them up and taking their lunch money. "That's very nice of you," I said aloud. "But I wasn't intending to stay, so we'll go as soon as the police are done. We'll just wait in a cafe until they can interview us. Me." I shot a glance at Ruiner, who squinted at me in a way that I'm sure was an alternative to eye-rolling.

"Nonsense. I'm not hearing any more about it."

I looked at Ben a little desperately, hoping for an ally, but he just smiled and said, "It's all sorted. Don't worry."

"Right," I said. "I mean, thank you, but there's the cat, too. No one's going to let me stay with a cat."

"Petunia will be fine," Ben said. "Just as long as your cat doesn't eat her frogs."

"Sorry? She has frogs? Like, she collects them or something?"

"Something like that. No eating the frogs, and no parties after 10 p.m., and you're all good." He smiled at me, showing those dimples again, and somehow I'd just been talked into staying at the B&B. I wasn't even sure if it was the dimples or the fact that I just really needed a shower to get the scent of dead bodies and aniseed off me. I looked at Ruiner, who glared back at me, but it didn't matter how much he hated the idea. We had to stay. We couldn't walk away when the police were going to need to talk to us. Or me, rather.

"Right," I said. "In that case, thank you very much." Ruiner bared his teeth, and I smiled at him. "You're not going to eat any frogs, are you, Ruiner? You'll be a good cat."

He looked away with such enthusiasm he almost fell off the windowsill.

"Ruiner," Isabella said. "That's a very interesting name."

"It's a very apt name," I said, and this time Ruiner hissed. I ignored him and said, "Do you have the address?"

"I'll show you," Ben said. "It's just down the road."

I was more than happy to follow him out of the shop and onto the pavement. The afternoon sun was growing low and rich, but the day was still heavy with heat. Isabella stayed behind, still examining the cauldron, as if curious.

"Is she really the mayor?" I asked Ben.

"Yes," he said and hesitated before adding added, "Has been for quite some time now."

"She's unusual."

He laughed. "Yeah, everyone thinks that when they first meet Isabella. She's definitely different. But she's fair, and she's going to be on top of all this. You really don't need to worry, not about the B&B, or … anything." He waved at the shop vaguely.

"I hope you're right." That wobble was starting in my voice again. I've never been very good with people being sympathetic. It's not something I've been used to.

He pointed down the road. "Go straight to the end, turn left, then keep going for two blocks. It's called The Witchinn', and there's a sign outside. You can't miss it."

"Thanks," I said, taking my keys from my pocket.

He looked as if he was going to say something else, paused, then said, "Mystic Munchies does really nice meals. And they're cheap. I often go there for dinner."

I nodded, and we looked at each other for a moment before he said, "This'll all work out. Theodore's a good … man." The pause was weird, and he added hurriedly, "Police officer. You'll be okay."

I didn't have any answer for that, so I just said, "I better grab my cat."

"Okay," he said, and pointed back inside. "I'll see if Isabella needs any help." He gave me an awkward little wave, winced, and spun around to head back into the shop.

I waited until I was sure he'd gone, then peered down the little alley that ran along the side of the building and called, "Here, puss, puss."

"Puss puss yourself," Ruiner said, trotting out of the shadows to meet me. "What were you *doing?* Running off without me and bringing the bloody mayor and some Boy Scout back with you?"

"I don't know, dealing with the *dead body*, perhaps? The one we've now got to talk to the police about?"

"And whose fault's that? If we'd just left when I said—"

"I'm trying to do the right thing! You're the one that brought us here. And if I get bloody well arrested, I'm never forgiving you."

Ruiner looked like he was about to start arguing, then he looked at me a little more closely and said, "Fine. I'll admit, this has not gone entirely as I expected. But it'll be fine."

"Nothing *ever* goes as you expect. And you better hope it'll be fine," I told him. "I can't believe you've dragged me into your mess again."

"I just want to not be a cat. I had nothing to do with the body."

"My name was on a note," I said. "How can you not have had anything to do with that?"

He looked away, then said, "I need you to help me grab something."

"What?"

"Just come with me."

I glanced around to make sure no one was watching us through the shop windows, then followed him down the right side of the building, along a narrow walkway just wide enough to allow foot access. Weeds grew along the old stone sides of the shop and the building next to it, and the ground underfoot was dusty.

Ruiner led me to where two bins were tucked tidily behind a wooden shelter. There was a lavender one with a large rune on the side that looked faintly threatening, and another that looked no different from the one I used to have at my house before I left everything with Jason. I had a momentary pang of homesickness.

A chunky book lay on the ground next to the bins. It wasn't large, no bigger than a diary, but it was a lot fatter, and the cover was formed from leather of such a deep red it was almost black. Embossed patterns crawled across it, and it was hard to be certain exactly what they were. The more I tried to focus on them, the less distinct they seemed to be, forming vines or tendrils or even tentacles. The first word that popped into my head as I stared at it was *grimoire*, even though I had never seen a grimoire before, so my identification could've been off. Although if a grimoire was a very old, scary book, this did fit the brief.

"Where did that come from?" I asked.

"It's probably best you don't ask too many questions," he said. "I'm not going to be able to answer in any sort of way that makes you happy."

"You stole the book." I pointed at him. "You *stole* the book from a *crime scene*."

"Yes," he said. "And you removed a note from a crime scene."

We looked at each other. "You think there's a cure in there?" I asked him.

"I really hope there is."

I sighed again. "Fine. *Fine.*" I picked up the book, the cover oddly and unpleasantly slippery underneath my fingers, both cool and hot all at once. I wanted nothing so much as to just drop it back to the ground again, but I tucked it under my shirt as we walked back to the car.

Isabella was leaning out the front door, and she gave me a questioning look.

I pointed at my brother and shouted, more loudly than necessary, "He needed to use the litter box."

"Oh, thank you very much," Ruiner hissed. "Thank you so much."

I ignored him as I climbed into the car. Any victory's a victory, no matter how small. We headed off for the B&B with the grimoire looking like a black hole at the bottom of the passenger side footwell. I almost fancied I could smell it, heavy with old skin and older secrets, and I don't know why, but it felt like we were getting deeper into something rather than clawing our way out.

FIVE

Frogs before princes

BEN CERTAINLY HADN'T SENT us to the posh side of town, in as much as Hollowbeck had such things. It wasn't like we were heading into the depths of a council estate, and there was no graffiti or abandoned shopping carts lurking about like the discarded skeletons of old hunts, but the few gates sagged and the low garden walls were crumbling, and there were more semi-detached bungalows and rows of terraces with pocket-sized gardens than big houses and sprawling cottages. The buildings themselves were haphazardly maintained, and the gardens, where they were big enough, looked a little more *survival of the fittest* than *Chelsea Flower Show*. It was kind of comforting, to be honest, to find somewhere that was free of all the twee tidiness. My old car didn't even seem out of place here.

We pulled up in front of a weathered two-storey house, its white walls pocked with dark-framed windows. There didn't seem to be straight line or a right angle anywhere, and the walls bulged slightly, giving the impression the whole place was on the verge of collapsing under its own weight. The roof had a slightly swaybacked look, as well as a couple of dormer windows that suggested attic rooms, and the garden was a jumble of vegetables and herbs and flowering plants all rubbing shoulders with each other and vying for space between the shadows cast by heavy-trunked, mature trees. Paint peeled gently on the window frames, and a sign that was in much better condition than the house proclaimed it *The Witchinn'*. The sign had a picture of a frog on it, and I wasn't sure if that was a threat toward misbehaving guests, or simply evidence of the owner's love of amphibians. There were cast metal frogs capping the leaning gate posts, too.

We looked at the house for a moment without moving out of the car. It didn't exactly look well-inhabited. A car of an even older vintage than mine squatted on the road outside the gate, leaning to one side wearily on a terminally flat tyre. It probably would have been called a classic except for the fact that it was some obscure make I'd never even heard of, and all the proportions looked a little off, as if it wasn't quite designed for today's humans. Otherwise, the street was empty, no one in the gardens or walking down the cracked pavements, and for one moment I considered that Ruiner might be right, and that we should just make ourselves scarce, dead bodies or not.

Then the house's front door opened and a small, shrunken woman who had the fine-boned look of the very, very old came tottering out onto the veranda. She was clad in a multicoloured, tie-dyed dress that stopped just short of a pair of heavily worn motorcycle boots, and she waved at us enthusiastically, her short white hair bouncing.

I waved back, a little more hesitantly, and looked at Ruiner. "We're here, then."

"This place is a dump."

"Cats can't be choosers," I said, getting out and grabbing my backpack from the back seat. "Especially not on our budget."

He grumbled and followed me out of the car. Birds were singing enthusiastically, but as I let us through the gate, they fell silent, and I looked up to see a row of crows glaring at us from the fence. Ruiner hissed at them.

"Behave," I told him.

"What? I can't help it." He kept his voice low enough that the woman on the porch — presumably Petunia — couldn't hear him.

"You know you're not actually a cat, right?"

"It's instinct. Stop cat-shaming me." He sat down abruptly and scratched behind his ear vigorously with a back paw.

"Cat instincts don't come with fleas," I said, pausing to wait for him.

"I don't have *fleas*," he said, pausing mid-scratch to glare at me.

"I'm getting you a flea collar."

"You are *not* putting me in a collar. I've only done that once, and it's not something I'm repeating with my sister."

"*Eww.*" I wrinkled my nose. "I didn't need to know that. It'll have to be flea drops, then."

"I don't like the sound of them." He went back to scratching.

"And I don't like the sound of you shedding fleas all over me," I replied, starting back up the little, partly over-grown path.

"Hello, love," the woman on the veranda called.

"Um, hi," I said, giving her a little wave. "I'm Morgan. Ben and Isabella sent me."

"Yes, yes." She waved me up the steps eagerly. Close up, she smelled of laundry dried in sunlight and warm baking, and old, faded tattoos crawled up her bare arms.

She was as diminutive as she was skinny, her head level with my chest, and her eyes were milky with the onset of cataracts. But there was a raw sort of strength couched in her stance, too, and her skinny shoulders were braided with muscle. She looked from me to Ruiner, her gaze bright despite the cataracts. "And you brought your kitty!"

"I did. I hope that's all right."

"Of course, of course." She bent down and examined Ruiner from close quarters, and Ruiner stared back at her blankly. "What's your name, kitty?"

"Ruiner," I said.

"Oh, that's unusual. Hello, Ruiner. I'm Petunia." She straightened up and reached into a pocket that was hidden in the voluminous folds of the tie-dyed dress, producing a large, watery-eyed frog. It goggled at me. "This is Clarence. Clarence, say hello to Morgan and Ruiner."

The frog licked his lips as he stared at me, then Petunia tilted him toward Ruiner. His eyes bulged at the sight of the cat, and he lurched off her hand, splatting into her chest and diving out of sight, presumably back into another pocket.

"Oh, *Clarence,*" Petunia said, and gave me a regretful smile. "Dreadfully sorry. He's a little bit shy around new people."

"Of course," I said, trying to contain the twitch in the corner of my mouth.

Petunia looked at Ruiner. "You seem like a very well-behaved kitty. You're not going to eat any frogs or birds, are you?"

"I promise he won't," I said, as Ruiner made a gagging sound.

"Well, that's *perfect,* then," she said, smiling brightly at both of us. "Everyone needs to get along, don't they?"

"Absolutely," I replied, giving in to the smile.

She clapped her hands lightly. "Come in, then. I've got some elderflower cordial that's in need of drinking. Do you like cordial? I've also got vodka if you'd prefer."

"Um, no. Cordial's fine," I said.

"Suit yourself," she replied, and her friendly smile suddenly blossomed into something much wider, her eyes crinkling deeply at the corners. "I usually go for both." She cackled with delight and headed for the open door, trotting into the shadows beyond with her laughter trailing behind her. Ruiner and I looked at each other.

"Mad as a literal box of frogs," he whispered.

"More so than anyone else here?" I asked, and he acknowledged that with a tilt of his head.

Inside was just as disasterous as the outside, crammed with slumping, threadbare furniture and floating dust. The scuffed wooden floors creaked underfoot, and the wallpaper was ancient, deeply floral, and peeling in places. Every spare bit of wall space was crammed with old portraits of both humans and animals (mostly frogs) and faded photographs in ornate frames, and the whole place smelled faintly of furniture polish and jasmine. It was both less creepy than I'd thought from outside, and oddly comforting. It was the sort of place you imagined your grandmother might have, full of old memories and old love that lived as close to the skin as the present, but I wouldn't really know. Our family had never been that kind of family.

We followed Petunia through to the kitchen, which was at the back of the house and bright with afternoon light. A kettle steamed gently on top of an old wood-fired cooking range, and the windows were open to the garden. Everything smelled of fresh baking.

"Your timing's perfect," she said, opening a cabinet to reveal a clutter of mismatched glasses. "I told Isabella I'd known someone was on their way. I just made Victoria sponge cake."

"It smells amazing," I said, and when she pointed me at the table I sat down gratefully. It was big enough to sit a dozen people and made of bare, scrubbed wood, but a clutter of jars and abandoned knitting projects and newspapers and pinecones and a large tank full of crickets took up most of it. The wooden chairs were topped with cushions in sunflower print covers and were far more comfortable than they looked.

"You look as though you could use some cake," she said, pouring us each a glass of sparkling water and topping it with cordial.

"It's been a day."

"Benjamin did say. You poor thing." She grabbed a bottle of vodka from the freezer compartment of a surprisingly modern fridge in the corner of the old kitchen and waved it at me. I hesitated, then shook my head.

"I better not. We have to talk to the police later. Apparently they don't work in the day?"

"Oh, no," she said, adding a generous glug of vodka to her own glass. "That'll be Theodore. He has a condition."

"So I've heard." I watched her fill a bowl with milk, then place it on the floor.

"There we are, Ruiner. That's lactose-free." He wrinkled his snout, and she looked at me. "It's much better for them, you know. They get all sorts of smells with regular milk."

"I had noticed," I said, taking a sip of the cordial. There was lemon in it, lifting the sweetness of the elderflower, and it tasted of summer. Ruiner gave me a disgusted look and sniffed the milk, then sat back and did a passable imitation of a cat's meow.

"Yes, we'll get you some food as well," Petunia said,

fussing around with a teapot. She took the frog out of her pocket and put him on the worktop, where he sloped over to a large terrarium and climbed in. "Clarence does prefer that to my pocket," she said. "But sometimes it's good to have company."

"I imagine," I said, wondering just how much company a frog could provide. But then again, he was probably a better conversationalist than Ruiner the Whiny.

"Now," she said, placing a large mug that said *Frogs Before Princes* in front of me. "I've made up the attic bedroom. I hope you don't mind the climb, but it's by far the biggest and most comfortable."

"That sounds wonderful," I said. "But—"

"There are quite a few stairs, but for a young thing like you, that should be no problem."

Young thing. I was liking her more and more. "No, not at all, and I really appreciate you accommodating us on such short notice. But…" I hesitated, wondering how to basically say, *I can't pay.* "Isabella said the town would cover the cost?"

"Oh, we'll sort all that out later," she said, waving dismissively.

"I'd rather just confirm it now," I said. "This trip was a little unexpected, so I'm on quite a tight budget."

She leaned her forearms on the table, skin folding the old tattoos into new and strange forms, and said, "Everyone pays what they can afford, dear." For a moment, her smile was gone, her eyes sharp and young and coolly evaluating. I started to protest again, wanting to *know* I wasn't going to be stuck with an unexpected bill, and she raised a hand imperiously. "I *said*, everyone pays what they can afford, and we will sort it out later. Are we in agreement, Morgan?"

I opened my mouth to argue and was suddenly aware

that the kitchen had gone cold, and that the smell of baking had been replaced by something deep and earthy, like early morning forests. Clarence ribbeted in the corner, and I stared back at Petunia, but not for long. I couldn't hold that gaze. It had weight.

I looked away and took a bite of my cake. It still held a memory of warmth from the oven, the jam sweet and the cream collapsing softly. It was distinctly better than the bourbon creams from earlier, even though they'd been exactly what I needed at the time.

"All right," I said, faintly surprised that my voice didn't wobble. "Thank you very much."

"Of course!" she exclaimed, and all the smells and warmth of the kitchen came rushing back in, leaving me thinking I'd imagined the whole thing. She looked around, rubbing one hand through her short white hair. "Where's that damn frog? He was just here, I'm sure of it."

"He's in the terrarium," I said.

"Oh, of course. One does lose track sometimes." She went to pick him up, then wandered off, leaving us sitting in the kitchen. Ruiner and I stared at each other, his tail pouffed out and his pupils huge, and a moment later Petunia shouted, "Do come on, dear."

"Right! Sorry!" I gulped half my cordial, grabbed my bag, and hurried out, tea in one hand and the remains of the cake in the other, Ruiner trailing behind me. Petunia was waiting at the foot of the stairs, and she smiled brightly at me.

"Watch your step." She pattered off, and we followed.

She'd been right to warn us about the stairs, and I was more than a little worried following her up. Half of them seemed to be missing boards, all of them creaked dramatically, and, at one point, there was an entire step missing, which I had to jump over to get to safe ground on two risers up.

"You could just let us go up," I said.

"Nonsense," she replied, bouncing along happily and sounding less out of breath than I was. "I'm very comfortable with the stairs."

I wanted to say that I wasn't, but I could hardly complain when we were apparently staying rent-free, which was about what we could afford. On the first landing, she led us to the first door in the hallway and opened it to reveal a bathroom with dark green tiled floors, a freestanding toilet with one of those big old tanks and a pull chain high above it, and a huge claw-footed bath.

"I don't do showers, dear," she said. "They're terribly modern."

I made an agreeable noise, not quite sure how I was meant to respond to that.

"The bath is very comfortable. Your time slot is between 6 a.m. and 7 a.m., to ensure all guests get a chance to use it."

"Okay," I said. "And in the evening?"

"No hot water in the evening, unless you wait until after midnight."

Well, that that was slightly awkward when there'd been sweat dripping down my back all day. On the other hand, a cold bath didn't seem like such a bad idea either.

"Come along," Petunia said cheerily, and trotted off again.

We followed, swept on helplessly in her wake, and the next set of stairs delivered us straight to a heavy wooden door. It opened onto a slope-ceilinged chamber that ran the length of the house. It was bigger than my entire apartment had been, and while I'd been vaguely worried, given the state of the place, that we were liable to fall to our deaths through rotten old floorboards, they were solid and ungiving underfoot. The dormer windows let mellow afternoon light play over both the wood floor and big rugs in reds and oranges. The rugs looked handmade and as if they'd outlast all of us. The bed squatted against one long wall, king-sized and heaped with pillows and cushions, and at one end of the long room were a couple of low dressers. At the opposite end was a free-standing, Narnia-style wardrobe, and in between were scattered a clothes horse, a desk with a chair, an overflowing bookcase, and a clutter of floor cushions.

"There we are," Petunia said. "I think you can be quite comfortable here."

I stared around at it. "This is really too much. We don't need all this space."

"You never know," she replied. "It's best to be comfortable in case you stay a while."

"We're not, though," I said. "It should only be for the night."

"That's okay as well. Just make yourselves at home. You're very welcome to come and make tea in the kitchen, and there will always be cake. And if you need me, just shout."

And then she was gone, pattering down the stairs at a surprising pace. A frog remained on the top step, and I couldn't tell if it was Clarence or not. It stared at us, flicked its tongue a couple of times, then vanished into a gap in the stairs.

I watched him go, then looked at Ruiner and said, "Should we be worried that the frog just went in the wall? Or about this whole payment situation? Is that what happened to you and Norma? With the favours? Or are we just worrying about the whole you as a cat thing for now?"

"I think we should be worried about everything," he replied.

"Well, that's reassuring."

He ambled across the floor to flop down on a rug in the sunlight. "Have you got the book?"

I patted my backpack. "It's here."

"Right," he said. "Then it's time for some research."

I grabbed a couple of cushions off the bed and sat down next to him, taking a mouthful of my still-warm tea. I didn't recognise the blend, but it was warm and mellow and full of afternoon promises.

For a moment, I didn't even open the book. I just sat there, the sun warm on my back, the cushion soft beneath me, and the idea of dead bodies suddenly a long way away. The house was quiet around us, and bird song drifted in from outside. The sweetness of the cake seemed to have loosened something tight in my chest, and I took a deep breath before lying back on the floor, my arms wide.

I was homeless, jobless, and nearly penniless. My brother was a cat. We were in a town that no one was meant to be able to find, and nothing about it made sense. There were tentacles in bird baths and frogs in the walls. The sheriff only came out at night. The mayor liked poking around crime scenes. We'd found a dead body in a *cauldron*. And someone had left a note with my name on it right next to that body.

But right then, in the sunlight, with Ruiner purring unevenly by my side, nothing felt too bad. Nothing felt *insurmountable*. And all of it felt, somehow, better than my life had before.

Which didn't say much about my life, if I was going to be brutally honest about things.

SIX

Returning to the scene

I DON'T KNOW when I fell asleep, but I woke up with my hip smarting from the hardness of the floor beneath the rug, Ruiner snoring next to me. Petunia stood at the door saying, "Hello dear," at a volume which suggested she'd been saying it for a while.

Something green and slimy croaked a few inches from my face. I yelped as my vision cleared, revealing one of Petunia's frogs, before rolling over, and half-squashing Ruiner. He hissed and sank his needle sharp teeth into my arm. I yelped again, slapped him, and sat up while the frog jumped away rapidly.

"Oh dear," Petunia said. "I didn't mean to startle you."

"It's fine," I managed, my heart going too fast. "I didn't mean to fall asleep." The room was dark, the only light coming from the sturdy flame in an old lantern Petunia was carrying. I looked at it then up at her.

She followed my gaze to the lantern and said, "Oh, I know there should be electric lights on the stairs, but, you know. One can't keep up with all this modernisation. It's too much."

I wondered at just what point showers and electric lights had stopped being modernisation and started becoming what the rest of us considered normal life, but decided some things weren't worth the discussion. I got up, stretching. It was cooler at least, and I dug in my bag for my hoody.

"The sheriff's here to see you," Petunia said. "I told him you'd be right down, but take your time, dear."

"Thank you," I said. "I'll be right there."

She turned and pattered down the stairs, leaving us in darkness, and I groped for my phone, turned on the torch, then managed to find the switch for the bedside lights. I looked at Ruiner. He was sitting on top of the grimoire, his long grey fur spilling over the sides and obscuring it entirely.

"What're you doing?" I asked him.

"Well, I don't know. I thought maybe we shouldn't have the book that we stole from a crime scene just lying out in the open."

"I didn't steal it from a crime scene," I pointed out. "You did."

"Sure. But I don't think they're going to arrest a cat, do you?"

I sighed. "I hate you so much."

"I know," he replied, and he actually sounded slightly contrite, which seemed to go against both Ruiner and cat nature. I found my brush and ran it over my hair quickly before bundling it up into a ponytail that felt less than tidy, wishing I had time to at least have a quick wash. The cold bath wasn't sounding quite as appealing as it had earlier, though, and a few minutes later we were hurrying down the creaking stairs, lit by the cold light from my phone. We found Isabella sitting at the kitchen table, leaning over a mug of tea and sniffing it with great pleasure.

"Hello, Morgan," she said, smiling at me brightly. "Are you feeling a little more refreshed?"

"Yes, thank you," I said. I was fairly sure mayors weren't usually this involved in things, but Isabella certainly seemed to take a hands-on approach to government, and I couldn't decide if that was better than the usual way of things or not.

Seated next to her was a lean man with ridiculously good cheekbones and longish dark hair, which was combed carefully back from a high forehead. He got up as I came in and gave me a formal little bow, gracing me with the sort of dark-eyed smile that would've sent my thoughts to some really inappropriate places if I hadn't been a little distracted by something else. I couldn't tell if it was the light in the kitchen or not, but his skin was the colour of cheese puffs. I tried not to stare as he held a hand out to me, and I shook it carefully. It wasn't the light. My skin looked just as pale and freckled as ever, while his looked very much as if he'd been rolling in grated carrots.

"Miss Morgan, I presume?" he said. "I don't have your last name."

"Winters," I said.

"Miss Winters—"

"Theodore," Petunia said, her tone reproving, and he pressed his free hand to his chest, eyes closing. In his well-cut dark suit and dark tie, he looked like a distressed but highly photogenic undertaker.

"My sincerest apologies. I made an assumption. A terrible habit, which I am working to break. Morgan Winters, how should I address you?"

"Um. As Morgan?" I suggested.

"Morgan. It's an honour to meet you. I am Sergeant Theodore Ianculescu, but you must call me simply Theodore. Delighted to make your acquaintance." He bent over my hand, and for one horrifying moment, I thought he was going to kiss it. And, cheekbones or not, I had no idea what I'd actually do if he did. Slapping Hollowbeck's sole police officer seemed unlikely to be a good move when I'd already been poking around murder scenes, but I also didn't feel anyone should be going around just kissing the random body parts of strangers without some sort of consequences. But instead of kissing it, he just hovered over my hand for a moment, then straightened up again. I had the oddest impression that he'd *sniffed* me, which I suppose wasn't the weirdest thing to happen recently.

"I should like you to accompany me to the crime scene and walk me through what you found," he said.

"Really?" I asked, looking at Isabella, who just smiled encouragingly. "Do I have to?"

"I fully understand and sympathise with your reluctance," Theodore said, his voice all smooth curves. "But this is my *method,* shall we say? It allows me to see your initial reaction."

"Okay, but it's not my initial reaction," I pointed out. "I've already been in there. *Twice.*"

"That is unfortunate," Theodore agreed, looking at Isabella, who just smiled. "But I was not there when you did."

"I really don't want to see a dead body again," I said.

"Well, you don't have to look at it," he said, in a tone that suggested I was the one being unreasonable.

"Sure," I started, intending to add *but I'll still know it's there,* but Isabella interrupted me.

"It'll be quite all right, Morgan. I'll be there with you the whole way." She pressed her hands together and brought them to her chest as she spoke, and I could have sworn they passed straight through her cup, but that was impossible. Although I had a sneaking suspicion I was going to have to re-evaluate my definition of *impossible* if I stayed in Hollowbeck much longer.

I looked at Petunia, who spread her hands and shrugged in a *what can you do* manner, and I sighed. "Okay, I suppose."

"Thank you, Morgan," Theodore said. "I, and the entire town of Hollowbeck, appreciate your gracious assistance." He looked at Ruiner, and said in a slightly different tone, "And this is your cat."

"In a manner of speaking," I said.

"How handsome."

Ruiner purred, and I said, "Appearances and all that. It's pretty skin-deep. He's not actually a very nice cat."

Isabella laughed, and Ruiner hissed at me.

"Not many are," Theodore said. "But he will have to come with us also."

"My *cat* has to come with us? To the *crime scene*?"

"Yes, I should like to recreate the scene as much as possible as you found it," he replied, setting a flat cap on his head as he turned to the door. It should've looked incongruous with his suit, but he carried it off somehow. It must've been the cheekbones. "Come along, my friends."

So we came along. Ruiner and I climbed into the back of a plain black car while Isabella and Theodore rode up front, and a few moments later we were pulling up outside The Cosy Cauldron once more. I looked at the purple banner, hanging limp in the still evening air, and my stomach twisted. I really, really did not want to go back in there. There may be many things in life which become easier the more you do them, but one thing I didn't want to become easy was seeing a dead body.

I sat silently in the car, wondering how to prepare myself for The Corpse Take Three, and Ruiner nudged my hand with his head. I looked at him.

"Don't mention the book," he hissed. "Or the curse. Or the note."

I sighed, and jumped as Theodore opened the door. He gave me a little bow and I clambered out.

"What time did you arrive, Morgan?" he asked.

"Just after two o'clock," I replied. "I looked at the time."

"Ah-ha," he said, producing a little notebook and a fountain pen with a flourish of his orange hands. "And the door was open?"

"Yes."

"No one inside?"

"No one at all." I was trying not to look at the shop itself, concentrating on a dandelion growing out of a crack in the pavement, a grim splash of yellow determination.

"Not even, say, a rat?"

I looked up at him, startled, and found his warm dark eyes watching me intently. "There was," I started, and Ruiner batted my ankle. I shot him a glance and he shook his head just slightly. I coughed. "Um, taxidermy ones."

"Taxidermy ones?"

"Yeah, there's a bunch in there. Rats and stoats and … I don't know. Other stuff."

"Other stuff?"

"I don't know what they all are." He was still watching me intently, and I looked back at the dandelion, wondering where Isabella was. I felt she might've intervened in the rat interrogation.

"Not a real rat, then? A living one?"

"No, why? Oh, she hasn't … nothing's been eating her, has it?" I pressed a hand to my stomach, suddenly aware that I was once again both starving and queasy. Apparently, bourbon creams and Victoria sponge cake are not enough to settle an empty stomach when confronted with dead bodies. "Oh, please say she wasn't eaten by rats."

"Oh, no, no. I'm terribly sorry to have distressed you." He took his hat off and fanned me urgently with it.

I wasn't sure what that was meant to do, but just said, "Thank you." I couldn't work out why Ruiner was telling me not to say anything about the rat, but he seemed to know a whisker more than the nothing I did, so I was going to go with it. A rodent in an old shop hardly seemed important, anyway.

"And then you went in," Theodore said, putting his hat back on.

"Yes, then I went in."

He gestured at the door. "Please."

I sighed, then led the way inside. The door was still unlocked, which seemed pretty careless for a crime scene, and I wondered if there was someone inside guarding it. I hadn't seen anyone around, though. I stopped just over the threshold, and Theodore said, "And then?"

"I walked to the counter."

He gave me a little *carry on* wave, and I stared at him. This was starting to feel like school drama class. I'd always been terrible at that. I walked to the counter with him trailing half a step behind me, and said, "I called out. You know, hello, is anyone here, that sort of thing."

"Did anyone answer?"

"No."

"And then?"

I looked at Ruiner. "Then I tried the bell."

"So why did you go into the back room?"

"Because I heard something." Which was true enough. Or Ruiner had heard something, anyway.

"A rat?"

Theodore had quite the fixation. "No, not a rat." He

was still looking at me expectantly, so I added, "It was like something falling. So I thought maybe there was a problem, maybe she was hurt or something."

"Ah, of course," the sheriff said. "You had a humanitarian reason for entering."

"Um, yeah. Exactly. So I went through and then … I saw her."

"Please," he said, pointing at the beaded curtain behind the counter.

I started forward reluctantly, the long chains of wooden beads clattering over my shoulders.

"You didn't touch anything else?" he asked, following me.

"I don't think so," I said. "Just the curtains."

"Theodore, dear," Isabella called from the end of the little hall. "The poor girl can't be expected to have a photographic memory just because you do."

"I don't have a photographic memory. I have perfect recall. It's a skill and it can be developed."

"Yes, well, Morgan is much younger than us," Isabella said, waving me forward. I'd have to ask her about her skin care routine. There was no way anyone with skin that perfect was older than me. "And probably has better things to do than practicing memory tricks. Stop harassing her and get on with your investigation."

"Of course," he said. "Do forgive me. Did you go into any of the other rooms, Morgan?"

"No, just that one," I said, pointing down the hall.

"And how did you know to go to this one?"

"The door was open," I said, which was actually true.

"I see," he said. "And you called out as you went?"

"Um, yes. But no one answered, so I looked through the door, and … you know."

"I see." We'd arrived at the door to the big room, and I

was trying very hard not to look at the body. I could just see it out of the corner of my eye though, the hand that I'd touched still resting gently on the side of the cauldron. "And then what did you do?"

I took a shaky breath. "I panicked. I ran back outside. I thought I was going to be sick."

"And yet you went back in," Theodore said, sounding only mildly interested.

I shot him a sideways look, trying to avoid meeting those deceptively warm eyes. "I realised I hadn't checked if she was actually dead, and that she might need help. So I went back in." I swallowed. "Then I knew I needed to find a police station, but I couldn't because there aren't any signs. There should be signs." It was too hot in here, and I was sweating again.

"And," Theodore started, but Isabella talked over him. Her fingers brushed the back of my neck, feather-light and soothingly cold.

"Morgan very sensibly came to the town hall. Benji and I accompanied her back here, where we confirmed that Norma was dead, and secured the scene for you. It really was very unnecessary to put poor Morgan through this, Theodore."

He frowned at her. "It's my process. And you interfering with the scene has not helped my investigation."

She sniffed. "Someone else coming in and finding poor Norma in a pot would have interfered with it even more. I keep telling you to hire someone to do day shift."

"I work best alone."

"Yes, yes, you're positively Han Solo." She linked arms with me, somehow without actually seeming to touch me. "I forbid you to ask Morgan any more questions. I already advised you against bringing her back here."

I felt like I should probably be saying something in my

own defence, but they seemed to be keeping themselves occupied, and the aniseed scent was still lingering, making me queasy.

Theodore gave a humph of disapproval. "I'm only doing my job."

"As am I, caring for *all* the residents of this town."

There was a pause, then he said, "I suppose that shall do for now."

"There's no suppose about it," Isabella said, her tone imperious.

Ruiner had followed us in, and now he and the police chief stared at each other. "Was the cat with you when you found the body?" Theodore asked me.

Ruiner wrinkled his snout and looked at me.

"Yes?" I offered.

"Was he ever out of your sight?"

"Theodore, you cannot suspect the cat," Isabella said.

"This is not a familiar cat," he replied.

"Exactly," she said, and I gave her a puzzled look. She smiled at me. "This is finished, Morgan. It has been a terrible start to your time in Hollowbeck, but now it's done."

I couldn't even be bothered to point out that it was hopefully also the end of my time in Hollowbeck, and instead just hurried back down the hall, through the shop and onto the street, where I concentrated on taking deep breaths of night-scented air.

I hadn't heard her follow, but after a moment I realised Isabella was standing next to me, her arms crossed over her generous chest and her face tipped up to the sky. After a moment she looked at me and said, "You were very brave."

I blinked at her and said, "Thank you?"

"I am sorry your introduction to Hollowbeck has been so *fraught*. But you should be most proud of yourself for your actions. Many people would have just left, rather than take responsibility and do what they can to help."

"I just went to find the police," I pointed out.

"Yes. But in so doing you put yourself in the middle of an investigation. *And* you went back to check on Norma, rather than just walking out. The right thing is rarely the easy thing."

"Thank you," I said again. I didn't really agree with her, but for some reason, it was making my chest tighten. We were both silent for a moment longer, then I said, "I really need some food."

"Of course," Isabella exclaimed. "Mystic Munchies is open. Have yourself a bite to eat and tell Ruby to put it on the town account. Then go home, rest, sleep. Know you have done your civic duty for Hollowbeck, and that we are so happy to have you here."

I looked at Theodore, who had followed us out. "Am I free to go?"

"To dinner," he said. "I will need you to remain in town though." He sounded almost apologetic and kept looking at Ruiner.

"Great," I muttered. "Wonderful."

Isabella pressed a hand to her chest. "Are you not comfortable? I can ask Petunia to give you a better room. Or we can find somewhere else."

"No, no, it's lovely. I just, you know, have stuff to get back to."

"A job?" Theodore asked.

"Not right now," I admitted.

"A love whom you miss desperately?" Isabella suggested.

"Definitely not that."

They both gave me puzzled looks, and Isabella said, "I don't understand. You have a good place to stay. You have no job, no love that requires your return. Why would you not want to stay?"

"Um, well … I don't live here," I said. "I mean, I was only passing through."

Isabella gave a slight sigh and I had the absurd feeling I'd disappointed her. "Ah, well," she said. "We shall have to work on that." Her brilliant smile returned, and she pointed to a little restaurant diagonally across the street, its exterior festooned with fairy lights. "Off you go. I hear the tiramisu is particularly good." And then she was gone, vanishing back into the shop with that same there and then not motion.

Theodore gave me a solemn little bow and followed her. I looked at Ruiner. He shrugged.

We crossed the road, neither of us speaking until we were sure we weren't going to be overheard. "We need to get out of here," he said finally. "You've got the police, done your *civic duty* or whatever, and now we need to leave."

"We can't," I said. "Theodore told us to stay."

"So you think country cop there's going to chase after us? You're not a murderer. Just a witness."

"Given the whole finding the body thing, I think I'm a suspect, at least," I said. "And what happens if we can't get out? Like the way people can't find the town?" Which was impossible, but again, I was re-thinking that.

He hesitated, started to say something, stopped, then said, "Okay, well, I suppose it gives me more time to figure out this whole cat issue. And we haven't even looked at the note. We should do that now. Maybe it'll help."

"No," I said. "Oddly enough, I do not want to look at the note right now. I'd like some hope of sleeping tonight."

"Fine, the book, then. We can get takeaway and go back, see what we can find on curse-breaking."

"No," I said again. "This has been a *day*, and I want proper food in a proper place, probably with a very large glass of wine, and tomorrow we'll worry about notes and curses and dead bodies."

He shook his head. "Think you were on bloody holiday," he said, and I aimed a kick at him. He dodged it easily, baring his teeth at me.

"If I was on holiday, it wouldn't be with you," I pointed out.

"Agreed," he said, and we headed for Mystic Munchies, my belly already rumbling.

SEVEN

Dinner & a threat

MYSTIC MUNCHIES SMELLED of roasting garlic and crushed thyme. As we pushed through the door, I saw the tall blond man from earlier talking to a couple at a table, a tea towel slung over his shoulder. He glanced at me, and his white-toothed grin vanished so abruptly I looked around, wondering if there was someone behind me with a machete and a balaclava or something. Teeth and tentacles, maybe. When I looked back, he was pushing through a swinging door with a porthole window in it, presumably into the kitchen.

A pleasantly rounded woman with a high dark ponytail and a ring in her nose wound her way past the tables before I could think too much about the Viking's reaction. "Hi," she said. "I'm Ruby, your server for … well, always." She grinned, bright and infectious, and I grinned back.

"Table for one plus a cat?"

I looked down at Ruiner and said, "If that's okay. He can always stay outside."

Ruiner bared his teeth at me.

"Not *outside*," Ruby said, as if I'd suggested leaving him

out in a blizzard rather than a pleasant late summer evening. "We have some excellent sardines tonight, or, if he prefers, there is salmon. But the sardines are fresh, while the salmon's been frozen."

She leaned down to talk directly to Ruiner and held her hand out to him. "So my recommendation would be the sardines, handsome." He rubbed his face against her hand, giving his unpracticed purr. "I think that's a yes," she said with a laugh.

"I guess so," I said, wondering how much fresh sardines would cost, and also if she was likely to call Theodore to arrest me for cruelty to cats if I pointed out he'd be fine with some Whiskas. But then again, Isabella had said the town was paying, so…

Ruby straightened up and pointed to the little table in the window. "I'll get you a highchair."

"A what, sorry?" I asked. I turned to watch her hurry across the restaurant.

It wasn't large, and the low ceiling gave it a sense of cosiness. Booths ran along the walls, and the centre of the room was divided by free-standing partitions that created little nooks of privacy for the tables. Plants spilled from the tops of the divider walls, and everything was red checked tablecloths and tea lights in old jars and couples leaning toward each other to talk quietly. A woman ate alone with a large iguana sitting on her shoulder and a man dining opposite a bored-looking goat that was chewing on the tablecloth.

Before I could point them out to Ruiner, Ruby reappeared with a highchair, which she set at a small table in the window, opposite a single place setting. She put a menu down, then vanished again, promising to put a hold on the sardines so no one else could get them.

"She likes me," Ruiner said, jumping up to sit in the highchair.

"She likes a cat," I said, keeping my voice low. "She doesn't know you."

"I'm starting to see the advantages of cat-life," he said, looking around the room. "Hey, there's some guy with a goat over there. Freak."

I sat down, and we stared at each other across the table. I couldn't remember the last time I'd had a meal with my brother that hadn't either been Mum-mandated or ended in us throwing things at each other. Sometimes both.

"We shouldn't talk," I said to him. "Someone could overhear."

"They'll just think you're another crazy cat lady," he said.

"Fine, then *you* shouldn't talk."

"I don't think anyone's paying any attention in here."

He was right. No one was paying attention to the woman who was feeding her iguana slices of mango from a silver spoon she'd taken from her handbag, or another man who'd just walked in the door and was conferring urgently with his bat while Ruby waited patiently, or even to the goat-man, who was currently trying to pull the tablecloth back out of the goat's mouth. Hollowbeck was pretty non-judgemental, it seemed.

"Alright," I said. "So why are we being so careful, then?"

"Well, we just don't want a lot of questions, do we?"

"We, or you?"

He looked across the room, as there was a sudden commotion in the corner. "That bat just bit someone. I think they're sitting at its usual table."

"What happened when you were here before, Ruiner? Why are you so keen no one knows who you are?"

"It's embarrassing, isn't it? Being turned into a damn cat."

I leaned back in my chair. "Well. If you're happy spending life as a cat, I guess you don't have to tell me."

He glared at me. "I'm *not*. And I'm telling you all the important stuff, Morgs. I promise."

"Sure." I took a bread roll from the basket on the table and broke it in half, the crust crispy but the interior invitingly soft.

"We'll look at that book when we get back," he said. "We'll find the reversal, then get out of here, and I promise I won't ask anything else of you. Ever."

"A) that's such utter bollocks, and B) two promises in a row? You must be sweating in that fur coat of yours."

He growled. "Fine. You got me here. If you're going to be that much of a pain about it, leave. I'll figure out the reversal from the book myself and sort *everything*."

I snorted, then smiled at Ruby as she put a bottle of water on the table and a bowl of the same in front of Ruiner, then hurried off again. Her hand was wrapped in a handkerchief, so I guess the bat had taken its seating-based frustrations out on her too. "That's always worked really well for you in the past."

"And how do you think you're going to help with magic?"

"How do you think *you're* going to do it? Just stick a paw in the book and hope for the best? How are you even going to know what works? You're not a witch. You're not even a human anymore. You could end up freezing your-self as a cat forever, or turning your hairballs into weapons of mass destruction. Can you even *do* a spell in cat form?"

"I don't know," he snapped. "But I'll figure it out.

Better than we're doing right now, anyway, since you won't even *look* at the book."

"Sure. Once again, my brother in his endless optimism." I turned my attention back to my bread roll, which was *really* good, and comforted myself with the thought that at least we hadn't reached the throwing things point yet.

Someone came to the table and I looked up, expecting Ruby. Instead it was Ben, holding an open bottle of red wine and looking like he was already questioning his decision to come over.

"Hi," he said. "Can I join you?"

Ruiner and I looked at each other, and he hissed. I grinned. "Absolutely. It'd be a pleasure."

Ruiner growled loudly enough that Ruby, who had appeared with a second chair for Ben, gave my brother an alarmed look.

"Is everything all right?" she asked, apparently addressing Ruiner rather than me.

"Everything's absolutely fine," I said. "My cat just has a thing about men. He doesn't like sharing with them." Ben looked even more uncomfortable and I suddenly realised what that sounded like. "*No,*" I said. "No, I didn't mean … I just mean at the table. Sharing space. Attention. Not…" I couldn't figure out how to recover, so I just shook a finger desperately at Ruiner. "Bad cat."

Ben set his bottle down, grinning, and took the chair from Ruby, who looked for a moment as if she didn't want to give it up. "No, I get it," he said. "Cats. I'm not a cat person."

Ruiner growled, and Ruby gave Ben a disapproving look. "You should be," she said. "Cats are magical." She scratched Ruiner between the ears and he purred happily.

"That one isn't," I said. "That one's a knob."

Both Ruby and Ruiner gave me outraged looks, while Ben snorted with laughter and tried to cover it up with a cough.

"That's not very nice," Ruby said.

"Neither's he."

"I'm sure he has his moments," Ben said. He picked Ruiner's chair up and shuffled it around the table so that he had a bit more space. Ruiner tried his best to bite him, but Ben was too quick. He sat down and smiled at me.

"That was his spot," Ruby said. "He's further from his mistress now."

Ruiner and I gave alarmingly similar snorts, and I said, "He's his own cat. And he's just fine further from me."

Ruby *hmph*ed, but left to find another table setting for Ben, and I had the feeling I'd just gone right down in her estimation.

Ben and I looked at each other across the table. His glasses were still pushed up on his head, and he lifted the wine bottle, raising his eyebrows.

"Oh, please."

He leaned forward to fill my glass. "Did you speak with Theodore? Is everything all right? Are *you* all right?"

I decided to ignore the last question, as I didn't want to think about it too much, and definitely not in public. I'd already all but fainted on the library steps in from of him. I wasn't having any uncontrollable sobbing and potentially expletive-laden screaming on top. "He wants me to stay in town."

"Ah. Hollowbeck can be very hard to leave."

I frowned at him. "It'll just be until the case is sorted. It's not like staying forever."

"Oh, of course." Ben nodded, his eyes on his glass as he swirled the wine.

I picked up my own, imitating him and wondering if

he was going to start talking about bouquets and so on. I hoped not. I took a mouthful and said, "How did you end up here, then?"

"An advertisement for head librarian. Library jobs are hard enough to find, let alone a head librarian one. So I jumped at the chance to apply, and they got me in for an interview." He frowned. "I think I was the only person they interviewed. Maybe the only person that applied."

"How?" I asked. "If library jobs are so scarce?"

He finally took a small sip of wine and made an approving noise. "Hollowbeck is ... different. Other than the tourists, who think it's just some sort of theme park, only people who really *see* it stumble onto it."

"*See* it? What does that mean?"

He gave me an amused look. "You know. You were shocked by the body, but not by the cauldron. You haven't looked twice at the iguana."

"I have," I protested. "But it's just weird, is all. Lots of places are. Like Whitby or something."

"Do you honestly think that?"

"Of course." I tried to hold his gaze, then gave up and took another mouthful of wine. "Alright, it's weird like nowhere else. You don't mind that? You like it here?"

He shrugged. "It's a nice kind of weird. Maybe I was always looking for a place that was a bit different. You get used to it."

"I don't think I want to get used to it," I said. "I just came here because my brother—" I stopped, aware that Ruiner was staring at me.

"Your brother?" Ben asked. "Is he in Hollowbeck?"

"Um, no. I came here to get something for him."

"Oh. That's nice of you." He tapped his fingertips on the tablecloth, the skin warmly dark against the red and white checks. "So you'd never been here before?"

"No?"

"That's very unusual. I've…" He hesitated, looking at me almost shyly. "I've been making a bit of a study of Hollowbeck, you know. Because it isn't on any maps. None at all. The tourist season is very precise. It starts on the 15th of May and ends on the 15th of August, and there are no tourists outside those times. And the people that come outside those times are either invited or … Well, they *need* to come here, say."

I frowned at him. "Well, my brother told me about it," I said.

"I suppose that would count as an invitation," he said, almost to himself. "Was *he* invited by someone?"

"I have no idea," I said shortly, and opened my menu. "What's good here?"

For a moment I thought he was going to keep pushing, and honestly, I love libraries and by extension librarians, but this one was poking around crime scenes with the mayor and interrogating me over dinner. I was going off him, dimples or not.

But he just said, "The pasta's really good. Homemade."

"Carbonara it is, then," I said, and closed the menu. We sat in an uncomfortable silence, broken only by Ruiner chasing his fleas. "Stop it," I said to him, and he bared his teeth at me.

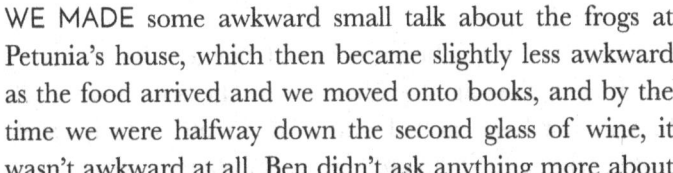

WE MADE some awkward small talk about the frogs at Petunia's house, which then became slightly less awkward as the food arrived and we moved onto books, and by the time we were halfway down the second glass of wine, it wasn't awkward at all. Ben didn't ask anything more about my brother, or suggest I was *meant* to be here somehow, and by the time he waved us off outside the restaurant, I was quite happy to agree to go to the library for a tea the next day. At least he wasn't sniffing my hand.

Ruiner and I walked the quiet, flower-scented streets back to the B&B, his tail swinging with his soft gait. There was no sign of Petunia as we let ourselves in, and we padded up the creaking stairs to the attic room. The bedside light was still on inside and on the stairs outside was a small pile of towels with a little note that said, *If you need anything, just let me know.* It was somehow reassuring that she'd left the towels there rather than going into the room. The grimoire was hidden and it wasn't like we had anything worth stealing, but it was still nice to know that we had some little space that was our own.

I thought about a cold bath, but in the end I just put my pajamas on and climbed into bed with Ruiner sitting on the pillow next to me. It had been a long time since we had shared a bed and there was something odd about it, even if he was in cat form. I set the grimoire on the bed and then picked up the envelope, which I'd fished out of the pocket of my shorts. The paper was heavy and softly textured, and I felt like I was leaving sweaty prints all over it.

"You have to read it," Ruiner said, his voice low. "We need to know what it says, who it's from."

I turned it over in my fingers. "You really don't know anything about this, about how she might've had my name, *anything?*"

"I don't," he said.

And for once I believed him. I opened the envelope, my fingers shaking. I wished it was because I was still hungry, but I was stuffed with a large plate of truly excellent carbonara, followed by a substantial serving of tiramisu which had been as good as Isabella had promised. I could see myself spending an awful lot of time in Mystic Munchies if we stayed in town. Not that we were going to stay, of course. That wasn't an option.

The paper inside the envelope was of the same heavy stock as the envelope, the sort of thing you find in expensive stationery gift sets that are never actually used. The writing was in blue ink, in a looping, curling hand. At the top of the note was just my name, *Morgan Winters*. No *dear* or *to*, just *Morgan Winters*. And underneath that, *Leave Hollowbeck. Your life depends on it.* Beneath that, *Your soul depends on it.*

And that was it. There was no signing off. There was no name, no stamp, not even a stray ink blob. There was no clue as to where it had come from whatsoever. I stared at it, then looked up to meet Ruiner's gaze.

"We've got the spell book," he said. "We should go."

"We can't," I said. "Theodore told us not to."

He looked at the piece of paper then back at me and said, "I think this kind of overrules that."

"What if we can't work the counter-curse?" I asked him. "Or even find it? What if we need an actual witch to do that?"

"Then we'll find one," he said, and I blinked at him. He sighed. "I know I'm a knob sometimes. I know I drag you into things, and you always help, and it's not fair. But this is different, Morgan. This is serious. We have to leave."

I turned the piece of paper over again, searching for some sign of what to do next, but there was nothing.

"Morgs? Are you alright?"

I folded the note, put it back in the envelope, and tucked it inside the grimoire, then lay down. Ruiner said something else, but I couldn't quite hear him, and after a moment he curled up next to me. The warmth of him was oddly reassuring, even if he was my idiot brother. I closed my eyes.

I didn't sleep, though. Sometime after I heard midnight chime on a clock deep within the house, I got up, went down to the bathroom, and ran a bath. The water was steaming hot as it chattered into the tub, and there were bottles arrayed along its side. I sniffed a few of them and chose one that had a soothing rosemary and lavender scent, then sprinkled a few drops into the bath. They curled and foamed, chasing each other up and down with the movement of the water — or I hoped it was with the movement of the water. Who knew in this house? This *town?*

A frog appeared from behind the toilet down pipe and nodded at me. I gave it a thumbs up and it vanished again, and I climbed into the bath. I lay there looking at the ceiling, which was mottled gently with damp and had decorative cornicing all around the edges and the light fitting.

Ruiner was right. The note was a threat, a *real* threat, and we needed to leave. We didn't have anything to do with the death, and I hardly thought the one-person Hollowbeck police force was going to be chasing us back into Yorkshire.

But at the same time, I was angry. I was tired of this. Tired of *everything.* I'd settled for a crappy job and a crappy apartment because they were still better than my crappy ex, and I'd even given up my own, non-crappy house just to get out of a very crappy relationship. Then I'd had to give up what little I had to help my crappy brother and chase around some wildly bizarre town that wasn't even on a map. And then, to add a cherry on my craptastic cake, someone was leaving me very not-crappy threats. It was ridiculous, and I was sick of it. I didn't want to run. I didn't want to be the one bending over and making allowances for someone else *again*.

And while I didn't want to think about it too much right now, something about Hollowbeck and its weirdness was oddly reassuring. The frogs watching from the drainpipes. The restaurant with its highchairs for cats. Our tattooed, vodka-and-elderflower landlady, and the out-and-out oddness of simply *everything*. So maybe I didn't want to *have* to leave. Maybe I wanted a choice, and for it to be *my* choice for once, not a choice made based on the needs of others.

Plus, I couldn't exactly go home at Christmas and tell Mum that my brother was now a cat. We needed to sort this, and our best chance of sorting it was staying in town. So that was what we were going to do. And once this was over, I was done with helping my brother. We were even. I'd had enough of picking up after him. After *everyone*.

That decision made, I slid underneath the water, lying there with my eyes closed and listening to the echoes of bubbles in my ears. It wasn't until I surfaced that I looked at the vials along the side of the bathroom and remembered the one at the murder scene. And I wondered that, if the vial had maybe been left by the murderer, then so might have the note.

Which seemed like a clue worth following.

EIGHT

Books against cats

I'D LEFT BOTH the curtains and the dormer windows open and the morning brought heavy, golden sun that cut across the room, carrying birdsong in with it. I ignored it for as long as I could, since my early hours decision to go hunting a murderer was starting to feel a little ridiculous with the morning light on it. Who did I think I was, Nancy Drew? I lacked the sports car and general teenaged perkiness, at the least. But the sound of Ruiner scratching had me sitting up before long.

"Get your fleas off the bed," I said to him.

"I don't have fleas," he said, swapping the scratching for chewing on his fur instead, sounding like he was trying to suck it out by the roots.

"Then you've got very poor personal hygiene," I replied, and picked up my phone from the bedside. I'd never been the sort of person who was glued to it, but I'd barely even glanced at it yesterday. I should've had at least ten newsletters I didn't remember signing up for, twenty-three marketing emails from companies I'd bought from once and never would again, and an offer of three million

78

dollars if I just supplied my bank account details to a nice gentleman in a country I'd never heard of. There was nothing. I stared at it, then checked the signal. Zero bars. We were in town, and the house was plain old brick, not a concrete bunker. There should've been *something.* I dropped it back on the bedside table with a sigh and went to brush my teeth.

The kettle was already on when we went downstairs, steaming softly on the old cooking range. A loaf of fresh bread sat out on the kitchen table, round and crusty and inviting, with a dish of butter and a pot of homemade marmalade next to it. Petunia was nowhere to be seen.

I busied myself with making a cup of tea since I couldn't find any coffee in the cupboards. There were various seeds and grains and powders and things in unlabeled jars stacked on the shelves, but I decided that it was probably best not to try any of them unsupervised in case we both ended up as cats for the next ten years, or however long a cat lived. I found a plate of fish in the fridge with a note that said "for Ruiner," with a little heart underneath, so I chopped some up and put it in a bowl on the floor for him.

"You're eating better than I do," I told him. "Can't remember the last time I had fresh fish."

He sniffed. "You get to use a knife and fork. You get to have cake. You get to have tea. I'm eating raw fish off the floor. It's hardly better."

I couldn't really disagree as I carved a large wedge of still slightly warm bread off the loaf. "Well, I suppose there's got to be some advantages to being a human," I told him.

"Put my plate on the table, at least."

"Best not," I said, thinking of the way the light had seemed to change last night when Petunia had suddenly taken a serious turn. "You can survive eating from the floor for a bit."

"You suck." But he went back to his plate, and we ate in silence for a moment while Clarence — or a frog, anyway, as I still hadn't quite worked out if there were multiple frogs or just one really mobile one — watched us from the terrarium. Finally, Ruiner sat back on his haunches and said, "We should get moving before Constable Carrot Cake turns up again. Get your bag."

"Sergeant Carrot Cake, and it's daytime. He's not turning up." I took a breath. "And I'm not getting my bag."

"Why not?"

"Because we're not leaving."

My brother stared at me, his ears twitching as if he were listening for movement deep in the house, attackers or stalkers or monsters. "Morgan," he started, the familiar irritation in his voice, then he stopped. When he spoke again his tone was different, edged with anxiety. "I told you, it's too dangerous. You can't stay."

This was not my brother, not with the concern in his voice and the way he was shifting his paws. My brother had never done guilt in his life, other than the performative, insincere sort. It made me more afraid than even the body had. "Tell me why not."

"Because someone left a note for you," he replied. "A seriously *threatening* note. You can't just ignore that."

"I'm not ignoring it. But we came here to get you out of cat form. If we leave, that's not going to happen. And besides, I've got a lead."

"A *what?*"

"A lead. To figure out who killed Norma."

"Oh, *well.* If you've got a lead. That sounds super

important, you know, figuring out who killed some bloody witch."

"It is," I replied. "Because the note was left with the body. And whoever wrote the note could also have killed Norma."

"Well, let Theodore sort it out, then," he said. "Or Isabella, or your stuffy new librarian buddy. They're all in the middle of it, and they're not being threatened. Leave it to Team Weird."

"You're a human in a cat's body," I said. "You can't call anyone weird." I spread marmalade generously on another slice of bread, finished off my tea, and got up. "Come on, we're going."

"Where? Since we're evidently not being sensible and leaving?"

"To do some research."

IT WAS WARM OUTSIDE ALREADY, promising heavy heat in the day to come, and the trees were weighted with sunlight and a very soft breeze that set the leaves whispering. A dog barked a few houses down, but otherwise nothing moved except the ever-present birds, singing with weary enthusiasm.

I took my phone out and checked it as we walked to the street, wondering if there was some sort of magical weather-generator sitting over Hollowbeck. Two days of this sort of heat wasn't exactly Cumbria's M.O.

"This is really strange," I said, tipping the screen so Ruiner could see it where he trotted next to me. "There's no signal at all. I thought there'd be some outside, at least."

"Not that strange. There's no phone signal in Hollowbeck."

I stared at him. "Nothing? That's impossible. Nowhere has no phone signal unless you're in … I don't know, the outer Himalayas or something."

"They've probably got more phone signal there," he said. "It's just another one of those Hollowbeck things. There's no mobile phones, no internet."

"No *internet?* How's that possible? What do people do if they want to…" I waved vaguely, suddenly unable to come up with a single important reason for internet. "Look at cat videos or check the weather or something?"

He snorted. "There's a weather clock in the town hall that's more accurate than anything outside town, and I don't think cat videos are as entertaining as magic-working. If you want internet, you've got to leave town." He looked at me pointedly.

I sighed, poked my phone a couple of times, and then put it back in my pocket. "Fine. In that case, we're going for tea."

"Going for tea where? And since when do you drink tea?"

"Since always," I said, which wasn't entirely true. Tea might be the national drink, but in my mind, it was a pale substitute for coffee, fit only for sick days and old ladies at afternoon knitting groups. "And we're going to the library."

"Oh, not the bloody librarian."

"Not the librarian, the library," I said, picking up my pace.

He trotted along behind me. "Hollowbeck is not the place to start dating. He's probably half-goblin or something."

"What—" I stopped myself. The goblin question was going to have to wait. "It's not a date. If we've got no internet, we have to go to the old-fashioned internet, and that means the library. It means books, Ruiner."

"I hate books," he said.

"Another reason to doubt you're my brother," I replied, heading down the street.

"Wait, we're *walking?*"

"It's good for you."

"I've only got little legs," he complained, and I picked up my pace. I intended to use every advantage the human form gave me.

THE LIBRARY WAS ALREADY OPEN when we got there, the lights glowing beyond the doors. Stepping into the cool, book-scented interior felt like stepping home, and I paused on the threshold to take a deep, slow breath. There were a lot of windows, both on the mezzanine and down on the main floor. With the wooden shelves and flooring, I had the sense that I was being encircled in the warm heart of a forest full of stories.

I savoured it for a moment, Ruiner silent next to me, and then padded down the steps toward the desk. It was empty today, no Isabella and no Ben, but as I hesitated, a woman appeared from behind me in the stacks. She was about my height, with thick dark hair, wearing a teal tartan dress and heavy boots.

"Oh, sorry — you can't have him in here," she said, pointing at Ruiner.

"He's an emotional support animal?" I offered.

"I'm terribly sorry, no exceptions unless you have a permit." She raised her eyebrows at me, and I shook my head.

"It's more of an informal arrangement."

"Well, then. I can't let him in, I'm afraid. The problem is, if we let one animal in, we have to let them all in, and the next thing you know we've got the baby alligator eating someone's poodle all over again. Not to mention the mess the cockatoo made in the rare books section."

I stared at her, wondering if any of that was true, but she just smiled.

"He can wait outside for you."

I looked at Ruiner, and he glared back at me. "Off you go. Wait outside," I said. He growled, tail flicking, then turned and stalked back up the steps and stood at the door, looking back at us. "Oh, right."

I ran up to let him out, and he hissed at me, "Don't hang around. Just do your bloody research and get back out here."

"Of course," I said and trotted back down the steps.

"Terribly sorry about that," the librarian said again.

"It's no problem," I said. "Nice to be free of him for a bit." She gave me a puzzled look and I added, "Is Ben in?"

She looked around vaguely, as if expecting him to materialize in front of us. "He should be around here somewhere. Shall I tell him he has a visitor?"

"No, that's fine. Can you point me to a section on runes or something like that?"

She directed me into the depths of the shelves off to the left of the desk on the ground floor and I pattered off, feeling both relieved and vaguely uncomfortable without my brother trailing along behind me.

The section on runes was massive, and it was next to the witchcraft section, which was even bigger. It seemed to sprawl through one entire wing of the library, shiny new paperbacks rubbing shoulders with feathery pamphlets with crumbling pages and great heavy tomes that looked like scaled-up versions of the grimoire still tucked under my bed at Petunia's. Everything smelt of dust and old stories and a strange crack of ozone, and I had the oddest sense that more than usual care should be afforded to these books. They had *presence*.

It was hard to tell where to start among the crammed shelves, but I supposed I might as well just take a stab at any of them. I pulled my phone from my pocket again and checked the photo I'd taken of the vial and the rune on the label, then chose a shelf and started pulling the books out one by one.

I'd been in there for about an hour, and I still hadn't found the exact rune I was looking for, even though there appeared to be about five treatises on each and every rune known to humanity in here. I was sitting on the floor with books strewn all around me, trying to narrow them down to ones that were almost right, but *so many* of them were almost right, just a small angle or extra squiggle out, when an amused voice said, "Finding everything you need?"

I looked up to find Ben leaning against the shelves with his hands in his pockets, smiling slightly. I looked guiltily at the books splayed face-down on the floor, and his grin widened. "Not really," I said. "And I'm also wondering if any of these are likely to bite me."

"Usually not," he said. "We keep the bitey ones down-stairs, mostly." He held up a hand, the fingertips bandaged, and I blinked at it. "What are you looking for?"

I hesitated. Ruiner evidently had his own reasons for being suspicious of everyone in Hollowbeck, but Ben and Isabella had been more than helpful the day before, and I wasn't going to get anywhere on my own. I wasn't even close to figuring out what the rune meant, and it was the only lead I had to who was threatening me. Besides, Ben was a librarian. If you can't trust a librarian, who can you trust?

I zoomed in on the rune on my phone and handed it to him. "Have you seen this before?"

He examined it, his face expressionless, then said, "Where did you find it?"

Saying *poking around at the crime scene* seemed like a bad choice, librarian or not, so I said, "It's just a thing I found."

"A thing?"

"Yes, it was at Petunia's house," I said, remembering the vials on the side of the bath. "In the bathroom. I wasn't quite sure if it was something I could put in my bath or not."

He smiled, crouching down next to me so that we could both see the photo. "It's pretty safe. This is a symbol for whisperwind."

"Whisperwind? What's that? Some sort of digestive relief?"

He laughed. "No, it's a sedative, basically. It makes all noises quiet as a whisper."

"She's leaving *sedatives* by the side of the guest bath? That seems risky."

"Well, it's not a sedative like we think of them. It's not Valium or anything. You put a couple of drops in the bath, or even your tea, and it just takes the edge off the world. It quiets everything down."

"That sounds like Valium."

"Maybe?" He looked doubtful. "A lot of people use it around here, anyway."

"A lot of people put some sort of esoteric Valium in their baths? Is life that stressful here?"

He snorted. "Don't ask about the herbs Petunia grows out the back if you're worried about a little chemical help. But whisperwind's safe enough — just don't put the whole bottle in. You'll be fine with a few drops."

"What would happen if I put the whole bottle in?"

"Well, it'd knock you out," he replied, giving me a puzzled look. "Why? Are you planning to try it?"

I ignored the question. "Would I wake up again?"

"Sure, but the bath'd be pretty cold by the time you did."

"Okay, good to know." I took my phone back, then looked at him, crouching in front of me with his hands hanging loosely between his knees. He was wearing a short-sleeved shirt with flamingos on it and his jeans were wearing through at the knee.

"You know quite a lot about these things."

He shrugged and waved at the shelves. "You've seen the size of this section. In most libraries, it's one shelf at the most. So even before I realised how odd Hollowbeck was, I started reading up on things. You have to know what matters to the community if you're going to be any good as a librarian."

"That makes sense." I looked around at the books on the floor. "I guess I didn't need to dig all these out, then."

"I'll help you re-shelve them." He started collecting the books, and I closed the one on my lap.

"Whisperwind, though — could it get confused with something else?"

"Why?"

"There were a lot of other vials in the bathroom, and, well … Petunia's a bit old. She could have got them mixed up."

"If you're worried, you can get some bubble bath from the grocery store," he said.

"I'm not worried exactly, just curious. It just seems a bit risky having a sedative by the bath in a guesthouse."

He nodded, picking up his pile of books and starting to return them to the shelves. "She might not have thought anything of it. As I said, lots of people use it here. The only thing you've got to be careful with is combining it with other substances, but that's the same as anything. You know, like bleach and vinegar can react to give you chlorine gas. Everything's dangerous if it's used in the wrong way."

I nodded, getting up and wincing as my knees clicked. "So don't mix my weird bath vials, then?"

"Exactly." He collected some more books from my hoard on the floor. "This seems like a lot of trouble to go to. Why didn't you just ask Petunia?"

"I didn't want to insult her," I said, slotting a book back into place.

"That's wise. You don't want to get turned into a frog."

I gave him a startled look. "A frog? Wait, you mean like all the frogs at the house?"

He grinned. "Do you want that cup of tea?"

"Yes. I also want to know more about frogs."

He laughed and handed me another pile of books. "Get these put away, and I'll tell you about frogs while we have our tea."

"Fair."

NINE

Dangerous optimism

WE SHELVED the books in companionable silence, although I didn't get mine back as neatly or as quickly as Ben did, and I saw him quietly re-shelving a couple that I'd put in the wrong place. But we were done quickly enough, and he led me deeper into the library.

"Where's your cat?" he asked as we walked.

"Outside," I said. "He wasn't allowed in."

"No, the books are a bit..." He hesitated. "We have to be cautious about animals coming in here."

I looked at him and said, "You were going to say the books don't like the animals being in here, weren't you?"

"Sort of. Which sounds like I've been sniffing too much book glue."

I raised my eyebrows at him. "You've just told me that my landlady is turning people into frogs, and I'm a bit worried because I don't know how long I'll be here, or how I'm going to pay her if the tab runs out. Stroppy books hardly rate a mention."

He laughed. "Just don't suggest that she's trying to kill people with the bath salts, and always compliment her cooking, and I'm sure you'll be fine. I stayed there for a while when I first got here, and I didn't get turned into a frog."

"Not even briefly?" I asked.

"Not that I know of," he said, and stuck his tongue out at me. He immediately looked mortified. "Sorry, that was meant to be a frog impression."

"You need to work on that," I said, grinning.

Ben led me into a clean, white-walled corridor with lights sunk into the ceiling, in the far corner of the library. From there he took me into a small, cluttered staffroom that was stacked with books in need of repair, piles of fliers for book fairs and library sales, and a noticeboard crammed with calendar pages, notes, and reminders. He ambled across to a kitchenette area and switched a kettle on, taking two mismatched mugs from a cupboard.

I picked up one of the damaged books, running my finger down its spine. "These look a bit well used."

"Yeah, they don't always get returned in the best condition. I seem to spend half my time repairing them."

"That's got to be frustrating. Don't you fine people or anything?"

"No," he said. "It's sort of an understanding that a lot of the books in this library get well used. We have a smaller fiction section and a larger…" He paused to search for the word. "A larger arcane section, shall we say."

"*Arcane*," I said. "So that's the fancy way of saying you've got lots of magic books like the ones with the runes and people go out and they try to do things with them, then bring them back looking like this." I shook the book slightly, and a piece of old bread and half a centipede fell out. We gave a simultaneous "*Eww*," and I put the book down hurriedly.

"That's pretty much it," he said.

I wondered if I should just say, *Look, I know Hollowbeck's a properly magic town, and my brother's been turned into a cat. Can you help me?* But Ruiner was trying, in his own ineffectual way, to keep me safe, and as much as my brother was annoying as hell, I needed to try and keep *him* safe. So all I said was, "Well, that must make the job a bit interesting," and took the cup of tea that he offered me. It was full of floating leaves and soft little flowers again, although I noticed today's blooms were blue rather than yellow. "Is this a mix from one of these books? Is it going to wipe my memory of ever being here?"

He sorted. "No, it's camomile."

I looked at the floating flowers. "I thought camomile flowers were yellow?"

He checked his own tea. "Oh, right. That's not camomile. It's deadly nightshade."

"*What?*" I just about dropped the mug and he grabbed it, laughing.

"Sorry. *Sorry.* Very bad joke. Terrible joke. I'm not used to having someone around."

"You've got the woman who works in the library," I said, examining my tea suspiciously. "I just saw her."

"Oh, Dee," he said. "Yes. Someone different around, then."

We looked at each other, and I thought again that I should just tell him. But no, I'd come in here for one thing, and that was to find out what was in the vial. And mission accomplished, although it definitely hadn't handed us either a murder weapon or a suspect. Windy whisper or whatever it was sounded like it was both common, and also shouldn't have done too much to Norma. Unless it had been a way to relax her enough that the killer could walk in unnoticed.

"Do you have a brother?" I asked him suddenly.

"Yes," he said. "Most annoying person I've ever met."

"Me too," I said. "Almost as annoying as cats."

He nodded. "Yeah, that's siblings."

And then the moment to say anything about cat transformations and murdered witches was gone, so we sat there and talked about broken books and overrated books and books we liked, and the annoyances of younger siblings. I couldn't remember the last time I'd sat down and talked to someone without wanting to break things or divorce them. Possibly both. It was both reassuringly normal and wildly uncomfortable, because through it all I knew I was going to have to go back to figuring out a murder and a cat-brother.

But not just yet.

∽

FINALLY, I finished my tea and stood up, thinking of Ruiner outside. "I should probably go. My phone doesn't work here, and I suppose at some point someone'll be looking for me about ... well, you know."

Ben nodded, taking both our mugs over to the sink to rinse out. "Yeah, the phone thing's annoying. You do get used to it, though."

"What about if I want to let someone know that I'm here?" I asked. "I didn't even see a phone at Petunia's." Not that I'd looked, but given the fact that showers and electric lighting on the stairs were considered a bit too modern, I wasn't holding out much hope.

"Like your partner or something?" Ben said, with a studied casualness that was almost as funny as the question itself.

I snorted loudly enough that he gave me a startled look. "No. But my mother may want to talk to me at some stage."

"Oh," he said. "Yeah, I quite like not having the phone because of that."

I laughed properly this time. "There are advantages, aren't there?"

He grinned and said, "Yes, there are. And there are landlines. You're welcome to use the library one if you need to call anyone."

"Thanks. For everything." For making me laugh in the face of the absolute madness of the last couple of days, and for making me forget for a moment that someone was threatening me, and for being an oasis of normality in the middle of chaos.

I dusted my hands off, looked at them, and then held one out for him to shake. Which immediately felt enormously awkward, and I don't know why I did it, but he took my hand gravely, and we shook. "I'll see you soon, I guess."

"Yes," he said. We were still holding hands when Isabella came through the door. Both of us yelped and jumped apart, and she lavished us with an enormous smile.

"Hello, dears," she said. "Are you getting on all right?"

"Good," I said. "I was just having a cup of tea."

"Morgan was wondering if Petunia was trying to kill her with bath salts," Ben said, and I scowled at him.

"I don't think so," Isabella said, her voice thoughtful. "You've only been there one night, so I don't think you've had time to upset her. Besides, if you're annoying her, she'll tell you, and if you keep annoying her, she'll turn you into a frog."

I stared at her, but she wasn't laughing. She just looked back at me with luminously dark eyes and gave me a reassuring smile.

"Good to know," I said. "I'll stop worrying about the bath salts and start worrying about the frog thing, then."

"I wouldn't *worry*," Isabella said. "Just keep it in mind." She pressed her hands together and added, "I just wanted to pass on a message from Theodore. His preliminary verdict is that poor Norma's death was accidental, but he'd rather like you to remain in town until he's absolutely sure." She thought about it. "Actually, I think he said you *must* remain in town, but there we are. His social graces are not always where one would like."

"Oh," I said. "Really? But we've answered all his questions."

"Theodore is quite the perfectionist," Isabella said. "I'm sure he'll come to a proper conclusion soon, though. He's very efficient."

I thought of the note and the grimoire, otherwise known as *items removed from a crime scene*, still tucked under the bed upstairs, and wondered if he was somehow aware that they were missing. Or the grimoire, at least. Witches were probably expected to have things like that on hand at all times or something. "He thinks it was an accident, though?"

"He does. What with poor Norma being in the cauldron, it seems likely she was overcome with heat and possibly a little chemical help while having a restorative soak. She was a habitual user of certain sedatives to help with her nerves." She said it with perfect sympathy, but I thought there was a touch of disapproval in her face.

"Okay," I said. "Is soaking in cauldrons common practice around here?"

"Sometimes a full-body immersion is simply what is required."

"And no one's heard of baths?"

She smiled. "Of course. But if the fire's going anyway, it's cheaper to heat a cauldron than run a boiler."

I couldn't really argue that, given energy prices at the

moment. "So Theodore thinks she took too much of this sedative?"

"It seems so."

"What was it?"

She gave me a curious look. "Whisperwind. It's very common around here."

"So I've heard," I said, looking at Ben, but he just straightened a stack of fliers on the table. "I thought it wasn't dangerous, though."

"So much depends on the dose," Isabella said with a little sigh. "One's resistance grows over time to anything that's used habitually." She inclined her head. "I am sorry that we must insist you stay, but I hope that you would choose to do so anyway. We do love having you here, and there is a place in Hollowbeck for you." She pressed her hands to her bosom, gave us both a nod, and then she was gone, presumably out the door, although I somehow wasn't entirely sure.

I looked at Ben. "I thought you said whisperwind couldn't kill you."

He shrugged. "Maybe it was a particularly strong blend, or she had other products in her system. She even could have had an underlying condition she wasn't aware of." He nodded as if to confirm it to himself, still looking at his fliers. "Probably that, in fact. That'd be my guess."

I waited, but he just moved on to sorting a jumble of old paperbacks, and after a moment I said, "Right. I better go, then. See how I'm going to pay Petunia."

He looked at me finally. "I'm sure Isabella will cover it for as long as you're not allowed to leave."

"Maybe," I said, and hurried out the door.

～

I FOUND Ruiner sitting on the grass under a tree, ignoring the crows that were screaming bird obscenities at him from the branches above. His ears were back, tail flicking irritably, and he stood up as I left the path to join him.

"About bloody time," he said. "Damn birds have been harassing me the whole time you were smooching about in there with your bloody librarian."

"We've got a problem," I said, ignoring his complaints.

"I don't want to hear about your love life," he replied. "I'm being *harassed*. By *birds*. And an old lady grabbed me and tried to stuff me in her shopping bag. I had to bite her."

"*Had* to?"

"If I didn't want to be taken home and forced to wear knitted bonnets or something, yeah."

I sighed. "Theodore's saying we still can't leave town."

"Theodore, the police officer who only comes out at night? Let me see how we might be able to get around that…" He trailed off, scrunching his eyes half-closed in what was probably meant to be a thoughtful expression.

"No, you muppet," I said, glancing at the crows, then lowering my voice. Not that they could *actually* be listening, but, well. Maybe they could. "I already said we needed to figure out who did this. Now we *really* need to, because if Theodore realises Norma's book's gone, and someone saw us take it…" I trailed off, looking at him with my eyebrows raised. A crow cawed, and I glanced at it, shivering.

Ruiner stared at me. "We don't need to figure it out. We need to *leave*."

I ran a hand back over my hair, then turned and headed toward the road, Ruiner trotting after me. Outside the library, the heat was already raising sweat on my forehead. "We can't. We need to find out who killed the witch."

"I heard a house fell on her." He bared his teeth at me in what was probably meant to be a grin. "Look, even if it wasn't an accidental death, Norma's not our responsibility."

"I know she's not, but people saw us going into the shop. It'd be easy enough for us to be blamed for it, and even more so if we run."

"Who saw us?"

"Anyone on that street," I pointed out, then remembered. "Also, there was a magpie, and the big blond guy from Mystic Munchies. The one that looks like a Viking."

"Asger," Ruiner said, then shrugged when I looked at him. "I've had a beer with him before. When did he see us?"

"When I was trying not to vomit on the pavement," I said.

Ruiner glanced behind us, but the crows had stayed in the tree by the library. "I don't think he's much of an issue, but I suppose you're right. Anyone could've seen us."

"I know." We were silent for a moment as we headed back in the direction of the guest house, then I said, "Also, behave yourself at Petunia's, because apparently if you don't it gets you turned into a frog."

"*What?*" He glared at me. "We *have* to leave. Being a cat is bad enough."

I spread my hands. "You know our best chance of changing you back to annoying human rather than annoying cat is by staying here."

"I'm not annoying. I'm entirely charming in any form."

"You keep telling yourself that."

"So what do you think we're going to do?" he asked. "A cat and a stranger in a magical town?"

"Find out who the killer is. And if they left the note."

"*How?*"

"I don't know. I'll figure it out."

"Figure *what* out, Morgan? How to get yourself killed?"

I stopped walking and looked at him. His tail was whipping from side to side, and his pupils were all but invisible in the bright sunlight. "What do you know about the note, Ruiner?"

"*Nothing.* But we should take the book and get out of here before you get arrested. There're witches in other places. We don't need to stay."

"Why are you so keen to leave? I thought you said you were all into this magic thing."

"Why are you so keen to solve the murder of someone you've never even met and don't even know?"

"Because I don't want it pinned on me due to you and your thieving bloody paws."

He sighed. "There'll be other suspects. *Better* suspects. She wasn't a good person, Morgan."

"What do you mean?"

He looked away from me, ears back, and I saw a sigh heave through his tiny frame. "I told you about the favours, right?"

"Yes." We'd stopped in the middle of the pavement, and now I beckoned him to a bench under a willow tree, where we could sit down next to each other and talk a little more easily. It was surprisingly hard to hold a quiet conversation with the height difference between a cat and a human. I checked for crows, then said, "Explain."

Ruiner jumped up next to me then onto the back of the bench where we could be more or less at eye level. "So the favours that she asks, it's not like, *get the groceries in.*"

"I had figured that," I said.

"I only had to take a letter, but the person I took it to vanished right after. I don't know if they left town, I don't know if someone vanished them, but the rumours were that they'd made a sneaky business deal and cut their business partner out of a load of money. It reverted to the business partner after they vanished."

"So the letter was a threat?"

"At the least. Norma brokered favours. She never got her own hands dirty, but if someone wanted something *fixed*, she called in various favours to do the job. She was always a couple of steps removed from everything, but that's also why I ended up seeing her. I owed someone money, and she took the debt on and got me doing favours."

I rubbed my forehead. "Ruiner—"

"I know, it was stupid. I've done a lot of stupid things. But I was just carrying notes. I didn't think it'd be dangerous to anyone."

"But how do you *always* do this? How are you *always* getting yourself in these messes? What d'you do — have a daily newsletter subscription to *101 Ways To Screw Up My Life?*"

He looked at me, then down at his paws. "I just always think it's going to work out. Sometimes it does."

"With my help," I said, and sighed. "Your optimism is bloody dangerous, Ruiner."

"I know." He sounded almost contrite again, and it made me vaguely uncomfortable. Cauldron baths and hungry books seemed much less strange than my brother being *contrite*. I shivered despite the heat, looking for crows again.

TEN

The shop will go on

WE SAT THERE in silence for a little while, before I leaned back in the bench, crossing my legs at the ankles and looking up at the dappled light coming through the foliage. There was no point dwelling on my brother's terminally foolish life choices, or how often they ended with me breaking up fights, paying someone off, or otherwise being dragged into things that really shouldn't concern me. At least I didn't have Jason to worry about now too. Let his younger, newer model tidy up after him.

I looked at Ruiner. "These notes — what sort of paper were they on?"

"The same as the one you got," he said.

"So it might've been Norma herself threatening me, but more likely it was someone who she was brokering a deal for? Someone else was meant to take the note to me as a favour?"

"That'd be my guess."

"But why? What do I have to do with *anything*, other than you?"

He shuffled his paws. "I don't know. And I swear I never told anyone about you, Morgs. Not anything about my family."

I'd closed my eyes for a moment, and now I squinted at him. "Mum?"

"No! And anyway, anyone who went after her would be defeated by the etiquette required to get in the door."

I gave a half-hearted snort of laughter. This was true. Along with our mother's obsession with European royalty went a fixation on The Way To Do Things, which involved convoluted place settings, guest slippers, and frequent reporting on the social failings of our neighbours. Which would have merely been eccentric if our family had come from some sort of old money, but as money seemed to be a mystery to all of us, it was just annoying.

"Why are you really so worried about being found as a cat?" I asked my brother. He didn't answer straight away, and I said, "Tell me the truth for once, Ruiner. Everything else is making zero sense, so at least give me that."

He stared down the street and said, "I'm not worried about being found as a cat. I'm worried about being found as *me*."

"Why?" I asked again.

"Because I did more than one favour in town," he said. "And I almost got caught doing the second favour."

"What was it?"

"There was a witch starting up a rival shop, and Norma wanted to make sure it didn't work out."

"Nice. She really does sound like a gem. So what did you do?"

He hesitated, then said, "Well, it was kind of a seduction thing."

"*Eww.* And that was going to help how?"

"It wasn't," he said. "It was a distraction, so I could plant some curses at Grace's shop. She lived above it."

"You know how to do curses?"

"They were already made. Norma gave them to me in little packets and I just had to leave them somewhere in the shop."

"And what happened then?" I asked.

"And then the shop burnt down," he said, and there was a catch in his voice. "I didn't know that would happen. I thought it was just a curse to stop her getting any customers. To drive people away or render her bankrupt or something. I mean, Norma just said that it would make sure she didn't succeed. I didn't think the whole place would burn down." He took a breath. "Grace got out, but she lost everything."

I thought about it for a moment and said, "And then she cursed you?"

"No," he said. "The cat thing is completely unrelated. I wasn't even in Hollowbeck."

"Wow. You've outdone yourself this time."

"Call it a talent," he said, and he sounded tired. "Seems like even when I don't mean to, I still upset someone."

"Yeah, well, burning down someone's home and livelihood will probably do that."

We looked at each other, and finally he said, "So you see why I don't want to be in town? People knew I worked with Norma. And Grace is still here, as far as I know. She's got friends. Being a cat is going to be the least of my problems if one of them catches up to me."

"Yeah, I do see that. But it doesn't change the fact that my name was on one of Norma's envelopes, and if what you're telling me about how she worked is right, someone gave my name to her. Someone really is after me, and that won't have changed because she's dead. Why me, Ruiner?"

"I don't know," he said. "And I really mean that. I never meant you to even know about any of this. I'm a knob, but I'm not that much of a knob. I wouldn't endanger you."

I looked up and down the street then back at him and said, "Frogs. *Frogs*, Ruiner."

"I didn't see that coming," he said. "I've never stayed anywhere where the landlady turns you into frogs."

"Neither have I," I said. "And I wouldn't have if you weren't around."

We sat for a little longer, silent on the park bench, and watched a stocky young man walking an ostrich on a leash go past. Then Ruiner said, "You're not going to give it up, are you? You're really not going to leave."

"No," I said. "There's no point. You weren't in town when you got turned into a cat. There's nothing to say that whoever's after me won't track me down outside Hollowbeck. Here at least we've got a chance of finding something out. Otherwise, they could just sneak up on me. I could be working at a bloody supermarket and someone'll come along and turn me into a frog."

"Stop obsessing about being turned into a bloody frog," he said.

"It's a little hard to stop obsessing about it. You've been turned into a cat."

We looked at each other for a long moment, then he said, "Right, fine, we're staying here. You'll get away with me following you around, at least, because half the town's got a familiar."

"Like the ostrich," I said, pointing down the street.

"That may be a fashion choice. I've never heard of an ostrich familiar. Seems risky."

"I've never heard of an ostrich as a fashion choice. Seems riskier."

"Whatever. You just pretend to be a bit magic, or at least aspiring to be magic, if anyone talks to you. How do you want to start?"

"I don't know," I said. "Ben told me that the mark on the vial was for whisperwind, which is just a light sedative. It can't kill you unless it's mixed with other things. But Isabella said Theodore thinks the whisperwind might have killed her."

."That doesn't make any sense," Ruiner said. "Whisperwind's really common, and she was a witch. She'd have known how to take it." He thought about it. "We could go back to the shop, see if there were any other vials about the place or anything."

I looked at him and said, "Finally, a decent suggestion. You can sneak in a window and let me in."

"It won't be locked," he said. "No one locks anything in this town."

"That seems very careless in a place where people can turn you into frogs," I said.

Ruiner growled and jumped off the bench, already starting to pad down the road. "I'm going to get very sick of this frog thing. It's almost as bad as the cat thing."

"Wait till I get turned into one," I said. "I'll follow you around ribbeting endlessly."

"Joy."

THE COSY CAULDRON, to our surprise, was open, and not just in the sense of being unlocked. The cart of books was topped up, a couple of rotating displays of sun-faded postcards printed with fairies and pixies were sitting to either side of the door, and the purple flag wilted by the roadside. The sign on the door read, *Come in and discover magic!* Which we did — the come in part, anyway.

Music was playing softly, heavy on panpipes and chimes, and the scent of incense was so strong I coughed. Otherwise, nothing had changed. The taxidermy animals still stared down from the walls, and the gruesome mobiles moved gently in the wake of our passage. The shelves were still lined with the same strange collection of voodoo dolls and books and souvenir magnets, and I found myself checking for the rat. It wasn't there, but the shop wasn't empty, either. A young woman with a tangle of heavy, dark blonde hair done up in one of those annoyingly effortless high buns stood behind the counter, sifting through paint swatches.

"Hello," she said, lavishing an enormous smile on us. "Welcome to the Cosy Cauldron." Her voice was almost unbearably bright.

"Hi," I said. "You're open."

"Yes, we're open seven days, or sometimes six or five. Four, if necessary." She looked around and said almost to herself, "I need to hire some help." She seemed to notice me again and went back to her bright tones. "How may I serve you today?"

Ugh. "Wasn't there a crime here yesterday?" I asked.

She clutched her chest with both hands, dropping the paint swatches everywhere. "Oh, you're ... *Oh.* Theodore mentioned you. You must be Morgan. Morgan Winters and her cat." She held her hand out to me. "Starlight Moore."

Ruiner just stared at her, not giving anything away.

"Um, hi," I said, shaking her hand. "Why would Theodore mention me?"

"Well, Ruby too," she said. "Ruby said you had dinner

in Mystic Munchies, and Theodore said you found poor, dear Norma. What a horror!"

So much for keeping a low profile. I supposed that sort of thing never worked in small towns. "You worked with Norma?"

"Yes. I was off with a cold yesterday, otherwise I would have been the one to find the body. I'm terribly sorry you had to deal with that."

"It was a bit of a shock." Which she evidently didn't share. She was very bright and breezy for someone who'd been too sick to work the day before. "Were you close?"

She hesitated for the first time, and the customer service smile slipped. "Not really," she said, her voice quieter. "I'm a trainee witch, and I was trying to learn as much as possible. Norma called it an apprenticeship, which meant she didn't let me do much but clean things. And she didn't pay me, so it wasn't great." We shared the sympathetic look of the terminally underpaid and overworked.

"What's happening with the shop, then?" I asked.

Starlight shrugged. "I guess I'll keep it open and see what happens. I don't know who's going to be taking it over or anything. She didn't have any family that I know of."

"So you didn't really have to open it today then?"

"No," she agreed. "But the shop's a landmark, and we don't sell just to the tourists. The locals come in for their herbal blends and tinctures as well. I'm going to get the pot on and start work on those as soon as everything's tidied up."

I flinched, thinking about the cauldron out the back and wondering if that had been *tidied up*. If not, I wasn't buying anything from this shop, ever.

Starlight seemed to realise what I was thinking, and put

both hands over her mouth then said, "No, *no*, the cauldron's gone. Theodore took it. I have a new one on order, and for the moment, I'm just using a couple of stock pots I borrowed from Ruby. They're small, but they'll do for now."

"Right." I took a breath, wheezed on the incense, and said, "Isabella mentioned it might've been whisperwind that ... did it. Did Norma use it a lot?"

Starlight nodded. "She did." There was a note of disapproval in her voice. "She used a terrible amount. I did tell her that, you know, using so much would lead to a dependence and from the dependence could grow an addiction. And then she'd need more and more for it to be effective." She shook her head. "It's terribly sad."

"It is," I agreed. "So you think it was an accident?"

"What else would it be?" She picked up the paint swatches. "She simply lost track of how much she was taking." She gave me a bright smile. "I should get on with things. I have people waiting on some balms."

"Of course," I said. "Um, can you tell us anything else about her? I mean, was there anyone that maybe might have wanted to do her some harm?"

For a moment, the mask almost slipped again, then Starlight smiled brightly. "Absolutely not," she said. "We're not that sort of town. I mean, people carry little grudges and so on. We're all ... mostly human. But, you know, part of it is simply not being exposed to the chaos of the external world. So we're much more peaceable here than in other places. Any trouble we have comes in from the outside." Her voice was still sweet, but I could feel my hackles go up almost as clearly as Ruiner's currently were.

"Right," I said. "So you don't think anyone would have done anything to hurt her?"

"Of course not. She served this community. Many people came to her for charms and help, and she was always so willing to extend different payment plans to those that needed it and maybe couldn't afford as much. If anything, she was a hero." She pressed her hands to her chest again, smiling at me brightly. "I really must get on."

"Sure," I said. "Well, it was very nice to meet you."

"You too." And she just smiled at me, painfully brightly, until eventually I turned around and walked out of the shop, Ruiner trailing behind me.

We stepped back onto the pavement and I took a deep breath of fresher air, looking further down the street to Bewitching Brews. I checked I had some money in my wallet, then marched straight toward the coffeeshop, with Ruiner trotting at my heel.

"What are you doing?" he asked, barely loud enough for me to hear.

"Coffee," I said, my voice low as well. "I'm doing coffee because I cannot think about any of this without coffee."

"Any of what?" he said.

"What she told me about Norma completely contradicts what you told me."

"Yes, but I'm your brother," he pointed out. "You know I'm telling you the truth."

"Do I? Your track record's not exactly great."

"That's unfair."

"It's not, though, is it?"

We walked in silence for a long moment, then he said, "Morgan, someone's threatening your life. Your *soul*. And that's something I wouldn't lie about.

I looked at him, glaring up at me with those strange eyes, my mouth suddenly dry. I swallowed with difficulty, looked away and said, "I really need coffee."

I marched on toward Bewitching Brews, because the answer to many things in life is coffee. I wasn't sure if magical towns and threatening notes were included in those many things, but it seemed reasonable to find out. It certainly seemed a better option that tackling them *without* coffee.

ELEVEN

An infestation

BEWITCHING BREWS WAS the kind of coffee shop that every coffee shop aspires to be. It was situated on a corner, and under the green canopy that stretched over the pavement to offer deep, inviting shade, vines climbed up the shop walls and draped themselves over the seating area. There were little Parisian-style tables and chairs clustered to either side of the door, chunky cushions softening the seats, and half of them were occupied. Behind one of the big display windows, I could see a roasting machine, silent now, but shining with well-kept stainless steel and promising caffeine of the best sort.

Before we even reached the door, the scent of fresh-brewed coffee washed out to greet us, warm and familiar and reassuring, as if we weren't dealing with frogs and cats and witches in cauldrons. There were a few more tables inside, and stools at the counter, but none of them were occupied. Everyone was out in the sweet-scented shade beneath the vines.

Behind the counter, a tall, well-built man a bit younger

than me scowled fiercely at the mug in front of him as he shook the milk out onto it. He swore, gave me a guilty look, then said, "I don't know why, but they always come out looking like something a fifteen-year-old boy would draw. Intentionally, I mean, not by accident. But I swear I'm doing it by accident."

I stepped up to the counter and looked at the pattern in the mug. He was right. I thought he might've been going for a four-leaf clover, but it would've raised giggles in any classroom in the country. "Well, it's a statement," I said. "Have your customers got a sense of humour?"

"Not these ones," he said, then dragged a toothpick through the silky foam, turning the design into a very lopsided heart or possibly a paw print, if you were being generous.

"It's the thought that counts," I suggested.

"Maybe," he said. "Except not with this table." He nodded at the windows, toward a table of four women who looked the least eccentric of anyone I'd seen in Hollowbeck. There wasn't an iguana or a bat to be seen between them, although one had a tiny poodle in a diamanté collar on her lap. They were wearing summer dresses in deference to the heat, but something about them gave the impression that they wished they were in twinsets, with pearls waiting to be clutched. In fact, they looked like any collection of women of a certain age who got together to disapprove of Things Today.

"Ohhh," I said. "Yeah, that's probably not ideal latte art for them."

"Are you any good at this?" he asked, putting the messy coffee on a tray and picking up another cup.

"Excellent at drinking it," I said.

"You're no good then," he said, and winked at me,

then started on the next mug. I watched, wondering what he was going to create this time, and just then an older woman with a soft, multi-coloured scarf over her hair came out from the back with a platter of delicate-looking cakes in her hands. She leaned next to the younger man, examining his work, then set the tray down and pushed him aside. "Honestly, James, how many times do I have to tell you? I do the latte art, particularly for the Upstanding Ladies."

"You were busy," he protested, but picked up the platter and hurried out the door, leaving her to take over.

"The what now?" I asked.

She looked at me and smiled, the expression lighting up her whole face and deepening the laugh lines in the corners of her eyes. "The Upstanding Ladies of Hollowbeck. That's the name of their group."

I turned and looked at the little table again. They were all staring at the cakes James had set on the table, displeased looks on their faces while he pointed to each one, apparently describing them all. "That seems like a really odd thing to have here," I said, then realised how that sounded. "I mean ... not that Hollowbeck's not upstanding ... just with the witch shops and things?" I could feel my ears growing hotter and hotter, but the woman just laughed.

"Everywhere has its moral police," she said. "The only problem is they've got nowhere to eat which fits their standards, so they just swap around all of us and complain about everything." She shrugged. "It's not like anyone's going to stop."

"Stop what?" I asked.

"Charms in the coffee and spells in the milk," she replied. "It's what we do." She showed me the cup, which was wearing a delicate rendering of a multi-petalled rose in the cap of foam. "Poor James has no knack, though. He's quite unmagical."

"Poor James," I echoed, and looked at Ruiner. He twitched his ears at me, which I took to mean he didn't think much of charmed milk either. "Is that safe, though?"

She gave me an affronted look, then set the last cup on a tray. This one had a daffodil on it, and now I looked, every cup had a different flower, all perfectly drawn. "We wouldn't get much repeat business if it wasn't, dear."

"Right," I said, my ears heating up again. "Sorry."

James came back in, looked at the tray, then at the woman behind the counter. "Thanks, Aunt Edith," he said. "I'll let you take those out. I just had to eat a brownie and two different cookies to prove they weren't poisoned, and now they want them replaced."

His aunt shook her head and came out from behind the counter. She picked up the tray, the soft folds of her long purple dress flowing around her. It had glittering trees embroidered on the bodice, and she'd folded the sleeves back over strong forearms.

"*Honestly.* As if I'd poison a whole batch when I could just charm one." She headed out the door, and I watched her go, wondering when anything was going to start making sense again, or if my mental break theory when Ruiner had appeared on my windowsill had been right after all.

"What can I get you?" James asked, wiping his hands on a towel.

"Um. Long black," I said. "Sans charms, if possible."

"Excellent choice. No latte art involved," he said, busying himself with the grinder.

"I didn't want to put you through it," I replied, finding a grin from somewhere. I looked back out at the table of Upstanding Ladies, where James' aunt was standing next to them with the tray in one hand and the other on her hip, smiling brightly. As I watched, she adjusted the crystal necklace she was wearing so the light caught it, scattering rainbows across the table and making the ladies flinch. One actually held up her fingers in a gesture that I thought might be to ward off the evil eye. I looked at James as he slid a cup of coffee in front of me.

"Is she doing that deliberately?" I asked.

"Of course," he said, tamping the coffee down with a practised twist of the wrist. "Aunt Edith can't stand them, and she gets all her best witchy gear on when they come in. She's usually in T-shirts and jeans, but she braves the lace and velvet when she knows they're going to be here."

"That doesn't seem very good for business," I suggested.

"No," he agreed. "But my aunt very rarely does things for reasons that are just good for business, or good for her. She prefers for the good of the town, and she doesn't believe that the Upstanding Ladies help the town very much."

"Moral police or something, I think she said?"

"That's them," he said. "But all that ever means is they're people who don't like that others do things differently, or believe differently, or live differently. And in this case, the Upstanding Ladies don't like the magic stuff, and Hollowbeck is all about the magic stuff, so, you know, instant clash."

"That seems unfortunate here. Not liking the…" I couldn't quite make myself say *magic*, as I was still entertaining the mental break idea. I waved vaguely. "Stuff."

The corners of his lips quirked up in a smile as he slid a cup in front of me. "The magic stuff?"

I nodded, leaning over the mug. It smelled of rich heat

and distant sun on hot earth and glorious, glorious caffeine. "So that's just a thing here then?"

He was still examining me, and suddenly the perplexed look on his face cleared. "Oh, you're her."

"I'm who?" I asked.

"You found Norma," James said. "You're Morgan … Morgan Winters, right?"

"How does everyone know my name already?"

"It's a small town," he said. "Everybody knows everybody, and everybody hears all the gossip. Theodore was in last night after work."

Great. Probably the lizards carried tales all about town or something. "Last night? How late do you open?"

"We have a night shift to cater for people like Theodore," he said. "I don't work it, but when I came in this morning, I heard all the gossip."

"Right," I said. "So zero privacy in this town then?"

"Pretty much," he replied, grinning. "Magical small towns are even worse than regular small towns for gossip." The grin vanished suddenly, and he added, "I'm really sorry though. It must've been a huge shock finding Norma."

"It wasn't great," I agreed.

He leaned his elbows on the counter in front of me, examining me with warm green eyes. "Would it help if I told you that sort of thing never happens here?"

"Well, it evidently does," I pointed out.

"True," he admitted. "But I've been here three years, and it's never happened before. Theodore said it was probably an accident though?"

"Maybe," I said. "I just talked to the woman running Norma's shop. Starlight?"

He snorted. "Is that what she's calling herself now?"

"It's not her real name?"

"It's Estelle, but she thought it wasn't magical enough. She changed it to Stella with an A, then she went to Stellar with an AR. And now I guess she's Starlight."

I nodded. "Well, at least she's being consistent." I gave him a sideways look. "So you know Starlight pretty well then?"

"Oh, we had a thing when I first got here. But she was always so hardcore into the whole 'I'm going to be a witch' thing. It gets a bit tiring if you stay over and wake up to newts in the bed, or the soup has bats' wool in it, or the table salt runs away from you, and eventually you start wondering if you're going to be turned into a toad if you have an argument."

"Or a frog," I suggested.

He thought about it. "She never threatened me with frogs. But you never know. It would depend how good she was at the toad, I guess."

I looked at Ruiner, who'd wandered to the door to examine the Upstanding Ladies, his ears back. James' aunt came in and stooped down to rub the back of Ruiner's ears.

"Oh, hello," she said. "Pleased to meet you, handsome. I'm Edith." She at looked at me. "I didn't realise you had company."

"I'm not sure I'd term him that," I said, and Ruiner bared his teeth at me.

Edith straightened up. "Pop him on the barstool, and James can get him some cat biscuits." Ruiner made a gagging sound, and she frowned at him. "They're very high-quality ones, I'll have you know. Grain-free." He wrinkled his snout, and she added to me, "They do make a fuss."

"This one especially," I said as Ruiner jumped up on

the stool next to me and looked at James expectantly. "He's never happy."

"Never mind, dear," she said. "As you and your familiar become more closely bound, everything will become much easier and clearer."

"I don't want to be closely bound to him. I'm doing everything I can to get *unbound* from him."

She frowned. "But he's your familiar."

"No, I just acquired him," I said. "Call it an accident of nature."

Ruiner hissed at me, and I stuck my tongue out at him.

"That's how familiars usually work," Edith said. "And you already seem very in tune. You might just need a little bit of time to get used to each other."

"We've had plenty of that. I think we're just not that compatible."

She put the tray back on the counter, smiled at us, and said, "Some things just take more time than you think." She headed into the back of the shop as James set a small bowl of cat biscuits in front of Ruiner. He sniffed them, then looked at me.

"You're a cat," I said. "Eat cat things."

He tried to bite my arm, and I pushed him off, looking at James. "Can you give him a coffee?"

"I'm pretty sure cats don't drink coffee."

Ruiner yowled and slapped the bowl with one paw, sending it spinning to the floor in a hail of kibble. He glared at James.

"Then again, sure." James turned back to the machine. "I'm not doing latte art for a cat, though."

"Do one of your special ones," I said. "He deserves it." Ruiner tried to bite me again, and I jerked my arm away. "Stop being such a cat!"

The coffee machine drowned out Ruiner's response,

which was probably for the best not only because of the whole talking cat thing, but also because it meant I didn't have to knock my brother off his stool and get done for animal cruelty.

James set a small espresso cup in front of Ruiner, replete with well-foamed milk and some slightly obscene latte art. Ruiner held eye contact with him as he carefully stuck his paw in the foam, then flicked it across the counter.

"Sorry," I said to James. "He's always like this."

James shrugged, wiping up the mess. "Cats are cats, especially in Hollowbeck."

I examined him. "You believe in all this witchcraft thing, then."

He rubbed his chin, which was thankfully free of the usual well-cultivated barista beard. "I know what I see," he said. "And Hollowbeck attracts a different sort of people, which means different things happen here."

"Different things?"

"Well, your cat, for example." He pointed at Ruiner, who ignored him, his snout stuck in the mug.

"He's not my cat," I said.

"Your familiar then."

"I already said he's not my familiar. He's just a cat that I've acquired along the way."

"Yeah, like Aunt Edith said, that's kind of how familiars work. But however you put it, that's not a normal cat."

I looked at Ruiner, who lifted his head, licking foam from his chops. He narrowed his eyes at James, then pushed the mug over with one paw, spilling the remains of the coffee onto the counter. I sighed. "Sorry. Should he even be up here? Aren't there health and safety regulations, food hygiene, that sort of thing?"

"Yeah, I thought that when I first got here as well," he said. "I've given up."

"Great." I shuffled my stool a bit further from Ruiner and his puddle of coffee. He was looking at it a little regretfully, but I wasn't getting him another one. "Right, so cats drink in coffeeshops. People do witch apprenticeships and threaten to turn their boyfriends into toads. And this is all perfectly normal."

"In Hollowbeck, perfectly," he said. "You'll get used to it."

"I don't plan on getting used to it. I'm only here to sort a couple of things out."

"What sort of things?"

"Just some stuff for my brother."

"Oh, is your brother from here?" he asked.

"Not exactly," I said. "He just needs me to … get something." I wished I hadn't brought my brother up, but I'd needed a reason to be here, or it had felt like I did. Anonymity seemed to be the only thing that Hollowbeck wasn't amenable to.

"Maybe I can help. What do you need?"

Ruiner gave a little growl and I looked at him. He shook his head slightly, so small you could almost have missed it.

But James grinned. "Not a familiar, eh? His communication seems a bit good for the average cat."

"He's not a familiar," I insisted. "He's just a very annoying cat who's kind of come along with me. And I can't seem to get rid of him. I'm working on it, though."

"Alright," he said, raising his hands. "It doesn't bother me what he is. So do you need help?"

I leaned back on the stool, scrubbing my hands through my hair. The rough ponytail I'd managed this morning (I hadn't been able to find my hairbrush and had a sneaking suspicion a frog had stolen it in the night) felt lumpy and uneven. I looked at Ruiner. We did need help if we were going to work this out. "Maybe," I said aloud. "What do you know about Norma? I spoke to Starlight, and she said Norma was tough but everyone in town loved her." I tried to remember the exact wording. "A local hero, that's what she called her."

"A local hero," he said. "Wow. I mean, I know you're not meant to speak ill of the dead, but that's pushing things. Especially coming from Starlight."

He glanced around the shop, but his aunt was still out the back, where the scent of baking was fighting with the ever-present aroma of coffee beans. No one else had come in, and three of the Upstanding Ladies were having a sword fight with their knitting needles, giggling uproariously. The fourth had a rose clenched between her teeth and was cantering an invisible horse around the table, tossing her head magnificently. Whatever charms were in the coffee, they were evidently strong ones.

James looked back at me. "Norma was the sort of person that could get things done. If you had a problem, you went to Norma."

"Okay. That doesn't seem so bad."

"Sure, but she charged for it."

"That's generally how these things work," I said. "Basis of capitalism and all that."

"Not quite," he said. "You paid your money, sure, but then there was always something else. This town works in many ways on a barter system."

He pointed behind him, to a sink with an empty draining rack on one side and neatly labelled soap and handwashing containers attached to the wall behind it. An overflowing bag of softly brown-capped mushrooms nestled next to a basket of luminously red tomatoes that were almost bursting with ripeness. "There's no cash point in town. We don't have card machines. There's a bank, but it's mostly for the tourists. Half the town at least has no bank account, and we do a lot by barter system. Part of the barter system with Norma was that at some point you would get a little envelope. In that envelope would be something that told you what you needed to do to hold up your end of the bargain. And you'd do it or else there would be consequences."

"What sort of consequences?" I asked.

He shook his head. "I don't know. As far as I know, everyone always fulfilled the bargain."

"How do you know about it? Did you do a deal with her?"

"No. But Stella — Starlight, whatever — told me a bit about it."

"So she was part of the deals?"

He hesitated, scratching his jaw. "I don't think Norma let her have much to do with anything, to be honest. She used to say she was just unpaid labour, and the most magic she did was cleaning the loo. But she did know about the deals. At one point there was an infestation moving from place to place around town, because the way Norma solved it was to give each person who came to her a charm to pass it on to someone else of their own choosing. It was just about civil war by the time it finally died out. Everyone blaming everyone else."

"An *infestation?* Like what? Rats or locusts or…" I couldn't think of what else might be termed an infestation. Politicians?

"Pixies."

"Pixies," I repeated, and Ruiner snorted so hard into the remains of coffee in his saucer that it splattered the counter.

"Gross," I said to him, but James just wiped the mess up with his cloth. "Sorry about him."

"You should see it when the ferrets are in here," he said. "There's at least three ferret familiars in this town, and the mess they make is unbelievable."

"The food hygiene thing really isn't an issue, is it?" I said.

"Not in the slightest."

TWELVE

Potatoes & day-drinking

I WAS quiet for a while as a tall, skinny man wearing a lot of Lycra came in for a takeaway tea, then hobbled out again. Only once he was gone did I say to James, "Pixies, though. I mean, really?"

He shrugged. "I never saw them, but that's what everyone was saying they were. I mean, maybe they were just rats. But they moved from one place to another for about three months, then finally vanished when Ruby over at Mystic Munchies had to do a different charm." He hesitated again. "Or I think that's what happened."

"What sort of charm?" I asked.

"I'm not *certain* this is what happened," he said, lowering his voice. "But she had the pixies, or whatever the hell they were, and then the next thing one of the Upstanding Ladies had a coffee at Mystic Munchies, decided she was a tree, and the infestation was gone."

"She what, sorry?"

"She decided she was a tree. Planted herself in the park, stark naked with her feet in a flower bed, and that was that."

"What was that? She's not still there, is she?"

"Oh, no," he said. "She left the park and seems to have taken to the deeper parts of the woods around town. Better trees for company, apparently. You normally only see her if you're looking for her now, and she's only naked on nice days."

"Right," I said, and looked at Ruiner. He arched his whiskers at me in an expression that was a very clearly a cat version of *I told you so*. "And you think that was due to Norma, what — charming her or something?"

"I honestly couldn't tell you. Nobody talks about it. It's just connecting the dots, you know." He shrugged. "The whole infestation drama was kind of my introduction to the place, really."

"Nice intro," I said.

"Better than a body in a cauldron."

"True," I admitted. "Why did you come here, anyway?"

"Aunt Edith used to do herbalism and all that, then one day she decided to chuck it in and set up this place. She didn't know anything about coffee, but I had a place in Leeds. I was a bit fed up of it, so I sold up and came over to help her out for a bit while I decided what to do next." He looked around. "That was three years ago, and somehow I'm still here."

"Worrying about being turned into a toad," I said, and he laughed.

"Exactly. But it's not a bad place, you know. It's got this weird microclimate going on, so it's always warmer than it should be in the summer, and the trees are better than anything I've ever seen in autumn, and winters are actually snowy, and spring looks like the whole town's a florist's shop."

"It's still weird, though."

He shrugged. "You get used to it. And making cat cappuccinos is better than dealing with half the customers I used to have to. I've never had to make a half skinny milk half oat milk chai and single shot decaf latte with whipped cream, half a pump of sugar-free caramel syrup, and half a pump of…" He trailed off. "I forget. There was something else as well, I'm sure. I must finally be recovering from the trauma."

I snorted. "Alright, fair enough. But still — those deals sound pretty dangerous."

He nodded. "Yeah, I'm glad Aunt Edith never got caught up in any." He pointed out the front windows, and I followed his gaze. The Cosy Cauldron was just across the road and a couple of shops down. He had a perfect view of anyone going in and out. "The amount of local customers Norma has — had — is pretty mad. I must've seen most of the town going in there at some point. She was like a spider, you know? Webs everywhere."

I shivered and looked at my mug, wondering if I should have another one. But as good as it was, it wasn't helping this place make any sense. "I don't get it," I said. "Deals and infestations and people thinking they're trees and pixies in the kitchen. I mean, none of that can really be real, right?"

He raised his hands and let them drop. "I only know what I've seen. And, like I said, I'm new here. Maybe there's some sort of explanation I don't understand yet. But things have their own logic, and Hollowbeck draws certain people to it, like me. Like you." He pointed from me to Ruiner, encompassing us both.

"I haven't been drawn here," I said. "I'm just here to help my brother."

"Okay, sorry. And sure, not everyone's meant to be here, and not everyone who comes, stays." He narrowed his eyes at Ruiner slightly, who squinted back. "But ... that's not a cat. I'm not even sure it's a familiar. I've spent years watching people. I *know* people, and I think you belong here more than you realise."

I scowled at him. I was definitely rethinking the second coffee. "I don't belong here. I'm just a visitor."

"And yet you're asking questions about Norma like you're her long-lost bestie. You'd think you'd want to get out of town as soon as you could after finding a dead body, wouldn't you?"

I didn't have an answer for him, and for a moment the only sound was Ruiner growling.

Then Edith hustled out of the kitchen, wielding a tray full of little plates of golden shortbread fingers. She slid a broken one onto my saucer and winked at me. "I need someone to test it," she said before I could protest, then hurried outside, circling the tables and dropping a plate off at each one.

I watched her go and said, "I suppose the Upstanding Ladies don't go to Mystic Munchies anymore."

"They still do. There's no proving what happened. But they want someone to test everything before they eat it now."

"Of course they do," I muttered.

James turned back to the coffee machine. "Another?"

"No?" I said, but there was a question at the end of it, and he set the machine running anyway. I examined the shortbread, but I couldn't see any mysterious charms wafting around it, so I took a bite, the dusting of sugar crunching lightly and the biscuit crumbling into meltingly soft crumbs. It was bright with lemon, like biting into a summer's day, and ridiculously good, like shortbread's idea of shortbread. I made a mumbled sound of pleasure.

James grinned at me. "Yeah, my aunt's kind of the queen of shortbread. "

Edith came back in as he spoke, swinging her empty tray. "I am," she agreed. "Do you like it, dear?"

"I love it," I said, with more feeling than I think I've ever had for baked goods.

"Wonderful." She looked at James. "Coffees are on the house."

"No, you can't do that," I said.

"I can do whatever I want," she said. "First visit, first day in town, coffees are free. Just make sure you keep coming back."

"But I'm not planning to stay," I said.

She tipped her head slightly, looked at Ruiner, nodded, then said, "You may well not be planning to." I waited for her to finish the sentence, but she just vanished back into the kitchen again.

James set the second cup of coffee in front of me, and said, "Well, the shortbread's good, right?"

"Fantastic," I said, because that at least was one thing I was sure of.

IT WAS ALMOST lunchtime when we finally headed back to Petunia's. We'd circled the town after leaving Bewitching Brews, checking out the various little shops, cafes, and bars. There were a surprising amount for such a small place, all of them with that little edge of tweeness, as if they were someone's idealized version of whatever they were.

If it was a cocktail bar, it was the perfect sort of cocktail bar. There were no TVs tuned to sports channels, no music videos, no neon signs, no QR codes to scan for your menu. Everything was blackboards and fresh cut fruit and mortar and pestles. If it was a takeaway shop, the containers were all bamboo leaves and recycled materials, and there was a sign on the door saying there was a discount for bringing your own. Even the grocery store had low lighting and a huge display of fruit and vegetables with the names of the local farmers on little signs hanging above them. As for the bookshop, well I didn't even dare cross the road to peer in the window, otherwise I knew I wouldn't leave until they kicked me out. I could almost smell old paper and stories from halfway down the street.

Everything was just somehow that little bit better than it was anywhere else, and a part of me loved it. But it was still *off*. Nothing should be that perfect. Nothing *could* be that perfect. I found myself looking continually for a tear in the stage setting, where the real face of the town could peek through. Plus there was the whole no internet, no phone signal thing. Like I said, I was never really glued to my phone, but I suddenly found myself itching to check Facebook or Instagram or even TikTok, although I still didn't quite understand TikTok. I had a sneaking suspicion I was too old for it.

Ruiner and I didn't talk as we walked back through the tree-crowded streets. There were more people out now, wandering to and from the shops. Couples strolling hand in hand, men lugging shopping bags, women in smart skirts or scruffy shorts or kaftans, kids running with dogs or riding bikes in packs like they were in a Spielberg movie.

Hollowbeck had its own rhythm of life, a sense of many quiet strands of living going on under the surface, but I could almost feel the insularity of it. With the dearth of TV or internet, and the fact that the only way out of here was through the strange forest and its winding, apparently shifting roads, it felt like we were entirely cut off from the rest of the world.

I had a moment of almost-panic, a sense of claustro-phobia that we were stuck here and there was no leaving. I couldn't help thinking that even when we were allowed to go, perhaps we'd try, but the road would just deliver us straight back into the middle of Hollowbeck.

I shivered despite the heat, as I led us through the gate to Petunia's. She emerged onto the porch as we started up the path and waved enthusiastically. I waved back, putting on my friendliest, least likely to be turned into a frog face.

"Hello dear," she called. "Did you sleep alright?"

"I did, thank you," I said.

"Wonderful." She turned and picked up a basket that was sitting behind her on the porch. "It's time for you to earn your board, then."

"Of course," I said, putting as much enthusiasm into the words as I could, and hoping it wasn't going to be anything frog-related.

"I need you to dig up some potatoes for me," she said. "I'm making potato salad for lunch."

"Of course," I took the basket and trowel from her and looked around the garden. "Where do I find them?"

"In the vegetable patch, of course," she said. "Out the back."

She pointed, and I trotted off around the house with Ruiner padding along behind me. The back garden was a vast labyrinth of untrimmed green lawn, chaotic flower beds, a duck pond (with more frogs than ducks), and a greenhouse with broken panes and sunflowers nodding through the roof.

Beside the greenhouse was a vegetable patch planted in surprisingly neat lines, the fluffy heads of unidentified plants protruding out of the soil, and herbs such as basil and rosemary and thyme that even I could recognize bundled about the place in tubs. There were bell peppers hanging from some of the bushes, fat and glossy, and others bowed under the weight of juicy-looking tomatoes. There were eggplants, luxuriously curved and royal purple. Rambling, furry vines sprouted a profusion of courgettes, and over them nodded the great blossoming heads of artichokes.

What I couldn't see were potatoes. I poked at a couple of things that I was almost certain were carrots and wandered up and down the rows for a bit while Ruiner watched me. After a while, he said, "You have no idea what a potato plant looks like, do you?"

"Do you?" I shot back.

"No," he admitted. "I'm not a gardener."

"Well, neither am I," I said. "And I don't want to dig up a perfectly innocent plant and kill it, or—"

"Do not say you're going to get turned into a frog."

"Well, I might. This is an actual real problem. Even Ben said it was."

"Oh well, if *Ben* said it was."

I made a face at him and stuck the trowel in the ground experimentally, turning up a minuscule purple carrot. "Oh, that's pretty."

"But it's not a potato," Ruiner pointed out. "And it's tiny. Put it back."

I squeezed the carrot back into the soil and looked around again, but none of the plants had a helpful *I'm a potato* sign on them. "You could help me," I said. "Do a little dig."

"*Do a little dig.* What do you think I am? An armadillo?"

"Do armadillos dig?"

"I have no idea," he replied. "Which is my point."

"You make even less sense as a cat."

He huffed and wandered up and down the rows for a bit, looking as confused as I did. Eventually, we both started digging in random spots, me carefully trying not to ruin any roots and him just kicking the dirt around wherever he felt like. This very soon led to him doing the digging while I followed, putting the dirt back, until eventually we struck gold. Or potatoes, more to the point, tiny, pale little globes like mud-encrusted quails' eggs.

I dug around them quickly, aware that we'd been out here for quite a while, and half-filled the basket before pushing the plants awkwardly back into place. I didn't know if they were going to grow more, or if I should be pulling them out and discarding them, or taking the stems as well. It was as mysterious as pixie infestations and magical deals to me, so I just patted the ground around them and hoped for the best, then lugged the basket back up to the garden.

"You took a while, dear," Petunia said as I walked into the kitchen. "I'm almost finished with everything else."

"Sorry," I said, then decided it was probably best to come clean. "I have no idea what a potato plant looks like."

She stared at me for a moment, then broke into great peals of laughter. "Why didn't you come and ask me?"

"I don't know," I said, because that sounded better than, *I was scared you'd turn me into a frog.* "I thought I'd be able to figure it out, and I did in the end, but do they grow again? I just kind of shoved the plants back into the ground."

"They'll be fine," she said. "Scrub them up, get them in a pot, and we'll be done in no time. I'm just finishing the rest of the salad, and I've got more elderflower cordial on the go. Would you like some?"

"Yes, please," I said, tipping the potatoes into the sink.

"Vodka?" she asked, and this time I only hesitated for a moment before I said, "Yes, please."

Lunch with Petunia was both alarming and surprisingly enjoyable. The potatoes were tiny, delicate, and set off by herbs, bright green beans, and the sharp, sweet bite of cherry tomatoes in the salad. Great wedges carved from the loaf of fresh bread were perfect for mopping up the last of the dressing.

She slopped vodka generously and repeatedly into both glasses, apparently not noticing when I said half-heartedly that I didn't want any more. By the time I left the table, my stomach was full almost to the point of discomfort but I topped it off with a slice of lemon drizzle cake that tiptoed along the line of tart and sweet with acrobatic precision.

"You do need to let me know how I can pay you," I said to her. "I mean, this is just too much. I'm not sure what Isabella's covering, but I don't think it's all this."

"You dug my potatoes," she said. "Saved my back and my knees. And there'll be another job tomorrow. We'll figure it all out, don't you worry."

I gave her a grateful look and headed slightly tipsily upstairs, planning to collapse on the bed and sleep off lunch. However, as soon as we got into the room, Ruiner went digging under the pillows and pushed the grimoire out with his nose.

"Come on," he said. "We need to try and find this curse."

"Do we have to?" I asked. "I'm really full and I don't think I can read anything in this state."

"We have to," he said. "You've spent the whole bloody day messing around taking tea in the library and flirting with baristas and day-drinking with little old ladies. We need to lift the curse and then we need to get out of here."

"I was not flirting," I said, smothering a burp with the back of one hand. "And also, no. We need to lift the curse, then we need to find out who's after me and how to stop them. *Then* we can leave."

He sat back on his haunches and looked at me. "You're right," he said. "I'm going to work on the you thing while you look for the counter curse.

I stared at him. "How're you going to do that, cat-boy? And how am I meant to know what a counter curse looks like, anyway? You need to help."

"You think I know? I'm not a bloody witch."

"Everyone keeps calling you a familiar. Doesn't that make you a bit familiar with this stuff?" I chortled at my own joke, which I felt was pretty good, considering all the vodka.

"You're terrible when you're drunk," he said.

"I'm not drunk," I replied, and burped lemon drizzle cake. "I might be a little bit tipsy, though."

"You think? Look, I'm going back to the shop, and I'll have a poke around, see if I can find out anything about who Norma was doing deals with. You look through the book, see what you can find that looks like it might be a counter-curse."

"You can't poke around the shop," I said. "What's her name's there. The star girl."

"I can absolutely poke around the shop. I'm a cat, she's not going to notice me."

Before I could say anything else, he jumped to the floor and stalked out the door. I watched him go, then sprawled back on the bed. I would indeed get to looking for counter-curses because that was important, but right now a nap seemed much, much more important and much, much more pressing. I closed my eyes, listening to the birds chattering outside, and within moments I was asleep.

THIRTEEN

Only mildly criminal activity

I WOKE WITH A SQUAWK, sitting straight up and clutching my stomach. It felt like someone had punched me in it, but the only person to be seen was Ruiner, who jumped away from me and onto the floor. The afternoon light had gone long and orange where it spilled across the room, and I took a wheezing breath, glaring at my brother.

"*Ow!* What did you *do?*" I demanded, rubbing my poor abused abdomen. "Feels like a bloody donkey kicked me."

"I said your name half a dozen times," he said. "But you were just snoring. So I jumped on you."

"You really are a cat."

"I'm only temporarily a cat."

"A heavy cat."

"*Rude.* And stop moaning."

"Well, what happened?" I asked, taking my water bottle from the bedside table. My mouth was reminding me about the foolhardiness of vodka at lunchtime (which I'm sure had never been an issue ten years ago), and I took a hasty swig. "Did you find anything?"

"I saw where all the ledger books and things are," he

said. "But they were too big for me to get hold of. Plus I got chased out by a bloody rat."

"You got chased out by a rat?" I asked.

"Yeah, I think it might be Starlight's familiar."

"Great, so you were seen by the witch's familiar. Well done. Very sneaky."

"Witch's apprentice's familiar," he replied, as if it made any difference. "It's just a rat. Anyway, if we go back in tonight, you can grab the ledgers."

I frowned at him. "Is breaking and entering really a good idea when we're already on the police's suspect list? Especially going back into a crime scene?"

"I told you, nobody locks anything around here. No breaking involved."

"I think you're arguing semantics."

He shrugged. "We need to get a look at those ledgers and see what deals she was doing. That'll tell us who's after you."

I groaned and flopped back on the bed. "I can't believe I'm going to say yes. *And* I can't believe you got busted by a rat."

"Yeah, not a pleasant experience. It tried to bite me."

"Serves you right," I said, and he growled.

"Did you even look at the spell book?" he asked. "Have you done *anything* on your side of things?"

"No," I said. "I was recovering. My nerves were shot."

"You were day-drunk, you mean." He sat down and started to clean between his toes, and I made a gagging sound.

"That's disgusting, Ruiner. How can you do that?"

"What other choice do I have?" he asked around a mouthful of fur. "Besides, it's a cat thing. I can't seem to help it."

"You're getting more cat-like by the moment," I said. "You're going to be stuck like that."

"I won't be if you find the counter-curse."

"Fine," I said, and sat up again, pulling the book onto my lap. "The last thing I need is to be cleaning up your hairballs for the next ten years."

He sat down next to me and we leaned over the book together. It wasn't a massive tome, not like the chunky volumes in the library, but it had a weight to it that belied its size. It was hand-written rather than printed, the pages crammed with tight, slanted writing in a number of different hands. It looked like the sort of recipe book that gets passed down from generation to generation, each person adding their own twists, their own notes, and their own dishes. There were scribbles in the margins, spills of something unidentifiable on the borders, and fingerprints and paw prints in what I hoped was ink smearing the text. It was definitely a well-used book, but what it didn't have was an index or any sense of order. Spells for repelling slug invasions rubbed shoulders with charms to ensure your bread rose, and next to that were instructions on how to stop your cat shedding, which Ruiner immediately put his paw on.

"Try this one," he said.

"We're not trying anything," I replied. "If we find a counter-curse, we'll research it carefully, and *then* we'll try it. I'm not trying to make you into a non-shedding cat. We might flood the whole country with cat hair."

"You suck," he said. "You should try having fur. It gets *everywhere*."

"Rather not."

We stayed bent over the book until I checked my phone and found that it was well after closing time for the Cosy Cauldron. Theoretically, anyway. Streetlights had come on outside, and when I peered out the window the sky was deepening to indigo. The air wafting past was still warm, and somewhere someone was having a barbecue. I could smell wood smoke and the faint scent of meat cooking. My stomach rumbled hopefully, and I patted it. After the size of lunch, I shouldn't need to eat for another week or so.

Ruiner put his front paws up on the wall and tried to peer out the window. "Lift me up?"

"Absolutely not," I said, and he stared at me with big eyes. I sighed and lifted him so he could look out into the oncoming night, his whiskers twitching.

He sniffed the air, then said, "We should go."

"And I think we should wait till a bit later," I replied. "We don't want to be seen by anyone."

He started to argue, but at that point Petunia shouted up that there was food downstairs. Despite my assertion that I'd eaten enough to keep me going for days, we headed down immediately. I nibbled on leftovers and strenuously objected to any more vodka, while Ruiner scoffed fresh chicken breast from a bowl.

"Are you alright, dear?" Petunia asked. "You look a little bit peaky."

"I don't think drinking at lunchtime agrees with me," I said to her, and she burst out laughing.

"You obviously need more practice," she replied, but didn't offer me anything more to drink.

We retreated afterwards as if we were going to bed. It was only later, when the last of the noise had vanished from downstairs, and the distant sounds of life in town had given way to the cries of night birds and the mumble of the wind, that I pulled my jeans and a hoody on.

We crept back down the stairs by the light of my phone as carefully as we could. The steps creaked in all the usual places, but there was no avoiding that. I was just going to say that I had insomnia and was going out for a walk if Petunia or anyone else appeared. Not that I'd seen anyone yet — given the fact that I had a one-hour time slot for bathroom use, I'd expected to be running into other guests everywhere, but I hadn't seen anyone. Which was one less thing to worry about, I supposed.

The night air was rich with the scent of sleeping trees and cut grass, and cooler than the day had been, but still warm and close. Even with the streetlights on, I could see stars spilled above us, and I kept looking up at them as we walked toward town. I wasn't sure I'd ever seen stars as they were here, spilled across the ocean of the sky like salt crystals scattered on a dark-swathed table.

It seemed natural to go on foot, even without considering the noise of the car. That was one good thing about this town — everything was walking distance, and it didn't take us long to turn onto the main street. I could see the tall blond man — Asger — cleaning down tables in Mystic Munchies, and there were low lights on in Bewitching Brews and quiet music coming from one of the bars. A few people peppered the pavement, ducking into shops or ferrying coffees about. We loitered our way casually through them, then, when I was as sure as I could be that no one was looking, we ducked into the alley that ran alongside the Cosy Cauldron.

The back door was locked when I tried it, and I raised my eyebrows at Ruiner. "I thought you said nobody locked anything around here."

"I guess murder changes things a bit," he replied, and padded around the building. I followed him, and watched as he jumped up to a half-open window that looked like it probably let onto a toilet or something. Before long he was back, an old-fashioned key gripped in his teeth, which he offered to me.

I used the key to let us in, reminding myself again that we weren't doing any harm to the place, we were just trying to find out who was trying to do harm to *me*. It was a very different thing. I lit the way with my phone as Ruiner led me straight to a little office section in one of the rooms off the hallway. It was cluttered with filing boxes and bulk lots of crystals and little jars waiting to be filled, and more taxidermy piled in one corner, most of them missing eyes or teeth or paws. I shivered and looked away from them, examining the desk instead.

There was no computer, just a large ledger book resting open with a pen lying across it. On the shelf above were more ledgers, each one neatly labelled with a year. I leafed through the one on the desk, frowning. The dates went right back to January, and finding what we needed wasn't going to be easy. There were so many notations written in such cramped handwriting, that I really needed some decent light and plenty of time to read it properly. But we couldn't take it with us. The entering I could almost justify, but stealing shop property felt like it might bring the long arm of Theodore down on us. I started to read, running my finger down the entries, searching for my name, or Ruiner's, or anything at all that looked like it might help us.

The setup was just like any basic ledger, a column for the date, another for names, then another with products such as *anti-rat charms* or *joint salve* or even *plant food* noted down. Beyond was listed a price, five pounds or ten, or something like *sausages* or *woollen socks*, which I supposed meant she was bartering for some stuff. Not what you'd usually put in a cashbook, and her bookkeeper would hate her, but I had an idea Hollowbeck didn't exactly follow the tax rules the rest of the country did.

I kept reading, Ruiner peering down at the page next to me. In some entries the notes were written in code or runes of some sort, and runes appeared in the price column here and there as well.

"*Three cabbages,*" Ruiner read. "Who needs three cabbages?"

"Maybe she really liked coleslaw," I said, turning the page. If my name was in runes, we were going to be out of luck. There didn't seem to be any sort of key for working out what they meant.

"No one likes cabbage that much," he said, sitting back on his haunches and staring around the room. "This place is giving me the creeps."

I glanced at the taxidermy in the corner. "I know."

"There," Ruiner said, turning his attention back to the ledger and patting one of the columns. "See that?"

"What are they?" The column he'd tapped was a small one, not used on all entries, but next to some there was a little squiggle, careless as a doodle. As I scanned the page I saw that not every entry had one, but probably a good quarter did.

"I reckon those are the ones that were doing deals," he said, and I eyed him thoughtfully.

"Why?"

He sighed. "Because I watched her write down mine, and that's the column she used."

"There's loads of them!"

"I know," Ruiner said. "And look. They're all different."

He was right. His cat eyes were apparently better than mine for this (I was going to have to go to the optometrist when we got done with this, as I swear all the writing everywhere was shrinking), but when I squinted, I could see that each rune had an extra dot, or smaller squiggle, or a second, tiny rune next to it, like a duckling. "D'you think they say what the favour was?"

"Got to," he said. "There's so many of them, she'd have needed a way to keep track of who was doing what."

I flipped to the front cover, then the back, but there was no key of any sort. "This is no good. We're never going to figure this out."

"Just keep looking for your name," he said. "And hurry up."

"I'm going as quick as I can."

I'd only managed to get through half a dozen more pages when a chittering sound stopped me. For one horrifying moment I thought the taxidermy were coming to life and swarming across the shop to attack the intruders in their midst, then Ruiner hissed, glaring at the doorway. I swung around to see a sleek, dark-furred rat on the threshold, reared up on its haunches and bearing its teeth at us.

"Ugh," I said. "The *size* of that thing." It gave me an affronted look, and I stared back at it. It was as big as the poodle at Bewitching Brews, and I had a feeling it was the one I'd seen up in the rafters yesterday.

"That's the one that tried to attack me this afternoon," Ruiner said, jumping up on the desk next to me. "Bloody horrible thing."

It chittered at us again, little eyes bright, and a thought suddenly dawned on me. "Is it *Norma's* familiar?" I asked.

It swung its head toward me, teeth bared, and Ruiner said, "I don't remember her having a familiar."

"You wouldn't really have a rat out in the shop, would you?" I replied. "Not great for business."

The rat hissed again, and Ruiner said, "Please stop insulting the big scary rat."

I made a comforting sort of noise at it and rubbed my fingers together. "Good boy," I offered. It dropped to its front paws, hunching its shoulders. "Good girl?"

The rat chattered its teeth and made a little dart

forward before scuttling back again, and both Ruiner and I yelped.

I poked him in the side. "Can't you deal with it?"

"I'm not dealing with it," he said. "It's gross. I can't stand rats."

"You're a cat," I said. "Just go and do cat things to it."

"I'm not doing *cat things* to it," he said. "What do you think I'm going to do? *Bite* it?"

"Use all those cat instincts you reckon you have going on."

"I definitely don't have any rat-related ones."

The rat gave another of those unsettling hisses, and we both yelped again. While we'd been arguing, it had crept even closer, and was hulking its shoulders as if intending to rush us.

"Is there something wrong with it? Has it got rabies? Oh, no — can you get rabies from rats?" I asked my brother, who was showing no inclination to get off the desk.

"I'm sure you can get *something* from them," he said.

"Fantastic." I looked around for something to throw, but the nearest thing was a taxidermy seagull with a missing beak. I shoved my phone into my back pocket, picked the bird up with a shudder, and brandished it at the rat. "Back off," I told it.

It gave one final hiss and rushed us. I squawked, hurling the seagull at it. The rat dodged easily, launching itself at my legs, and Ruiner jumped to intercept it as I snatched up the desk chair. My brother sent the rat rolling backward, but it came straight back to its paws and rushed me again. I flailed at it with the desk chair, sidling toward the door as I tried to fend it off without actually hurting it. It was only doing what it thought its mistress would have wanted, after all.

Ruiner danced around occasionally darting in for a clumsily thrown bat at the rodent while letting loose a torrent of abuse that did nothing to distract it. Every time it feinted at him, Ruiner would sprint off yowling, and if anyone was outside there was no way this was going unnoticed. We needed to get out.

I worked my way into the hall, and as it charged me one last time, I shouted, "Ruiner, out!"

He vaulted the rat and shot down the hallway. I hurled the desk chair back into the office and then slammed the door, holding the handle closed as if I thought the rat might just open it and waltz out after us. Sweat coated my shoulders, and my heart was going too fast, but all I could hear was the frantic scratching coming from inside the office.

Ruiner and I looked at each other. "I think it was rabid," he said. "It was pretty much foaming at the mouth."

"It's probably just allergic to cats," I said, letting go of the door handle gingerly and checking I still had my phone. "I'm starting to feel the same way."

"Try living as one."

I left the back door open, the key on the inside, in the hopes that Starlight would think she just forgot to lock it, and padded down the side of the building. I checked each way along the street before stepping out onto it. There was no one in sight, and we hurried back to Petunia's and up the stairs to our room, neither of us talking. I let us in with a sigh, turning to Ruiner to tell him that I didn't think we were suited to criminal activity. As I did so, the bedside lamp clicked on.

I gave a little scream that hopefully drowned out Ruiner's curse, and Theodore looked at us with a smile.

"Hello, Morgan," he said. "Where have you been?"

FOURTEEN

Clam juice & cocktails

"THEODORE," I said, trying for bright and breezy, or at least relatively calm. I wasn't actually sure if outraged might not be a better option, given the fact that a bright orange man was standing in the middle of my room with his hands behind his back. I couldn't seem to decide which was the least guilty-sounding option, so I think the word started out calm and ended outraged, with a bright and breezy syllable in the middle. The logical part of my brain was also asking how he'd been able to switch the bedside light on from his spot in the centre of the room, and why he'd been standing in the dark in the first place, but there was too much panic going on for me to think about that too much.

"How wonderful to see you again," Theodore said, giving me a very small bow, and I found myself bowing back on some sort of autopilot.

"Yes, you too." I tried to look for the grimoire without appearing as if I was looking for anything. I couldn't remember what we'd done with it. Under the pillows? The mattress? In the bedside drawers? It wasn't in the middle of the bed like a fat, leathery *guilty* sign, at least. "Can I help you?"

"I was in the area, and thought to pop in and see you," he replied, the *pop in* sounding weirdly incongruous in his deep, sombre tones, like a judge calling someone *a little naughty*. "I did not think you would be out at this time of night."

"Oh, I had a bit of a sleep this afternoon," I said. "Petunia fed me such a huge lunch that I ended up napping, so I really needed a bit of exercise this evening."

He looked at my jeans and said, "Did you get this exercise?"

"Just a walk. Ruiner insisted on coming with me, and it's very hard to run with a cat."

"Ah, I see. Yes, I notice some of our more active residents prefer dogs to accompany them." Theodore thought about it. "I'm not particularly a fan of dogs."

"No?" I said.

"No, they don't seem to like me." He looked at Ruiner, who tried to look as amiable as possible. "I'm not sure cats do either. Most animals seem to be uncomfortable around me."

I made an agreeable sound and wondered if he included human animals in that, because I was feeling distinctly uncomfortable around him. Although that was quite possibly to do with the fact that the spell book *had* been in here somewhere, and while I couldn't see it anywhere, he might have done. He might even be holding it behind his back, as he hadn't changed position since we got in, and who knew what he'd been doing here in the first place.

"Um, who let you into my room?" I asked, using the stern voice I usually reserved for people who phoned up wanting to know if I'd been involved in a car accident recently. "It seems like a bit of an invasion of privacy."

"Oh, I see. Petunia invited me into the house. Was it not appropriate for me to come up to your bedroom?"

"No," I said, moving out of stern and into indignation. "It was *not* appropriate, because I have certain expectations of privacy. You can't just walk into someone's room like that."

He pressed a hand to his heart and bowed again just slightly, the light sliding off his cheekbones. They'd have been quite astonishing if not for the carroty hue. "I'm dreadfully sorry. Is there anything I can do to make it up to you? May I offer you a beverage?"

I blinked at him. "A beverage?"

"Yes, I believe Bewitching Brews to be open, should you enjoy a caffeinated option, but perhaps that is unwise if you wish to sleep. The Witching Hour may be a better choice."

"The Witching Hour?" Either the conversation or the cheekbones seemed to have rendered me incapable of doing anything but parroting his words back at him.

"A most delightful establishment, and regularly frequented by those of us who keep strange hours. Perhaps you would accompany me?"

I looked at him for a long moment and said, "Um, sure. Thanks." Anything to get him out of my bedroom and, hopefully, away from the spell book.

"Wonderful. I will wait for you outside."

I stepped to the side of the door to let him pass, trying to see if he had anything in his hands, but somehow he moved in such a way that I just couldn't tell. I peered after him as he left, but his hands were in front of him now, so it was still impossible to know if he was carrying anything. He walked silently on the creaky stairs, and when I shone my torch down them a moment later, he'd vanished. Ruiner and I looked at each other, and I wondered if Theodore had heard us talking, but we'd been pretty quiet on the way up. We hadn't wanted to disturb Petunia and risk any frog-based incidents.

I hurried to the bed, sweeping my hands under the pillow and throwing the covers back. No grimoire. I dropped to my knees and peered under the bed, but there was nothing there either. I tried the bedside drawers, panic rising in my chest, then stared at Ruiner.

"Do you think he took it?" I whispered, and he shrugged.

"How do I know?" he whispered back. "But I don't like him."

"Well, he did say cats don't like him," I said.

"I'm just cat-*formed*."

"You're very variable on what cat attributes you have."

Ruiner huffed. "I can see why you're divorced, you know."

"Unfair," I said. "I'm *getting* divorced, and it's because Jason's a muppet. And he spent all my money. *And* cheated on me."

"Fair," he agreed. "He is a muppet." We shared a very short moment of sibling solidarity, then he added, "But I can still see why you're getting divorced."

I couldn't waste any more time looking for the grimoire, not without starting to look suspicious, so I grabbed a jacket and we headed back down the stairs. Theodore was waiting on the garden path, standing very straight in his dark suit, his tie gone and the shirt open at the neck to reveal more luminous skin. I wondered if that was his version of off-duty.

He held an arm out to me as I approached, and I

looked at it, then at him. "Ah, this is maybe not the way things are done," he said, lowering his arm.

"Sorry?" I said.

"Where I come from, it is expected that one offers one's arm to one's lady companion."

"Right," I said. "Not so much in Cumbria. And this one is not really comfortable with the lady label."

"I'm dreadfully sorry," he said. "I've made an assumption again. Isabella informs me that I am slow to adapt." He thought about it for a moment. "Are you perhaps a *they*, rather than a *she?*"

I gave a snort of laughter that resolved any doubt about my suitability for the lady label. "No, I just mean that *lady* has certain connotations. I don't wear petticoats or raise my little finger when I drink my tea."

He smiled and said, "I understand," although it was quite clear from his face that he didn't at all. He gave a flourishing sort of wave toward the gate, accompanied by another of those little bows. "Shall we proceed?"

"Yes," I said, "I think that's wise."

I led the way out onto the street, and we walked together down the pavement with Ruiner trotting behind us, the night rich with unseasonable summer heat and chattering with night birds.

"And how are you finding Hollowbeck?" Theodore asked, glancing at me. In the low lights of the streetlamps his eyes were dark and unreadable, and his skin looked almost normal.

"It's interesting," I said, with perfect honesty.

He smiled at that, and it warmed his whole face. "Many people do find it interesting, yes."

"And you?" I asked. "Have you always lived here?"

"No, no," he said. "But I came here some time ago."

He didn't seem inclined to be any more forthcoming

than that, so I said, "And you liked it so much you decided to stay?"

"Yes," he said. "I do indeed like it. The outside world is not always welcoming to those who are a little different. Which is why I try to learn how to be welcoming to everyone who comes here, even though some of the things that are normal to others are very different to me."

I looked at him again, examining the effortless way he wore his suit, as if the concept of *casual wear* had never occurred to him. He had a handkerchief in his breast pocket, which I don't think I'd ever seen outside of a wedding party. Not mine, of course. That had been in a city hall with my brother and Jason's drunken cousin as witnesses and sole attendees.

"Where are you from?" I asked. "I don't recognise your accent." *Plus you sound like you learned English from* Downton Abbey, I thought but didn't say. The last thing I wanted to do was offend Hollowbeck's law enforcement, although I was having doubts that it was linked to law enforcement outside the valley in any way.

"Ah," he said, "I am from *Europe.*" He smiled broadly, as if that should be not only enough of an answer, but quite impressive as well.

"Which part?" I asked.

That seemed to confuse him for a moment, then he said, "Wherever we chose. We were a nomadic people who are no longer known."

"No longer known? How?"

"We were absorbed," he replied simply. "We were fighters, but no great army. We served those who paid us, but when we fell out of favour, we found ourselves beset on all sides. We fought fiercely, but there were many who hated us, and none who would shelter us. There was no resisting the inevitable. Our people were swallowed by others, or scattered."

"That's *horrible*," I said. "What was the name of your people?"

"We had many," he said, looking up at the stars. "They were all unimportant. I roamed Europe for many years, and further afield as well. Then one day I found myself in England, and stumbled into Hollowbeck. It has been home ever since."

I could sort of understand Hollowbeck being appealing after all that. No one seemed likely to exterminate your family outside Bewitching Brews. Turn them into trees, maybe, but not exterminate them. "You must've been very young when that happened. You don't look any older than me."

"Oh, but I am," he said. "I am much, much older." He gave me that oddly lovely smile again.

I wondered just how much Botox they went through in this town, or if it was a case of more magical means of preservation. I quite fancied finding out, if it worked that well. But asking seemed a bit rude, so instead I just returned the smile and concentrated on not getting too mixed up when he asked me what my favourite star was, and I said Olivia Coleman, which he asked me to point out in the sky because he didn't know it.

Witching Hour was down a side street, tucked in between a florist called Bloomin' Magic, and one of those hardware shops that would sell everything from toilet seats to spark plugs to garden gnomes. Refreshingly, it was just called Stuff, although a sign in the window advertised imp traps and anti-fairy-circle lawn spray.

The bar was barely wider than its double doors, but it plunged deep into the terraced building, and had a sunken floor and high ceilings. Double-decker booths with low tables and floor cushions lined the walls, and at least half of them were occupied, the low murmur of conversation drowned by mellow music. Hookahs smoked on low tables next to candles in black-framed hurricane lanterns, and cocktail glasses of various sizes sported umbrellas and such a variety of fruit that they looked like a viable option for your five a day.

"Hello, Tanya," Theodore said to a young woman behind the counter. She smiled at us both, wiping strong-looking hands on a spotless dishcloth.

"How's it, Theo?" she asked, taking a jug full of what looked like Bloody Mary mix from under the counter and mixing it vigorously. "The usual?"

"Of course," he replied. "And my friend here will have..." He raised his eyebrows at me.

I remembered my decision not to drink after the vodka lunch and said, "Do you do non-alcoholic cocktails?"

"We do everything," Tanya said. "Are you sure you want a non-alcoholic one though? You look like a real one might do you more good."

I sighed. "Probably. Do you have a specialty?"

"I will make you a specialty," she said, and leaned over the counter, beckoning to me as if about to tell me a secret. I leaned forward hesitantly, and she gave a deep, long sniff. I jumped back, and she grinned, exposing canines that looked just a little too long. "Yes," she said. "I know exactly what you'd like."

She turned back to what she was doing and I looked at Ruiner. He just stared up at me with his eyes wide, and Theodore said, "What does the cat want?"

"Ruiner?" I asked, too confused to protest that he was a cat and in need of nothing. When Tanya had leaned close to me, I'd smelt something too, something deep and distant and wild. Dark forests and endless moors, paws running cold and fierce over hard raw ground. My heart was going too fast, and Ruiner stared around the bar, his tail pouffing out.

Tanya gave us both another grin and said, "Yeah, I'll get the cat something too."

"Come," Theodore said and gave me that little flourishing wave again. "I have a favourite table."

"Great," I followed him deeper into the bar and out a back door, my head swimming as if the building was suddenly too hot, too lacking in air.

The cooler night washed over me as we stepped outside, the air scented with night flowers and herbs that were arranged in planters scattered about a little beer garden. Everything was flower-encumbered trellises and deep soft cushions, with canopies pushed back to allow the night sky in, and unlit outdoor heaters waiting for colder nights.

I dropped into a seat at the table Theodore led me to and closed my eyes, leaning back with a sigh. For a moment there was nothing but low music drifting from speakers, a mix of acoustic guitars and soft vocals, and somewhere a ripple of laughter as a table shared a joke. It was exceedingly peaceful and felt nothing like any other bar I'd been in at midnight anywhere else.

When I opened my eyes again, Theodore was examining me intently, sucking on a metal straw stuck into a pint glass of the Bloody Mary mix. A chunky tumbler of pale, cloudy liquid had appeared in front of me, a stalk of something green and leafy sticking out of it.

"What's that?" I asked.

"Your specialty," he said. "Tanya is very talented. She knows just what every person needs and wants."

I took a tentative sip, expecting some lemon and gin thing, going by the colour. But instead, an explosion of honey and ginger washed over me, followed by a spike of fresh pineapple, tasting of distant, sun-soaked beaches, which gave way to a note of something bright and crisp and floral. I couldn't have even said what alcohol was in it, let alone anything else, and I gave an involuntary *hmm* of pleasure. "That's incredible. What *is* it?"

Theodore shrugged, still sucking enthusiastically on his straw. "I'm not sure," he said around it. "As I say, she's a most excellent alchemist."

I wondered if that was what Hollowbeck called bartenders, or if she was an actual alchemist, and looked at Ruiner. He was settled into the soft cushions of the chair next to me, sniffing at a small bowl that had a couple of clam shells stuck in it for decoration. If nothing else, there didn't seem to be much chance of us going hungry or thirsty in this town.

FIFTEEN

A suspicious date

We drank in companionable silence for a little while, then Theodore said, "I must ask you something, Morgan."

I braced myself. Here it came. He was going to ask about the spell book, or taking the note from the Cosy Cauldron, or, worse, he knew we'd *broken in* to the Cosy Cauldron and was going to arrest us on the spot. Although he could've done that without taking me out on the town first. But I nodded and smiled as brightly as I could, not trusting myself to speak.

"Why are you still here?" His voice was mild, curious rather than accusatory, and I hesitated. He looked at Ruiner and said, "Is it because of him?"

"Ruiner?" I said, aiming for startled, although I don't think it went that well. "No. You told us not to leave town."

"Evidently I am very persuasive," he said, and gave me a sudden grin, slightly too toothy but so warm that I had the sudden thought that the cheesy puff hue wasn't insurmountable.

"You are police," I pointed out.

"I am," he agreed, leaning back from his drink finally.

"Did you have a personal connection to Norma, perhaps? Is that why you sought her out?"

"No, it was business," I said. "Isabella said you thought it was an accident."

"I do," he said. "But sometimes what we see is not exactly what *is*. And I hear you have returned to the Cosy Cauldron since our visit, which seems to me curious behaviour. You were not eager to revisit the scene with me."

"No." I took a careful sip of my drink. "I hoped I could still get help with what I came for."

"And that is?"

"Just a favour for my brother."

"I see. And he knew Norma?"

"He did," I said around my straw, trying not to look at Theodore. He was staring at me altogether too intensely. Did the man not blink?

Theodore nodded. "A deal, perhaps?"

I wrinkled my nose. "Something like that."

"And with Norma gone, you think you will find the details there, perhaps from Starlight, who you spoke with today? Or James and Edith?" He smiled at me as I flinched. "Ah, small towns. You cannot keep anything secret in small towns."

"Evidently," I said. "And yes, I thought Starlight might know about the deal that my brother had. I just spoke to James and Edith because I wanted coffee."

"And did you find anything out?"

"I didn't really get a chance to ask Starlight," I said. "She was quite busy. She seems to be running the shop now?"

Theodore nodded, slurping on his straw and making an apologetic gesture. "She is. For the moment, anyway. Norma had no family, so there is no one else to take the shop on. Unless there is anything to the contrary in Norma's will, Starlight may well be able to step into running it."

I nodded. "So she'll take on the shop and the income from it. And all the customers? Or will the customers go somewhere else? Do people trust her?"

He smiled at me. "Do you doubt my investigations, Morgan? Do you think my skills are maybe not up to those of the outside world?"

"No," I said. "But it's just odd, isn't it, that she's open straight away the next day? You'd think it would be closed for at least a day or so, wouldn't you? In mourning?"

He folded his hands around his glass. "One might," he said. "But humans are very strange creatures. They all deal with their grief in different ways, and many of those ways make no sense to those on the outside."

Theodore was a strange creature himself. Maybe whatever people he had come from in Europe didn't consider themselves human like the rest of us. "Well, I really do need to know about this deal my brother had," I said. "Because he's in a bit of a bind."

"A bind how?" Theodore asked. "Surely if he talks to Starlight, she will help him?"

"It's a bit tricky," I said. "But I suppose I could try. Any deals with Norma would be over now, anyway, wouldn't they?"

Theodore made a thoughtful noise. "Things are rarely so clearcut. It may be that such things are held by the shop rather than the individual."

Ruiner shifted uneasily next to me.

"So Starlight would inherit all of those too?"

Theodore gave a fluid shrug. "It is possible. The ways of witches are unclear to me, but anyone who deals in favours knows that their best protection is that any deal persists after their death. It rather removes temptation for those who find themselves deeply in debt."

Which meant Starlight had just become the most powerful witch in the village. One who'd been desperate to be a witch for years and forced into menial tasks by Norma. "You don't think that makes Starlight a bit suspicious, then?" I asked.

He smiled. "Are you sure you do not doubt my investigative skills?"

"No, just … that's got to be tempting, right?"

"Perhaps," Theodore said, going back to his drink. "But so too might be removing the holder of a deal to the uninitiated. Someone working on behalf of a loved one, perhaps, who does not know the ways of magic. Who thinks that removing the dealer stops the game."

I just stared at him, my heart going too fast, and after a moment he added softly, "I do recommend that you stay in town, Morgan."

"Okay," I managed, and we were silent for a long moment. I drained my drink, willing the alcohol to work its magic, but it didn't taste quite right anymore. I was really, properly a suspect, and the reality of it seemed to be robbing me of strength, making my fingers slip on the smooth sides of the glass. Theodore leaned over and caught it before it could escape me entirely.

"Isabella will be very happy," he said conversationally. "She does so love to have new life in town."

I nodded, my neck too stiff. "Yes. Um. She does seem very enthusiastic. Very involved in everything."

"Oh, she is. In fact, she will probably be along soon. We often meet here."

"Right." I took a deep breath. "And why have you invited *me* here again?" Why not just drag me off to whatever passed as a police station in Hollowbeck?

"I thought you would like to experience Hollowbeck's nightlife," he said, waving at the empty seats around us and the couple of occupied tables. Two men were seated at one, arms entwined as they stared up at the sky, and at the other three women were whispering softly to each other, a pot of tea on the table in front of them.

I looked back at Theodore and, because I couldn't think of anything else to say and my brain had apparently disengaged itself from my mouth, said, "Yeah, it's *pumping*."

Theodore nodded, examining the end of his straw as he tried to tap a blockage out of it. When he looked up, there was a smile quirking up the corners of his lips. "It does get busier on Fridays," he said.

I burst out laughing, hearing the ragged edges of hysteria in my voice, and Theodore gave me a bemused look, as if sure that he *should* know what the joke was, but equally sure that he wasn't going to get it. Ruiner watched me with his ears back for a moment, then got up and put his front paws on my leg, his claws pressing through my jeans. It wasn't much, but it was enough that I managed to get the laughter under control, winding it down to a few uneasy hiccoughs.

Theodore gave me another smile and went back to his Bloody Mary, and then there was nothing but the smell of night blooms and cooling stone, while I tried to swallow the last of the hysteria. It wasn't helped by the realisation that it was somehow less uncomfortable sitting here with the sole, nocturnal police officer of a creepy little town, drinking a nameless cocktail that someone had created by *sniffing* me, than I had been on the few blind dates I'd had in the city.

Although the fact that he thought I was a murderer wasn't exactly a mood-setter.

ISABELLA ARRIVED while I was trying to figure out how to leave without seeming rude, Theodore was still slurping steadily through his pint of Bloody Mary. Just as he'd said, she appeared to be completely delighted we weren't leaving just yet. She fussed around the place, talking to us, admiring the flowers on the tables, greeting the other drinkers, pointing out a particularly nice piece of fruit on someone's glass, then rushing back to our table again with her long skirts swirling around her so enthusiastically that it was a good thing the seating out here was all low pallets and heavy cushions. She'd have left a trail of devastation in her wake if they'd been lesser furnishings.

Tanya brought her a cocktail that steamed and smoked, and Isabella clapped her hands over it delightedly, complimenting the bartender on the floating motes that glittered and shone in the low light like captured stars. I noticed that she didn't drink it, though.

Instead, she settled herself next to us like a hummingbird coming in to roost and asked how the stay at Petunia's was going, what I intended to do while I was in town, if I was eating enough, how I liked my cocktail, and then proceeded to rhapsodize about the hiking trails, the cheese experience, the llama farm, and the local botanical gardens, and how I should explore all of them and experience everything that Hollowbeck had to offer.

I'd never met a mayor before, so maybe they all really are in it for the love of their towns, but I was fairly certain most were more about business deals and fancy luncheons. Isabella, on the other hand, should've been the one on the billboard on the way into town, rather than the freaky magician. She was a one-woman advertisement and welcome party rolled into one.

But of course, we weren't here for sightseeing, so I just nodded politely and promised I'd think about it before accepting a second drink so it didn't look like I was rushing off the moment she'd arrived. And also because they were *really* tasty, despite my good intentions following Petunia's impromptu lunch party.

By the time I finished, it was past one in the morning, and Ruiner was even more restless than I was. We needed to get back and have a hunt for the spell book. Theodore had done nothing to give away if he knew about it, or had taken it, but who knew with him. He was a cop to start with, so one assumed he'd be pretty good at hiding such things, plus there was no way to know if he was acting weirdly when the benchmark for that was already pretty high.

So I finished my drink (which had had the same *feel* as the first, all wide open spaces and wild skies, but not the same taste, and I couldn't quite figure out how that worked), then had a brief argument about paying, in which Theodore announced, with some of his Bloody Mary smearing his chin and his eyes bright in the dark, that he was the law in town and if he said I didn't pay, I didn't pay. Isabella glared at him so furiously that he immediately apologised, but then she turned around and told me that it was her treat.

I gave up. I was hardly in a position to argue with free drinks, anyway. I stood up instead, Ruiner jumping to the ground and stretching with his bum in the air. He was really getting far too comfortable with the whole cat-shaped thing.

"Do you need an escort?" Theodore asked.

I shook my head. I'd spent years walking around Manchester after dark. I wasn't about to worry about Hollowbeck. "It seems pretty safe here."

"Indeed," Isabella said. "What happened to Norma was a sad exception to our norm."

"Exceedingly tragic," Theodore added, slurping noisily on his straw. "But we shall be happy to accompany you home, should it make you more comfortable."

"That's alright," I said. "We'll be fine."

Isabella smiled down at Ruiner and fluttered her fingers at him. "And of course you have your staunch defender to accompany you."

Theodore raised his well-groomed eyebrows and looked at Ruiner, who glared back, baring his teeth. Theodore grinned, showing his own teeth, and Ruiner's ears flattened against his skull, hackles going up. I nudged him with my foot. "That's one way to describe him," I said. "Come on, staunch offender."

"Defender," Isabella said, and I just gave her and Theodore a little wave then headed back through the bar and onto the quiet streets, Tanya calling a cheery farewell as if I'd been coming in every night for the last twenty years.

It was still oddly warm, Hollowbeck's strange little microclimate defying the reality of English summer weather in a manner than made it very easy to believe in magic. It was cool enough I was glad of my jacket, though, and I tucked my hands into my pockets as we walked back the way we'd come, pausing where the side street joined the main one. Turning left would have taken us straight back to Petunia's, but on impulse I went right instead.

"What're we up to?" Ruiner asked as he trotted next to me. "We need to get back and find the grimoire."

"Some of the shops are open," I said.

"We're *shopping?*"

I shushed him with a wave as we approached a very small man stomping down the street, an enormous watermelon clutched to his belly. He nodded at us, I nodded back, and he strode off into the night with his fruit. "I want to see if the Cosy Cauldron's open," I said.

"Why? How's that going to help us?"

"I don't know," I admitted. "But the whole Starlight thing's interesting. She gets to just take over the whole business, and it sounds like that means all the deals that Norma had made, too. Including whoever's behind the note. Maybe we can talk to her and see if she knows about it."

"That seems like one of your worse ideas. She could be *behind* the note, as well as Norma's death, no matter what your orange bestie back there says."

I made a noncommittal sound. He was right, of course. But all poking around had got us so far was attacked by a rat and a glimpse at a ledger that had done zero to help us. We weren't getting anywhere, and the longer this took, the greater the chances that someone was going to discover Ruiner was more than just a cat, or that the threat in the notes might be carried out. So we had to do *something*.

Not all the shops were open, but some of the ones that had been shut when we'd been in here in the daylight were, such as a clothing shop called A Witch in Time. The grocery store was open, as was Bewitching Brews, and low, warm lights shone behind the windows. People browsed clothing racks, or bought milk, or sat down with a large latte and a scone, just as they might have during the day. There was no sense of it being some special sort of late-night shopping event, or a shadowy version of life, somehow divorced from the day and robbed of colour. It was simply business as usual, without the sun being out. Hollowbeck had a better nocturnal life than some of the big cities I'd lived in.

The Cosy Cauldron was open too. Starlight stood in the doorway, talking to an older woman who had the twisted hands of arthritis. She was gingerly cradling a shopping bag with the handles over her wrists, her shoulders stooped but her eyes bright as she talked earnestly to the young woman.

We stopped outside a shop called Family Familiars, close enough to hear but not so close that Starlight would notice if she looked around, and I pretended to be engrossed in a display of dog toys. The night was quiet, and I heard her say, "Make sure you rub it in really well. I've introduced a few little tweaks of my own."

"Are you sure?" the older woman asked, frowning at the tub Starlight was holding out to her. "I've been using Norma's for years. I can't afford to pay for something that's not going to work."

"It'll work. I promise."

"I hope so. I think it's getting worse, you know. I've been having to buy more and more to get the same relief."

"Yes," Starlight said, her tone flat. "That seems to happen with a lot of things. I suppose we all build up resistance, don't we?"

"Or I'm just getting older," the other woman said with a sigh, and started digging in her purse.

Starlight held up a hand. "No, take that for free. You can see how it works for you, then we'll work something out."

"Oh, thank you, dear," the older woman said. "But I must give you something. What is it that you need?"

"I don't need anything," Starlight replied, and I could see tight lines digging at the sides of her mouth. "Just use that and let me know how the new formula goes."

The older woman took the tub and tucked it into her bag, bowing her head in thanks, then turned and hobbled off into the night. Starlight watched her go, frown deepening, and I couldn't quite read the expression. She was unhappy that the woman hadn't wanted her new formula? Unhappy that the old one hadn't been working? Wracked with guilt about the murder? There was no way of telling, and while I wondered what to do next, she turned and went inside, leaving the pavement empty.

I looked at Ruiner, about to suggest that we may as well go home, and the sound of raised voices washed out of the Cosy Cauldron. We moved toward it without so much as a querying whisker raised between us.

SIXTEEN

Progressing backward

RUINER and I scurried down the pavement to loiter just out of view of the Cosy Cauldron's display windows. I picked up a book titled *Clean Your Aura* from the cart outside and pretended to read the back.

"But do you have it?" a woman's voice demanded.

"No," Starlight replied, her voice cool. "Norma's organisation wasn't great. I'm still trying to find it."

"But I need my charm," the woman said. "This was part of the deal. I need a constant supply."

"And I will get it to you," Starlight said. "But I've never made that particular charm, and I have to find the book to get the recipe. I can't just pull it out of thin air."

There was a long, still pause, and then the other woman said, "You have to find it. The deal goes to whoever holds the book, and I need to know you have it."

"I'm going to find it. But the deal can change depending on who has the book, too."

That pause again, and it raised the hairs on my arms, then the woman said, "Are you saying you want to change it?"

"I'm saying that right now, I can't help you. But I will as soon as I find the book. You're just going to need to be patient."

"I don't have time for that."

I barely had time to turn my back, still engaged in an enthusiastic perusal of *Clean Your Aura*, before the woman marched out the door and into the road, not stopping to look around. It was Ruby, and as she headed toward Mystic Munchies, I spotted Asger peering through the window as he placed a plate on a table. He saw Ruby and waved cheerily at her. She hesitated, put a bright smile on, and waved back before continuing across the road a little more calmly.

I put the book back and retreated to the dog toy display, whispering to Ruiner, "What do you know about that?"

"Nothing," he said. "It'll be another one of Norma's deals. Maybe it's to make sure their tiramisu is worth the truly disturbing noises you made eating it the other night."

"I did not. But it was really good tiramisu."

"So I heard."

We waited a little bit longer, but no one else seemed to be coming into the Cosy Cauldron. I was going to have to buy a chew toy in the shape of a magic wand if I hung around here much longer. I compromised by buying a bag of cat treats, much to Ruiner's disgust, and when I came back out of the shop, Starlight was locking up. She glanced across at me and frowned slightly.

I waved my bag of treats at her, grinning brightly, and she gave me a very small nod as she climbed onto a bike. It was glittery pink with a basket on the front and flowers woven around the handlebars. She switched a little head-light on and peddled off into the night without looking back.

"That seems very on brand," I said.

Ruiner nodded. "Yeah, full commitment."

We were silent for a moment, then I said, "When she said she has to find the book…?"

"I think that's the one we might've just lost."

"Awesome."

There didn't seem to be much to do after that. We'd already broken into the Cosy Cauldron once that night, and twice seemed to be pushing it, even if we hadn't managed to get anything from the ledger. We needed to see if we could find the spell book.

WE WALKED HOME through the quietly busy streets, peopled by the same mix of the everyday and slightly odd as the daytime had been. To be fair, some of these people looked a bit paler than the daylight inhabitants did, but no one was flouncing around in cloaks and pointy hats.

Well, one woman was, accompanied by a bored-looking black cat, but she was also pointing a multi-coloured feather duster at things and shouting, "*Bam!*" to no obvious effect, so I think she was just everyday odd.

There was nothing threatening about anyone I saw, nothing that even made me look over my shoulder. No wonder Theodore was hanging out in a cocktail bar. There wasn't much for him to do.

We sneaked back into the guesthouse and tip-toed up to the attic bedroom. Everything was as we'd left it. As far as I could tell, no one had been in since our unexpected visit from Theodore earlier.

I hurried to the bed, stripped off the covers and shook them out, before pulling the rest of the sheets and pillows off, dropping them on the floor. Still nothing. I hefted the mattress up and flipped it straight off the bed and then finally dropped to my knees to check under the base, as if all the activity might have scared the grimoire out of hiding. It hadn't.

"Did he take it?" I asked Ruiner. "Theodore?"

"Maybe," Ruiner said. "I mean, he was in here. I didn't see him carrying anything, but he could have been."

"Well, what does that mean? Why would he take it? And why did he take us out for drinks?" I dropped onto the bed, running my hands back through my hair. "If he knew what it was, he'd have accused us — me — properly, wouldn't he?"

Ruiner sighed. "I don't know. But that was our best chance of breaking this counter-curse, and now we're back to square one." He sounded less furious than I'd have imagined. This was a man — well, previously a man — who'd once called me in a rage because a girlfriend had used his favourite nail scissors to cut a clothing tag. He didn't do measured reactions.

I looked at him for a moment and said, "If we're assuming it was Norma's missing spell book — wait. Did you know that's what it was?"

"I guessed," he admitted. "I never saw her use it, but I knew it had to be around somewhere. I hunted about until I smelled something that made my fur stand up."

"Right. So can anyone use a witch's spell book?"

"Wouldn't have been much point me taking it if not."

"Did you know that or guess that too?"

He sighed. "I guessed that too."

"Alright. But say you're right — who else would've wanted it?"

"Anyone she was making spells for," Ruiner replied. "I told you, she's expensive."

"And the whole thing Ruby was saying about the deals going with the book?"

Ruiner gave me a blank look. "No idea."

I frowned at him. "Really? After what Theodore was saying about deals outliving the dealer?"

He shrugged. "He said they'd stay with the shop."

"He may not have known."

"Pretty poor police officer if that's the case," he said, looking around the room with studied casualness.

I sighed. "Fine. Who would know we had it?"

Neither of us spoke, but the answer to that was pretty clear. Isabella had seen us coming around the side of the shop after Ruiner stole it, and Ben had been there too. Petunia had been in the room when we'd had it out. And Theodore had been poking around in here earlier. None of the suspects filled me with conviction, but the book was gone. We'd lost our best hope of changing Ruiner back, and we had no idea where to go from here.

"I'm going for a bath," I announced, abandoning the deconstructed bed.

Ruiner was already bedding into the crumpled sheets and barely looked at me. "Eww, water," he said, mostly to himself.

The post-midnight bath was quickly becoming a ritual, and I wasn't sure if that was a development I liked or not. I examined the shelf of jars and bottles as the water gurgled into the tub and found the one with the same rune as the vial from the Cosy Cauldron. Whisperwind. I eased the cork out and sniffed cautiously. It had undertones of lavender and a whiff of camomile, and made me think of soft, deep pillows and rain on windowpanes. I considered dropping some in the bath, but no matter how safe Ben said it was, I could still see Norma in her cauldron. I popped the cork back in and went with the bath salts instead. They looked pretty innocent.

Before long I was clambering into deep, warm water, scented with roses and jasmine, watched by two frogs who had emerged from under the door. I waved at them.

"You weren't staying in the attic room, were you?" I said. "You didn't accidentally dig up any potato plants you shouldn't have?"

They looked back at me, unblinking, and I sighed and lay back in the water, staring at the ceiling. We had no book, and no leads — or too many, if we were thinking anyone Norma had done a deal with was a possible murderer. And I wasn't a detective. I didn't even know where to start.

I still didn't know when I got back to the room and clambered into the dishevelled bed. I shoved my hands under the pillow to adjust it and encountered a piece of paper. I pulled it out, wondering if it had come from the spell book.

It hadn't. It was a now-familiar sheet of heavy note paper, but it wasn't the same note. It was new and uncreased, and printed on it was, *Leave now. Your life is in danger. Your soul will be forfeit.*

I stared at it, my stomach rolling over and the work of the bath salts very much undone, listening to Ruiner's cat snores. It was a long time before I finally fell asleep.

I HARBOURED some small hope that the note had been a dream, but when I sat up the next morning, Ruiner was staring at it, his ears back.

"Can you tell anything about it?" I asked him.

"Looks the same as the other one," he said. "Where was it?"

"Under the pillow," I said, and he hissed. "Can you smell who might have left it?"

"I'm not a *dog*." But his protest was half-hearted. "Morgs—"

"I know," I said, getting up. "Come on. I'm hungry."

Downstairs, Petunia was once again nowhere to be seen. The loaf of fresh bread had been replaced by a large jar of homemade granola, with a note saying, *fruit and yoghurt in the fridge*. I found them next to Ruiner's plate of fish and its heart-studded label. I put the plate on the floor and said, "Don't get accustomed to this. I'm not buying fresh fish."

"You should," he said. "You're my sister."

"That's why I'm not buying fresh fish. I don't like you enough for that."

He bared his teeth at me and I ignored him, busying myself with the granola and yogurt, which was thick and creamy and looked homemade, and soon discovered I could easily have eaten the whole jar in one sitting. I restrained myself, though, and before long we were heading back into town, the route starting to feel well-worn and familiar. This place was growing on me, maybe too much. It wasn't like I could stay here. Never mind the threat — I hadn't exactly seen anywhere advertising for out-of-work bookkeepers.

I'd skipped tea with breakfast, since the coffee at Bewitching Brews had been more than good enough to warrant a return visit. We arrived with the morning rush, people brandishing thermal mugs for takeaway coffees and grabbing brown paper bags that smelled enticingly of warm bread and bacon grease. All the tables outside and inside were full, but the stools at the counter held only an older man with a long goatee and a miniature horse sitting on the floor next to him with its legs splayed. I took the furthest stool from them, and Ruiner jumped up on one next to me.

"Don't take a seat," I told him. "It's too busy."

He twitched his ears at me, and Edith smiled. She was executing a delicately detailed dragonfly on top of some-one's takeaway coffee mug. "Good morning, dear," she said. "Lovely to see you both back."

"Thanks," I said, looking around. There was no sign of James. "Is it just you this morning?"

"Oh, no, James is out back doing breakfasts," she replied. "I can't be doing with swapping around every time he needs someone to draw a flower on a coffee."

"That's fair enough," I replied, and watched her drawing with some fascination. She really was *very* good at it, and I wondered if it was magic or just artistic talent. Or if maybe that was the same thing.

A few minutes later, she set a long black down in front of me. "Anything for the kitty?"

"He's fine," I said, and sipped my drink while I waited for things to die off a little bit. Bewitching Brews was evidently the place to be on a Thursday morning.

I'd almost finished my coffee before the rush began to ease away, and Edith started wiping down the coffee machine, which was already cleaner than a lot of places I'd been in.

I nodded down the road toward Mystic Munchies. "They seem to do good business."

"Yes," replied Edith. "They're quite new, but they defi-nitely seem very popular." There was a certain reserve in her voice.

"You don't like it?" I asked.

"I don't go there," she replied. "All that foreign food. It's not for me."

"It's *pasta*," James said, coming out of the kitchen, carrying two plates of golden-hued scones with tubs of cream and jam nestled next to them. He paused at the counter and said, "And you can get other things too." His aunt shrugged, and he said to me in a stage-whisper, "Aunt Edith's got a bit of a thing about Mystic Munchies. She thinks they've been up to corporate espionage." He winked at me and hurried off.

I looked at Edith. "But they're not a coffee shop?"

"Not against me," she said. "Some of the other shops."

"Okay. Why do you think that, though?" I was wondering about Ruby saying *I need it* last night. Could Ruiner be right about the tiramisu?

Edith gave me a thoughtful look. "They didn't do terribly well when they first opened. Asger was doing the cooking, and he was very keen on lutefisk and things like that."

"Eww."

"Well, quite. That's what I mean about foreign food. I'm sure it's fine if you're used to it, but for the rest of us…" She wrinkled her nose. "Even after they decided to go down the Italian route, no one was too keen, just in case there was fermented shark in the gnocchi or something."

She shook her head. "Then suddenly, everyone in town started having trouble of some sort. Beth's juices down at Joo-Joo-Juice kept fermenting. She'd make the drink, give it to the customer, and halfway down the glass they'd come back and say it was off. Someone accused her of trying to get their kids drunk on fermented juice, of all things. And at Spiffing Sarnies, all Bert's bread went mouldy. He couldn't keep it fresh for more than ten minutes. Even the Cult of Cupcakes had a problem with exploding icing."

"I'm sorry, *exploding?*"

"Exactly. It was a *spate,* and the only place that wasn't struggling was Mystic Munchies. They got a lot of business because of that. Of course, they *were* hit by the pixie infestation, so it looked as though they were having as much trouble as anyone else, but still."

I stared at her. "But how would anyone do that? How *could* anyone do that?"

She smiled at me, tipping her head slightly. "How do you think, dear?"

"Right," I said. "A curse?"

"Exactly. Now you're getting the hang of Hollowbeck."

"But that's madness," I said. "Surely people can't do that, can they?"

"They *shouldn't* do it," Edith replied. "But there's no law, is there? Magic has rules, and if you break those, then things are likely to get very uncomfortable and involve tears in dimensions and people being turned inside out. But there aren't any *laws.* Generally speaking, magical folk just do what they can to get along. It's a balance, a social contract, but very few things are forbidden, and we can't prove anything."

"So how did everyone get their business back to normal?"

She gave a very small shrug. "Norma was always very happy to help out, for a price."

"They all struck deals with her?"

"There wasn't a lot of choice."

"Would a lot of people have had a grudge against Norma, then?"

Edith smiled. "She wasn't anyone's favourite person," she said. "But somehow, I don't think any of us would have done anything to harm her. I mean, it's no different to paying an exterminator if you get rats, is it? Everything has a price."

I wanted to say that most prices didn't include setting curses on people, but just then a group of five wizened old men came in and started arguing about whether to have hot chocolate or chai, demanding Edith explain the advantages of each. I'd learned as much as I could, anyway, so I slipped off the stool and headed for the door, not even complaining when Ruiner jumped to my shoulder.

"Where are we going?" he hissed.

"To see Starlight," I said. "We need to find out more about these deals."

"Oh, fun," he said. "I'm sure she'll be really open to that discussion."

SEVENTEEN

A whiff of aniseed

STARLIGHT WAS NOT OPEN to that discussion.

I mean, she might've been, but I went through the annoying bloody tinkling bells on the door of the Cosy Cauldron to an empty room and the scent of something burning deeper in the building. There was no one behind the counter, and the shop itself was so still and silent it might've been caught in amber, like the dragonflies and rhinoceros beetles for sale in a box on the shelf by the door.

"Hello?" I called, and no one answered. The burning smell was strong and astringent, making me wrinkle my nose, but there was no smoke, at least. I ventured to the counter and tapped the bell, hating the way the whole place had the same suspended feel as when we'd arrived and found Norma. I swallowed hard, listening to the echoes of the bell die away, and started to shout again when there was the slam of a door from the back of the shop.

"Starlight?"

Still no answer, but there *was* someone back there, or

there had been. I swallowed a groan and let myself around the counter.

"What're you *doing?*" Ruiner hissed into my ear.

"She might be hurt," I whispered back. "We have to check."

"What, do you just love finding dead bodies or something?" He was too close for me to be able to see if his tail was doing that bottle brush thing, but the way his claws were digging into my shoulder, I thought it probably was.

"Don't say that. I'm sure she's fine." I called her name again as I slipped through the beaded curtain. All the doors coming off the hall were open. "Starlight? It's Morgan? I was in the other day?" My voice kept going up into panicky questioning tones, and I peered into the office we'd been in the night before. The ledgers were scattered over the floor, and the taxidermy animals were jumbled everywhere, as if we'd interrupted them in some arcane dance.

"Morgan, we have to leave." Ruiner's claws were digging in so deeply that I shoved him off. He squawked, turning his fall into a graceful jump and giving me a dirty look. "Did you forget about the rat?"

"Shut up and help me find Starlight."

"*She's not here.* She'd have answered if she was here."

I waved at him impatiently, already peeking into the next doorway. It was a downstairs loo, looking sufficiently un-witchy with a bottle of toilet cleaner and a basket of spare loo rolls cluttering up the floor. The next door held stairs that climbed up to the top floor, but I ignored them for now, bracing myself to venture into the big kitchen and living area. The burning smell was stronger back here, and I coughed.

"Starlight?" I peeked around the doorframe. My eyes went straight to the hearth, but there was no cauldron and no body sprawled in it. There were just two blackened stock pots, smoking amid the embers.

I hurried over to them and grabbed an oven mitt that was hanging from the mantelpiece before pulling the pots off of the heat. There was no fire left, but the embers were still more than hot enough, and whatever had been brewing was boiled away to a gunky collection of twigs and scorched sludge in the bottoms of the pots. I wheezed a couple of times, hoping it wasn't some sort of magic nerve agent, and opened the back door to try and air the place out.

"Crisis averted," Ruiner said. "Can we go now?"

"Where's Starlight? She wouldn't have just left those on the fire," I said, waving at the pots smoking on the flagstones in front of the hearth. "And *someone* was here. We heard a door, right?"

"Right," Ruiner said, shifting his paws. "Presumably the same person who trashed the office and scared off Starlight. And you want to meet them?"

I opened my mouth to ask where his sense of responsibility was and heard a thud from the stairs. We both stared at each other, and for a moment I considered running straight out the open door. But if something *had* happened to Starlight, we needed to help her. Besides, in this bloody town, someone would definitely have seen us walk in, so there was no point trying to pretend we hadn't been here.

I tiptoed back into the hall and edged through the door, peering up the stairs. "Um, Starlight?" I tried, the words sticking in my mouth. I was rewarded by another thud, and I crept up the stairs, wishing I'd picked up a taxidermy ferret or something in case I had to hit anyone.

But no one rushed around the turn of the stairs to meet us, and a moment later I was standing in the upstairs hall, lit softly by light washing through one of the doors that lined it. The walls had evidently been painted at some point, old, embossed wallpaper showing through under the coat of white, but the floor still wore a threadbare dark green carpet, making it dull and murky up here. Starlight was sprawled on the floor on her stomach, arms out in front of her as if she'd ben crawling along the hall when she collapsed. I couldn't see any injuries from here, but I still hesitated, looking around. Any one of the doors leading off to either side of the hall could hide her attacker.

There was another *thud*, and I let out a little scream, jumping back and slipping on the top step. For one moment I wobbled on the edge of balance, then grabbed the banister and staggered back to safer ground.

Ruiner hissed. "It's that bloody rat."

I peered down the hallway, catching a glimpse of movement on an old dark wood sideboard. There were a few ornaments lying beneath it, and I heard the rat chitter. "Well, unless it attacked her, it's not really our problem," I said, and hurried forward to kneel next to Starlight, trying to keep an eye on the doors at the same time. There was no sign of movement from any of them, though, no clicking latches or turning handles, and I touched Starlight's shoulder, giving her a gentle shake. "Starlight? Are you okay?"

"I'm sure she is," Ruiner said. "Just having a little lie-down."

"Shut up," I hissed at him. Starlight gave a little whimper, pulling her hands in and tucking them under her. "Starlight?" I pushed her hair carefully off her neck so I could see her face where it was turned to the side. "It's Morgan. Can you sit up?"

She groaned, a little more loudly, and her eyes moved behind their lids, but she didn't open them. I tried patting her face, like people do in movies, but she just whimpered again, and I leaned a little closer, intending to shout in her ear. Instead, I got a whiff of scent off her, incense and patchouli and...

"Is that aniseed?"

"What?" Ruiner asked. He was stalking along the hallway, peering at the gaps beneath the doors. "I don't see anyone."

"Can you smell aniseed?"

"I can't smell anything over that bloody burning stink from downstairs."

It hardly mattered right now, anyway. I pulled my phone out, looked at the missing bars, and swore. "Is there even such a thing as emergency services here?"

"I've never seen any," Ruiner said.

"Great." I got up. "Stay with her. I'm going to get help." I ran for the stairs, ignoring him shouting after me.

"Wait! What'm I meant to do? I can't even *talk* to her! And there's a rat! *What about the rat, Morgan?*"

I lost the last of what he said as I ran out of the shop and into the street, hesitating for a moment. Mystic Munchies was closest, but Ruby and Starlight had been arguing. I turned and ran for Bewitching Brews, waving wildly when I saw James outside.

"Help!" I shouted. "Starlight's been attacked!"

James dumped his tray on the table and sprinted toward me, and I turned back to the Cosy Cauldron in time to see Asger hurrying across the road. It looked almost as if he'd come out of the alley next to the shop.

It turned out that James was not the sort of person you really wanted around in a crisis. He and I exchanged increasingly desperate questions about who to call if there was no way to get an ambulance until Edith strode in. She ordered James to put the still-unconscious Starlight on a bed, and fussed around her for a few moments, checking her pulse and prying her eyes open, and eventually saying, "She'll be fine. James, go back and mind the shop, will you? Old Art will've helped himself to about five free cappuccinos and all the sandwiches by now."

"But," James started, but Edith just raised her eyebrows at him and his mouth snapped shut. Her hands were planted on her hips and she was wearing scuffed trainers, old worn jeans, and a T-shirt with a futuristic-looking coffee grinder on it. The coffee grinder was shrieking *caffeinate!* and the whole outfit was somehow more witchy looking than her dress yesterday had been.

James subsided and hurried out, and Edith turned her attention to me. "You'd better go, too, dear."

"But I found her," I said. "Shouldn't I stay around until … well, I don't know. What happens now?"

"You did find her," Edith agreed. "So once Isabella gets here, she'll want to know why you were snooping around the shop *again*, after already finding one body here. And what Isabella wants, Isabella gets, and it all goes straight to Theodore." She gave me a thoughtful smile. "I don't think you want anyone asking too many questions of you and your cat, do you?"

Ruiner and I looked at each other, then I said, "But I haven't done anything wrong."

"That's rarely a good defence, even in Hollowbeck. Off you go, dear. Out the back. I'll field any questions." She shooed me, and I let myself be shooed, my chest suddenly too tight and hot. No one would really think I'd attacked Starlight, would they?

Would they?

~

OUTSIDE, without really thinking about it, I found myself heading back toward the library. There's always peace to be found among the books, if nothing else, but that aniseed smell was also niggling at me. I was sure it was the same scent as I'd caught when we'd found Norma, and I wanted to see if I could find out what it was.

Ruiner, predictably, complained as soon as he realised where we were going, then as I started up the library steps, he stalked off in the direction of the town hall, claiming he was going to snoop around and see if there was any news about the investigation. I thought it was more likely he was going to try and catch a glimpse of Isabella's cleavage. My brother has no class.

The librarian in the same teal tartan dress was at the desk, checking the cards in the backs of the books and I was quite abruptly seven years old again and terrified of late fines.

She looked up as I came in. "Morning," she all but shouted. A cadaverous man in a bowler cap popped his head around a shelf to stare at us both, frowning. "I'll have to get you a library card if you keep coming in this often."

"Oh, no thanks," I said. "I don't need a library card. I just wanted to do a bit more research."

She shrugged and waved vaguely at the stacks. "Suit yourself. Do you want me to let Ben know you're here?"

"No, that's fine." I said before heading toward the extensive arcane wing.

I poked around the shelves as I searched for the right section. It took me a little while to find the books I needed among the recipes for good weather (that explained a lot), guides to dowsing, breeding newts, and reading tea leaves, and an alarmingly large collection that all seemed connected to raising the dead. But finally I found what seemed to be a health section (much smaller than the section on curses, which I also made a note of — I needed to come back to later to see if it also covered counter-curses). I grabbed a hefty encyclopedia of magical medicines and sat down on the floor to hunt for whisperwind.

I was still sitting there, frowning at the five-page entry, when Ben appeared, ambling out of the stacks with his hands in his pockets. "Back again," he said. "What is it this time?"

I resisted the urge to shout *it wasn't me!* like I'd been listening to too much Shaggy, and instead said, "I wanted to know more about whisperwind. I still don't understand how Theodore said it was the most likely the cause of death if it's just a bit of muscle relaxant."

He shrugged, taking a book out and re-shelving it half a row over. "Well, like I said, she might have mixed it with something else. Magical stuff's not that much different to regular meds. It might be like having sleeping pills on top of alcohol."

That made sense. "Was she a drinker?"

"I don't know," he said, crouching down next to me and tipping his head so that he could see the page.

I pointed to the passage I was reading. "It says here that even with an excess dose, you should be responsive. You shouldn't be able to just drown in a cauldron."

He looked at me, his eyes a still, warm brown, but there was just a touch of irritation in his voice when he spoke. "That's straight whisperwind, though. Who knows what else she took at the same time?"

"True." I closed the book with a sigh. "What does it smell of?"

"It's a floral scent."

That was what the vial at Petunia's had smelled of. "Not aniseed?"

He frowned. "No. Nothing like that."

"Did you notice an aniseed smell at the shop? When you went to look at … her?"

"No." He was looking at me as if he thought I needed a bit of whisperwind myself. "Why?"

"There was super-strong smell when I found her." *And on Starlight.*

"Maybe it had gone by the time we got there," he said. "Plus it was a pretty stressful situation. You could have imagined it."

"I'm pretty certain I wouldn't have imagined that. I don't even like aniseed."

"Well, I imagine you probably don't like dead bodies either," he replied. "Maybe it was an association."

"Aniseed equals dead bodies?"

"I can't stand the smell of bananas because they remind me of dentists," he said.

"What?"

"My mum used to buy me those squishy banana sweets to bribe me to go to the dentist. Put me right off."

I stared at him for a moment. "They don't even smell like actual bananas."

"Association." He grinned at me, then stood up and held a hand out. "Tea?"

"Tea," I replied, taking his hand. He looked at it for a moment, then helped me up and held his other hand out for the encyclopaedia. "*Oh.*" I handed it over, trying to will the heat out of my cheeks as he re-shelved it, then followed him to the now-familiar staff room.

Ben brewed more herbal tea, and while it steeped, he showed me one of the books he was working on. The spine had just about been cracked in two, and pages stuck out of it at weird angles. Someone had tried to repair it, apparently with dinosaur-print band-aids and paste made from flour and water.

"Poor thing," I said, stroking the cover with one finger, then shuddered and wiped my hand on my jeans. "Eww. Why's it slimy?"

"Best not to ask." He pointed at another, sitting on its own in the bottom of a large plastic tub. "Check this one out."

I peered down at it, keeping my hands away this time. The cover was warped and water-stained, and the title was impossible to make out among all the foliage that coiled over it. It looked a lot like it had fallen into a cluster of grapevines, to my experienced horticulturist's eye. *Ha.*

Ben touched a vine lightly, and it immediately let go of the book and wrapped itself around his finger, squeezing so tightly that the fingertip went red. He pried it off again, not without some difficulty, and all while fending off another couple of vines that sprouted up to join the fight.

"It took us three days to get it out of the return box," he told me. "Dee had to threaten it with secateurs."

I stared at him. "I'm guessing librarian training doesn't usually cover this, unless I know a lot less about libraries than I thought."

He grinned. "These aren't even the books you have to worry about. These are just books that someone's spilled a bit of magic on."

"Right," I said and picked up a slightly tattered bodice ripper from the table. "And this?"

"Very popular among some of the older witches," he replied, his grin widening. "But you don't want to see those ones when they've been magicked."

"Right," I said, and dropped it quickly. I'm all for embracing one's sexuality, but not if the book's going to embrace you back. Ben laughed and went to pour the tea.

EIGHTEEN

A very bad plan

BY THE TIME I'd finished my tea and eaten half a dozen custard creams (they're small, okay?), I was starting to feel slightly more human, and slightly less like I was about to be taken out by some sort of magical neighbourhood watch. Ben had a way of making things feel a little more manageable, and with some tea and sugar in me, it seemed ridiculous that anyone could really suspect me of attacking Starlight. I put my mug in the sink and said to him, "I think I'd better head off then."

"Sure." Ben picked up my mug and rinsed it out. "As in leaving Hollowbeck, or…?"

"Not just yet," I said. "I haven't quite finished this thing for my brother."

"Of course. Can I help you with that at all? Any research you need, or local knowledge, or anything?"

I hesitated, but Ruiner would vomit in my shoes if I told Ben anything. Plus, while he did make things seem *better* somehow, something about the way he'd dismissed the aniseed thing so quickly annoyed me. Just because he hadn't smelled it didn't mean *I* hadn't. It was a fickle thing to withhold trust for, but there it was. Sometimes instincts were louder than logic. "No," I said aloud. "Thanks anyway, though."

He nodded. "Well, if you need anything, you know where I am."

"Repairing bodice rippers with great caution."

"And fending off triffid-books."

"I bet more people would be librarians if that stuff was in the curriculum."

He laughed, and I left him tidying away the last of the custard creams, presumably before Isabella could come in and disapprove of them.

Ruiner was waiting on the path outside, sprawled on the stone to soak up the sun.

"What, no bird attacks today?" I asked him.

"I told them I'd pluck them, stuff them, and roast them for Sunday dinner if they touched my tail one more time," he said. "It seemed to work."

"Always making friends and forming connections."

We headed back to Petunia's, my legs heavy and my head fuzzy with weariness. The route was starting to get so well worn into my brain that my feet just followed it on their own, my head drifting in the weird, close heat of the village. I was exhausted. Which made sense. Everything that had happened since Ruiner had turned up on my windowsill was completely against the way the world should work. My head needed a break as much as my body did.

We got back upstairs without being waylaid by vegetable gardening duties or offers of a day-drinking session, and I dropped onto the bed with a sigh, flinging my arms wide. The room was warm but not stuffy, and the bed felt like an embrace.

"What're you doing?" Ruiner asked, jumping up next

to me. "I've got an idea. I don't love it, but I think it's our next best move."

I squinted at him. "Really? You have an idea you don't love?"

"Shut up. Look, Theodore's the most likely person to have taken the spell book, right?"

"Well, he was here, but why wouldn't he confront me about it last night?"

"Because he has his *methods* and he's waiting for you to incriminate yourself further."

"Oh, *super.*"

"Or he fancies you, for some unfathomable reason that's probably related to toxic shock from overuse of fake tan."

"You think he fancies me?"

"*No, Morgan.*"

I scowled at him. "You said it."

"You cannot be interested in him. He looks like he fell in a tub of custard."

"I didn't say I was interested," I protested.

Ruiner bared a tooth at me. "*Anyway.* We should at least rule out the possibility of him having the book, then—"

"Please tell me you're not suggesting we break into a police officer's house."

"The town hall. I snooped while you were swapping tea leaves with the librarian, but I couldn't open the door to his office."

"*No,*" I said, with as much heat as I could manage, which wasn't a lot. I closed my eyes. "We're not breaking into the town hall. And I need a nap."

"What's wrong with you?" Ruiner asked, pawing my arm. "We need to get on this while it's still light."

"I'm tired. Running around trying to solve all your problems does that."

"*My* problems? It's whatever you're up to with the bloody librarian that's wearing you out."

"I'm not *up to* anything," I said, but it was barely a mumble. It was too warm to be irritated with him. I wondered vaguely if I'd inhaled a bit more smoke from the shop than I'd thought.

"Morgs. Morgs. *Morgan.*"

"Shut up," I said, or thought I did.

I WOKE up with the light at a different angle on the walls, my mouth sticky but my head distinctly clearer. I yawned, licked my lips, and looked around to see Ruiner sitting next to me, front paws pressed tightly together as he glared down at me with his tail flicking.

"What're you doing?" I asked.

He huffed. "What're *you* doing? Napping half the bloody day when you're likely to be arrested for assault *and* murder."

"We didn't have anything to do with either," I said, pushing myself onto my elbows. "They can't arrest me with no evidence."

"Just how much do you think this town runs according to the rules of the outside world? And how much do you think that applies to the outside world anyway?"

I wiped my mouth, not looking at him. "Fine. But what do we do? We're not breaking into the bloody town hall. That *will* get us arrested."

He growled. "We're not getting far like this, though, are we?"

"No," I admitted, rolling over to reach for my water bottle. "We need to try to get another look at the ledgers, I suppose. Why don't we just ask Starlight? We helped her today, after all. She might be ready to help us."

"Finding the spell book's more important."

"Why? Just so you can be changed back?"

He growled. "No. This is about who's after you, and ledgers are just records. The spell book has power."

I watched him for a moment. "Is this because of what Ruby said? About the deals going with the spell book? It doesn't matter, does it? We just need to find out who has a deal out regarding me, not who holds it now."

He hesitated, his tail twitching. I knew this hesitation. It was less about being unsure, and more about choosing what he was going to tell me. I sighed. He wasn't going to answer. And, sure enough, when he spoke again, it wasn't about the spell book. Instead, he said, "Ruby was kicking off last night. What if she attacked Starlight?"

"Or Asger," I said, suddenly remembering him hurrying across the road. "I saw him leaving the shop this afternoon."

Ruiner looked at me, his ears back. "You're just remembering that now?"

"Oddly enough, I was slightly distracted by trying to help the unconscious woman. But yes, he came out of the alley down the side of the shop, same as he did when I found Norma. What if he killed her? Maybe that was who we heard when we found Norma, and you took the book before he could get it. So today he was back there looking for it?"

"Seems reasonable," Ruiner said. "But that means he doesn't have it if he was looking for it today."

"Oh," I said, deflating suddenly. "Right. But we need to tell Theodore about him being there."

He made a non-committal sound, then we were both

silent for a bit. Finally, I said, "So we've got no lead on the book, or on the note. Nothing at all."

"I still think—"

"We are *not* breaking into Theodore's office."

"Then we should leave."

"Theodore said not to."

"Do you think he can stop us?"

I thought about it. "I kind of feel like he might be able to, somehow."

He looked at me, arching his eyebrow whiskers. "So we're back to looking for the book, which means checking the most obvious place while the sun's still up."

"Really? But what if we get caught?"

"That's entirely the wrong attitude to take in life, you know."

"I'm sorry, who's been turned into a cat?"

He huffed. "Fine. Then we try the others. Isabella's in the same building, so I suppose she's out too, if you're being this picky. We could try your library bestie, or Petunia. You can ask her, see if you get turned into a frog."

"Fantastic," I said. "Thank you for reminding me of that. Those are all terrible ideas. I'm sure Ben has nothing to do with any of it—"

"Huge surprise."

"—and Petunia ... well, frogs."

"Right. So, since you hate all those ideas, what's *your* plan?"

I got up and stretched. "You're being oddly calm about the whole missing spell book thing. I was expecting more of a tantrum about the cat thing, to be honest."

"No point," my brother replied, as if he hadn't always treated every minor inconvenience as a personal affront. "No *time*. If someone's after you, Morgs ... I mean, I didn't *do* anything, obviously—"

"Obviously."

"—but if someone's after you, it's my fault. We need to figure that out, then we can get back to finding out how to turn me back into a person."

"You are a person," I pointed out. "Just a small, furry person."

"This is not a person. This is a cat."

"Cats are people too," I replied, grinning, and he hissed at me as I pulled my shoes on. "D'you think we should ask Starlight about the deals, then? See if she'll help?"

"I think we check on the last person at the murder scene. That note was displayed very nicely for you to find. Norma didn't leave stuff like that lying around. It was all locked in her office. It's no accident it was on the fridge."

I stared at him. "You want to talk to Asger? But he's…" I waved wildly, trying to encompass just how tall and broad-shouldered and generally much, much bigger than either of us he was. "A Viking! And Ruby was arguing with Starlight before she was attacked — they're probably working together. How can we talk to *Asger?* Do you *want* me to get my soul forfeited?"

Ruiner sighed so deeply his whole body heaved. "No, you muppet. Not *talk* to him. They'll be cleaning down from lunch and getting Mystic Munchies ready for dinner. They live not far out of town. All we have to do is nip out there and have a look around, see if he has any more notes hanging about. At least then we'll know who we're dealing with."

"Oh, that's all, is it?"

"Other option is looking for the book at the town hall."

"I'm starting to feel you're less invested in my well-being than you should be."

"Unfair."

I considered it. "Alright, a bit. But you're certainly a bit careless with it." I got up, sighing almost as deeply as Ruiner had. "*Fine.* Let's go."

"Really?" he asked, jumping off the bed and watching me take my jacket from the back of the door. I was still waiting for normal summer weather to reassert itself.

"Why not. May as well get the soul-forfeiting over with." I looked around the room thoughtfully. "Do you think we should wait and talk to Theodore about seeing Asger first?"

"Well, A) even if Theodore didn't take the book, he already thinks you're meddling in this investigation and second-guessing him, which isn't likely to make him too receptive. And B) Theodore only comes out at night."

"Do you really think he has a sun allergy?" I asked. "And it's not just him, either. Half this bloody town only comes out at night. *Why?*"

Ruiner arched his whiskers at me. "Gee, I don't know, Morgan. What only comes out at night and drinks gloopy red cocktails?"

I looked at him for a long moment, then said, "No." I headed for the door, skirting five frogs gathered around a smooth grey stone on the landing, all of them goggling at it with great concentration. It hardly seemed worth noticing, which I felt was a bad sign regarding how comfortable I was getting with life in Hollowbeck.

"You can't just say no," Ruiner said, trotting after me. "Saying no doesn't stop it being real."

"No," I said again and hurried down the steps with him following me. At least we were doing something. The question of the nocturnal cop and his gloopy cocktails could wait.

~

I'D HALF-HOPED, given all the other weirdness around here, that my poor old Volvo would somehow catch a bit of magic and rediscover her lost youth, but no such luck. She coughed and spluttered, and it took about half a dozen attempts to start her, and another few minutes before I could put her into gear and pull away from the kerb, accompanied by a large belch of exhaust smoke.

Ruiner coughed dramatically, and I scowled at him. "Some of us don't run up massive debts and then have our fancy cars impounded," I told him. "Some of us make do with what we've got."

"It's hardly making do when the car's terminally ill, is it? Besides, *some of us* have images to uphold."

I ignored him, and patted the dashboard lightly. "Good girl."

After a few false starts (Ruiner had never been good at directions when he was human, and being a cat didn't seem to have improved matters), we were rolling out of town in the opposite direction to the one we'd arrived from. I couldn't help but be tempted to just keep going, to see if we could drive straight out the other side of the valley, leaving suspicious police and murdered witches and charmed coffee, good as it was, behind us.

But it wasn't that easy, especially not with the second note appearing mysteriously among the bedclothes. That note meant it wasn't Norma writing them, and also that the person behind them was still following me. Following me closely enough to be in my *bedroom*. Maybe I should let myself be warned off, but there was still a corpse and an attacked woman out there, with witnesses putting me slap-bang in the middle of both. Plus Ruiner needed my help, and that was all tied up somehow with the bloody notes and my name. It was like an itch I just couldn't scratch. I needed to figure out what was going on.

And had the note-leaver also been the spell book-taker? It seemed likely, and if it wasn't Theodore, then the most obvious suspect was Petunia. I hated to think that it could be her, frogs or not, but she'd let Theodore right into my bedroom. She was hardly the most upstanding of landladies.

I pushed the thoughts down, leaning my arm on the open window and breathing in the fresh air washing past the car, redolent of hot ground and soft grass and more farm-y smells. Thinking about it wasn't changing anything. At least we actually had a lead and something to investigate, and it felt good to be doing something, even if, admittedly, it wouldn't have been approved by Theodore or Isabella. And I also wasn't sure *I* even approved of it, but there we are. It was something.

It wasn't far to Ruby and Asger's house, which was a weathered wooden cabin nestled into a rocky, multi-level garden crowded with herbs and flowers and, for some reason, miniature lighthouses and windmills.

I parked outside the gate and looked warily at the other houses further down the street. There weren't many, just a scattering, like a clump of the village that had drifted away down the road one night without anyone noticing. All it would take was one person looking out a window to spot us. Even as I thought that, I was sure I saw a curtain twitch in the downstairs window of the bungalow diagonally across the road.

"I don't like this," I said.

"So we leave. There's still plenty of time to get out of town before dark."

I shivered slightly. The idea of being hunted through the night as we tried to make a run for it in the tangled, shifting woods of the hills was enough to make my knees a little wobbly. But that was ridiculous. No one was going to be *hunting* us. "Do you think it'll let us go?"

"I've never heard of people not being able to get out. Just not being able to get in."

Which wasn't an answer. I opened the door and got out, letting Ruiner jump out after me before I closed it again and let myself in the gate. The path was jumbled grey pebbles, and they crunched under my trainers as I walked to the front door, sounding as loud as smashing glass in the stillness. Certainly no point trying to sneak in.

I knocked firmly, waited, then put one hand up to my ear, cocked my head, and shouted, "Around the back? On the way!"

Ruiner stared at me. "What's wrong with you?"

"We're being watched," I said, and headed down the path around the side of the cabin. "I'm making it look like we're meant to be here."

"Because whoever's watching won't have seen Ruby and Asger leave?"

"They might not have," I said, dodging a sprawling lavender bush that was spilling scent and bees all over the path.

"Brilliant," Ruiner breathed, then spat at a bee that bumped into his ear. "Ugh. *Nature.*"

The garden washed around both sides of the cabin and into a backyard that was so crammed with plants there was barely room for a fishpond capped by a little bridge, a summer house, and a patio holding a table and a clutter of chairs. There was also a small wooden building with no windows that looked like a garden shed, but had a chimney on it for some mysterious reason. A magpie fluttered down to land on its ridge line, tipping its head from one side to the other as it examined us. There was no one here, though, so I tried the back door. It was unlocked. I looked down at Ruiner.

"Go on, then," he said.

"I really don't want to," I said, but I pushed the door open onto a bright, white-painted kitchen. "Hello?"

There was no answer, and I stepped over the threshold, smelling herbs and woodsmoke and warm wood, and looked around at the shelves. "Where do we start?"

Ruiner miaowed, sounding almost like a regular cat, and I looked down at him. "What?"

Which was when a heavy hand landed on my shoulder and spun me unceremoniously around to face a very large, very displeased Viking, his body blocking the doorway as he loomed above me.

NINETEEN

A stroppy book

"WHAT ARE YOU DOING?" Asger demanded, his accent making the words clipped and sharp. "Why are you in my home?"

"Why are you *naked?*" I blurted before I could engage my brain enough to think of anything better to say.

He looked down at himself. "I was in the sauna." He pointed at the garden shed. That explained the chimney, at least.

I kept my eyes firmly on his shoulder. That seemed safer than any further south, and his expression was too furious for eye contact. The magpie cawed from behind him, and Asger looked over his shoulder. "Yes, thank you, Ulf."

"You talk to your magpie?"

"Don't you talk to your cat?" He walked past me into the kitchen, taking an apron from a hook on the wall and pulling it over his head. It had a sexy witch on it, winking and blowing a kiss as she zoomed off on a broomstick. "And answer, please. Why are you in my home?"

I ventured eye contact with him. He looked less angry

than bewildered now, probably because he'd realised he was dealing with idiots. "Sorry," I said, and looked at Ruiner. I hadn't had time to come up with a story to explain our presence, so I just said, "I saw you outside the Cosy Cauldron today."

"Yes?"

"And the other day, too. When I'd just arrived."

He folded his arms, which made his shoulders and biceps bulge alarmingly. I glanced at the door, wondering if I could make it out before he shoved us in the sauna and steamed us alive or something. But he just said, "Yes?" with that same questioning tone.

Ruiner took a step toward the door, and the magpie cawed. He hissed back, and the magpie reared up, beating its wings furiously. Ruiner's hiss turned into a yowl, his hair standing to attention along his spine and his tail pouffing out.

"Ulf, you cannot eat his eyes," Asger said conversationally. "It is in bad taste."

"Yes, behave yourself, Ruiner," I said, and both my brother and the magpie glared at us.

"Also, you cannot eat her eyes," Asger added. "You must stop with the eyes."

"Please do," I said.

He looked back at me. "You are the new keeper of the book."

"I am?"

Ruiner hissed, and I glanced at him. He lifted his chin slightly, which I decided to interpret as approval.

I turned back to Asger. "I am."

Asger sighed and waved at the table. "Sit. I must find pants." He left, the floorboards creaking under his weight, and after only a very small peek after him to check what the apron didn't cover, I started for the door. The magpie opened its wings, blocking my way and tipping its head one way then the other as it examined me with glittering eyes. I stopped short, staring at it, and after a moment sat down in one of the pale wooden chairs. I wasn't getting into a battle of the wills with anything that had a fetish for eating eyes.

Asger came back a moment later in jogging bottoms and a white T-shirt that was being tested to the limits of its endurance on his shoulders. "Coffee?" he offered. "Or no. You English and your tea."

"Coffee, please," I said, and he gave me an approving glance, then busied himself with a grinder and a stovetop espresso pot. He didn't speak again until he set a mug in front of me, and we stared at each other. There were shadows under his eyes, and he looked wary.

"What do you want?" he asked me. "How much?"

"Um…" I looked at Ruiner for help, but his ear wiggles weren't as effective as he evidently thought they were. "How much did you usually pay?"

"Two hundred pounds a month plus favours," he said, frowning. "But you know this?"

I tried the coffee, which was dark and rich and so strong it made my eye twitch. "Of course. Just, um, confirming."

"So what happens? I must swear on the book again?"

"Swear on the book? The spell book?"

Asger folded his arms on the table and stared at me. "You do not know?"

I took a breath, started to say that *of course* I knew, then gave up. "I have no idea," I confessed. "This is all new to me."

Behind me, Ruiner groaned and flopped onto his belly on the floor. Ulf cawed and hopped forward a few steps, tweaking Ruiner's tail. Ruiner didn't even move.

"Ulf, no," Asger said, then added to me, "But you do have the book?"

I eyed him over the table, not answering. If I threw my coffee in his face, I might have a small chance to leg it. "Yes," I said, since it was clear he didn't have it, and I *could* still have it. As far as Asger knew, anyway.

Asger took a sip of coffee and said, "And you do not know how to use it." It was impossible to read his tone. He might've been angry, or amused, or just bewildered. All possibilities were on the table.

"I only came to Hollowbeck to help my brother," I said. "I took the book when I found Norma because he, um, mentioned it. Said that it was to do with his deal, so I thought it might be helpful."

"You took the book," Asger said, and this time I could read his voice. Astonishment, and not of the admiring sort. "You took it simply because it was there? A book like that? I think maybe you do not even know what it really is."

"Not entirely," I admitted.

Asger looked at me for a long moment, then abruptly burst into a great roar of laughter that made Ruiner roll back to his feet and Ulf bounce anxiously around the kitchen, cawing wildly. I just stared at the huge man, waiting for him to finish and throw me in the fishpond. It took some time, but finally he chuckled himself to a stop, wiping his eyes. "This is very funny."

"So glad it's entertaining for you."

"I have been very worried. I thought that the new keeper of the book might ask for terrible things. Norma asked for unpleasant things, but not truly *bad*."

I considered this for a moment. "So whoever has the book owns the debts, and that means they can ask for other things?"

"Yes. The deals are open-ended. Or maybe not all, but

201

mine was. She could ask me anything, and I must do it, or she would take back the deal."

"What would happen then?"

"Everything would go back to as it was before, but worse. If one had wished for good crops, all would rot overnight. If one had wished for the business to do well, it would burn down, or be torn apart by debtors. The debt *must* be paid. The book insists."

"Just like that? Couldn't you talk to her?"

"The book has power. To make a deal, one swears on the book. Bleeds on it."

"*Eww*," I said.

"Yes. But then the book takes charge. Only once the keeper of the book releases the debtor can they escape. Otherwise, the book will destroy them no matter where they run. The consequences become worse and worse the more they try to resist."

I stared at him. "And how many people in town have these debts?"

He raised his big hands and let them fall. "Many. For some it is just a little payment, soon forgotten. For others, such as me, the deals are ongoing. There is maybe no escaping them." He sighed, the breath shaking his whole body.

"Unless the new owner of the book releases you," I said.

He looked up sharply. "You would do this?"

"If I can."

He started to say something, then shook his head. "But no. I still need the charms. So there is no escaping. You will be able to provide the charms?"

"I am working on all aspects of this book keeper thing with a look to resolving it in the near future," I said with as much dignity as I could manage. He didn't look particularly impressed by that, not that I blamed him. Management speak didn't hold for much when it came to curses and deals and magical books. "Can I ask … why were you at the shop the other day? When I found Norma?"

He rubbed a hand through his mane of still-damp hair and said, "I went to collect a new charm. I always go to the back door, but when I knocked, Norma didn't reply." He hesitated, not looking at me. "I opened the door and I saw her in the cauldron. I would have helped — I *should* have helped — but I heard someone come in the front. I panicked and hid in the pantry until you left, then ran. I thought I might be blamed."

I glared at him. "Well, now *I'm* getting blamed."

He grimaced. "Sorry."

"And the note?" I asked.

He frowned. "What note?"

"She didn't give you a note?"

"She was in the cauldron. Dead. Not in a condition to give me a note."

"Right," I said, while Ruiner sighed deeply on the floor next to my chair. I scowled at him. I'd like to see *him* do better. "So you don't know about any notes for me?"

"This was not my deal."

Dammit. "And today? Why were you there?"

"I went to see if Starlight was going to do the same deals. I thought she was the new keeper of the book. But she wasn't there."

"She was upstairs. Unconscious."

"Ah. I did not do that."

"Me either," I said, then finished my coffee. "But now I think I'm a suspect in both."

He looked at me for a moment, then said, "Maybe I can help. If you will help me with the charms?"

"No promises on anything, but if I can, I will."

He leaned over the table, holding his hand out. I took it gingerly, and we shook. "Deal," he said.

I examined him for a moment, then said, "You're not going to ask me to give you the book so you can use it yourself?"

He shrugged. "Not everyone can use a spell book. They have ... personalities. I do not have the experience to try. Particularly not with Norma's book. She was not enthusiastic about men."

Great. The book had a personality now, as well as being missing in the wilds of Hollowbeck. I found myself hoping Theodore really had taken it. If anyone could deal with a stroppy book, I had a feeling he could.

❧

WE LEFT NOT LONG AFTER, much to the disappointment of Ulf, who was apparently trying to collect enough of Ruiner's tail fur to make a nest. Asger promised to talk to Theodore as soon as he was up, and we left to head back into town.

Back in the car, I looked at Ruiner. "Right," he said. "Town hall, then? We've still got time to try and dig up the book before Theodore starts glowing about the place."

"Not so fast," I replied. "You knew that was Norma's spell book when you took it."

"Alright, yes," he admitted. "But it was just the spells I wanted."

I frowned at him. "Really? You didn't give a single thought to clearing your own debt *and* taking on all the others? Seems doubtful."

He bared his teeth at me. "I didn't *know*, okay? I might have guessed a bit, because of the whole bleeding on the book to seal the deal—"

"Again, eww."

"Exactly. But the most thought I gave it was that I might be able to get free of *my* deal. I just want to not be a cat anymore. That's kind of a big deal for me right now. And that book's the most powerful thing I've come across."

"I don't believe you," I said. "I think you knew perfectly what having the book meant. And now you've gone and lost it to someone else who knows that as well."

"*I* didn't lose it."

"Well neither did I," I snapped, and we glared at each other. "And now whoever's got it can force you to do things for them, or else have your deal revoked." I frowned. "What was your deal?"

"It doesn't matter."

"It does."

"It *doesn't.*"

"It *does.*" I shoved both hands against the steering wheel, hard, aware that the curtain-twitcher in the house opposite was likely still spying, and it probably looked like I was sitting in the car arguing with myself.

"This is just … so bloody *you*, Ruiner. You run to me asking for help, but you don't tell me anything. You just *lie*. You lie all the time." I started the car and jammed it into gear more roughly than was really fair. It wasn't the car's fault, after all. "Why can't you just for once tell me what's actually going on?"

He looked as ashamed as any cat, which is to say not at all. "You don't need all the details," he said. "And you know, I'm not proud of everything I've done."

"You shouldn't be," I said, pulling away from the kerb. "You really shouldn't." I swung the car into the gateway to a field to turn around, then we headed back toward town at a sedate pace. I really wanted to floor it, but the car didn't deserve such treatment.

"Look, I'm sorry," Ruiner said. "Yes, I should have told you about the deal and the book. But I didn't think it would be this complicated. My plan really was to go to Norma for help, and when she turned up dead, I thought we could take the book and leave. We'd find the counter-curse, and you wouldn't need to know anything else. I mean, you're not really equipped for all this magic stuff, are you?"

"Such absolute bollocks," I said. "You just can't help yourself. You always think you're going to get away with *everything*. And what were you going to do with the book after we'd got the counter-curse? Use it? Sell it?"

"No," he said, but he was looking at his paws.

"You *were*. You were going to sell it to someone." I shook my head and revved the engine, despite my best intentions. "Honestly, Ruiner, I can't believe you're my bloody brother half the time."

"Slow down," he said, peering through the windscreen. "Last thing we want to do is run over someone's familiar."

"Don't tell me how to drive," I snapped, although I also eased off a bit. He was right. Adding another crime to the list wasn't going to help the cause much.

"You shouldn't drink so much coffee. It makes you grumpy. Well, grump*ier*."

I took one hand off the wheel to flick his ear.

"*Hey!*"

"I've got every right to be grumpy. My brother is an idiot. And also, given that the deals are still in play, it means anyone could still be after me."

"I know," he said, and hesitated. "I'm really sorry, Morgan."

"You're not," I replied. "You're never *really* sorry. You only *think* you're sorry when things catch up to you, when you don't get your way and it's convenient for you to be sorry. You've always been like this." I was aware my voice was starting to rise, and I stopped, swallowing hard. The road was suddenly blurry, and I pinched the bridge of my nose. Someone was *threatening* me, and my brother couldn't even be honest with me to save my life. "You suck," I said, a little unsteadily. "This is a *disaster.*"

"It's not a disaster."

"It is."

Ruiner sighed. "Why do you always have to be so dramatic, Morgan?"

"I'm not being dramatic, Ruiner. You've stolen some sort of sentient witch's book that binds half the town to it, which means half the town *wants* it, and now we've lost it. Someone's threatening me, and that book might've really helped us sort that out, but you didn't even tell me what it really was. And I know you stole it so you could use it. So, yeah, it's a disaster. I don't even know why I'm still helping you."

"Because I'm your brother, and also infinitely charming?" he suggested.

This time I tried to slap him instead of flicking his ear, but he jumped into the footwell before I could reach him.

"I also have cat-like reflexes," he told me from a safe distance.

My brother the Ruiner.

TWENTY

A bad trip

I swung the car onto a different road rather than heading directly back to town. I didn't know where to go from here, so there didn't seem much point in rushing back. While plenty of people had been in debt to Norma, it seemed it was common knowledge that the book held the debt, not her. So there was no reason for any of them to kill her unless they could also control the book, and it sounded like that wasn't something just anyone could do. Which would certainly stop anyone who had a slightly lower opinion of themselves than my brother — in other words, almost everyone.

We needed to look at magic-workers. There was Petunia, who certainly seemed to have some power and may have seen the book. Theodore I wasn't sure about, but he could've taken the book for safe keeping even if he couldn't use it. Starlight would presumably be able to use it, but she didn't know we'd taken it. Although she knew we'd found the body, as did Ruby, so perhaps one of them had stalked us to find it? I shuddered. That was a horrible thing to imagine.

I could've shared these thoughts with my brother, of course, but I wasn't talking to him. It wasn't like he'd have anything useful to add, anyway, other than something along the lines of *it wasn't my fault!*

Ruiner had never been good with silence, though, and he was making up for my not talking by standing in the passenger seat with his paws on the door handle, giving me a running commentary on the scenery of Hollowbeck.

"That's a nice cow," he said. "It's fluffy. Highland cows, right? Or *coos*. They pronounce it *coos*. Nice horns, too. I mean, you wouldn't want to be on the wrong end of them, but they look cool. If I was a cow — a coo — I'd want horns like that. Must make the regular cows jealous." He glanced over his shoulder at me. "Why couldn't I get changed into a coo? You could really make a statement with those horns. Instead, I get *whiskers*."

I concentrated on driving, not looking at him, and he went back to the window.

"Birds over there. Don't think they're crows or magpies, but even so, I'm not a fan. Nasty beady little eyes, and those *beaks*. Just made for poking an eye out."

I was starting to consider poking my ears out.

"Oooh, rabbit! Little fluffy bunny. Isn't that a good luck thing? Don't you make wishes on rabbits? I'd wish to be a Highland coo if I have to stay stuck as an animal. I mean, obviously, I'd wish to be human again first, but if there wasn't a choice—"

I just about hit my forehead on the steering wheel. "Ruiner, *shut up!* Just for once in your life, *shut the hell up!*"

He gave me an affronted look. "I'm just trying to lighten things up a bit. You know, give a little perspective. You take everything so bloody seriously, Morgs."

"Of course I'm taking it bloody seriously," I snapped. "Your debt is now owned by person or persons unknown, and who the hell knows what they might force you to do, or what the consequences might be if you don't do it. This is presumably the same person leaving me threatening notes, so they could just as easy turn around and make *you* attack me." I stopped short. I hadn't realised I'd even been thinking that until I said it. I looked at Ruiner. "Couldn't they?"

"Yes," he said, his voice quiet, and I knew he'd already come to the same conclusion.

"Why didn't you tell me?"

"Because I'll know if it happens, and honestly, Morgan, it's better if they *do* try to make me do something. You can stop me. You might not know who else is coming for you."

"Bollocks," I said, but I could hear the unevenness in my voice. "You just can't be bloody honest with me about anything, can you? And here we are with no idea who's behind it all, or who can help us, and this all started with you being you and getting yourself turned into a bloody cat. Honestly, I think you probably deserve just to stay as one for a while. And *not* a Highland coo." I managed to get a good glare going. "I don't even know why I'm still here."

"Why *are* you still here?" he asked. "I said we should leave. You're the one who didn't want to."

I growled. "Sibling loyalty, I suppose. I mean, I've always had to get you out of these things."

"That's not a good enough reason," he replied. "I don't think that's it."

"Oh, well, you'd know. You're so up on human behaviour."

"What's that supposed to mean?"

"You're a *cat*," I replied. "And even when you were a human, you didn't care what anyone else was doing or feeling. You only ever cared about yourself and what you wanted."

"That's not true," he said.

"Of course it's true. When was the last time you thought about anyone but yourself? I mean, you stole that book, and you knew other people would be coming after it, which was hardly going to end well. But you did it anyway."

He bared his teeth at me. "Okay, maybe I did know. But better I own my debt than anyone else. Especially when it might protect you, as well. And I've been trying to get you to leave, Morgan. I don't want you in danger. I never meant for that to happen. But you're the one who won't go. And I don't get it — these people are *witches*, they're magic workers, and you're waltzing off to bloody cocktail bars with vampires. I mean, I know why *I* got involved. But how come you didn't run screaming the first time you saw a cauldron?"

"Seriously?" I asked. "I'm not some maiden aunt, fainting at the sight of blood. You're the one who chucked up." Although, admittedly, it had been an act of herculean willpower not to do so myself.

"Yeah, but you never exactly had the imagination in the family, did you? I mean, *bookkeeping*. Such a safe and sensible little thing to do. And you didn't even get as far as accountancy, or go off to uni to study. You just did some basic little night class course, then kept books for some basic little companies paying basic little wages and called it good enough. You've got no imagination. You've got no ... You've got no *ambition*."

I stared at him, started to say something, stopped, then just said, "Look where that got you."

"Sure, I'm a cat. But I *try*. You just go about making this big fuss about how you have to look after everyone, you have to be sensible, you have to be the adult, you have to do all these *things* that no one asks you to do—"

"If I don't, who will? Who's going to keep you from being arrested, or stop Mum bloody freezing because she's spent all her pension on a sodding *commemorative plate?* You?"

"It's not your job. You just *made* it your job, and all it is, is a way to stop you having to do anything for *you*. A way to stop you from achieving anything."

"That's utter bollocks," I managed. My eyes were stinging, and I glared at the road, blinking hard. My horrible, entitled, spoilt little brat of a brother, and he had the cheek to call *me* out? "Just because I don't run from one ridiculous, hare-brained scheme to the next like you."

"But they're not, are they?" he said.

I risked a look at him, raising my eyebrows.

He huffed. "Okay, yes, fine. Some of them are. But at least I'm *doing* something. You're sitting there being all self-righteous about it, but you don't dare try anything. You married a boring, needy man because he was safe, because he needed looking after, because you could blame him for everything and just say, 'Oh, I couldn't change anything because Jason needed this, Jason needed that.' But what you were actually saying is that *you* couldn't do any of it because you were scared. And he was a convenient excuse."

I slammed the brakes on and brought the car to a screeching halt in the middle of the road, the violence of the stop pitching Ruiner off the seat and back into the footwell with a yowl.

He glared up at me. "What're you doing?"

"Get out," I said.

"What?"

I opened my door, grabbed him by the scruff of the neck, and turfed him out of the car before he could say anything else. "We're done. I'm leaving."

"Really? We're not finished."

"Oh, we *are* finished," I replied. "We're so finished, Ruiner. I've never done anything but look out for you. And now you're going to give me all this crap like I *wanted* to be your bloody babysitter? No. No, I've had enough."

"We still don't know who's after you," he pointed out.

"Maybe no one is," I said. "Maybe you set the whole bloody thing up to get me involved."

"I was trying to get you to leave," he said, far too reasonably.

"I don't care. I absolutely do *not* care." I slammed the door, jammed the car into gear, and drove off, not looking in the rear-view mirror. He'd just be sitting there, looking small and pathetic, and I wasn't going to give him the chance. I was *done* with my brother.

I went straight to the B&B before I could change my mind, threw my stuff into my bag, and ran back downstairs. Let him explain it to Petunia. Let him sort this out on his own. Let him take some bloody responsibility for once.

I was out of the house and back in the car before I could even think about calming down. I headed for the main road out of town, the one we'd come in on, which would lead me up into the forested hills and down the other side, back to a world without charmed coffee and vampire bars and frog-infested accommodation.

I still had a sneaking concern that the road would somehow double back on itself and deliver me into the centre of Hollowbeck again, or the old car would start sliding backward as soon as I hit the hill, or, I don't know — fairies would swarm it and fly me back. Anything was possible. But there were no obstacles on the road as the town gave to farmland, and the slope as I changed down a gear and rumbled through the first of the trees was plain and tarmacked and devoid of trickery. I kept a good pace on, partly to escape any enchantments, but mostly because she was a heavy lump of a vehicle, and if I didn't maintain speed, I'd be crawling by the time we hit the top.

I rumbled through the first couple of turns, cranking the wheel over and trying not to lose too much speed, and she responded readily. She might not be fast, but she'd always been trustworthy. So when I hit the third curve, which was a little tighter, and went to change down a gear, it was somewhat of a shock when the gear stick flopped like a dead thing, and the clutch did absolutely nothing. Not only that, I was speeding up without my foot being on the accelerator. I tapped the brakes experimentally, but nothing happened. I jammed my foot down with rather more enthusiasm, but the engine just kept rumbling more and more loudly, the car gathering speed despite the steepening slope.

I thundered toward the next curve, trying the handbrake, the brake, the clutch, anything, then abandoned all attempts at slowing, braced myself, and hauled the wheel around, hard. I muscled through the turn, arms shaking with effort. We were going *uphill*, and steeply at that. With the decrepit engine and the weight of the car, we should be slowing down by now even if I'd had the accelerator mashed to the floor. But somehow I was still picking up speed, as if the physics of the place had turned upside down.

I had no time to wonder if this was *don't leave town* magic or a curse or just Hollowbeck being bloody Hollowbeck. I was bearing down — or *up* — on the next turn, still accelerating, and I tightened my grip on the wheel, hauled the handbrake on, and jammed the brake pedal to the floor with one foot while bracing myself with the other. I cranked the wheel over, silently pleading with the engine to stall out.

It didn't. I didn't slow, didn't stop, and didn't make the turn.

It was a close thing, the wheels screeching on the tarmac and the scent of burning rubber washing in the windows, my shoulders screaming protests as I fought the car, but she was too heavy and going too fast, and my stomach flipped as the tyres lost their grip. The old Volvo plunged straight off the road and roared into the trees, with me still clutching the wheel desperately, hoping I was going to bounce into a ditch before I ran into a tree trunk or, worse, off a cliff.

A tree loomed up in front of me, and I wrenched the wheel over, side-swiping the trunk neatly. For a breathless moment, I thought that was going to be enough to stop me, that the undergrowth and the rough ground would bring the car to a halt. But no, we were still accelerating, bucking and bouncing wildly though the forest like the old estate had delusions of being a quad-bike.

We had slowed, though, and I ripped my seatbelt off and forced the door open, throwing my full bodyweight at it. I tumbled into the moss-scented air, hoping I wasn't going to brain myself on a rock or impale myself on a fallen branch. I let myself roll as I hit the ground, tucking my legs in so that I didn't end up run over *and* impaled.

I tore my jeans, whacked one knee painfully on a rock, skinned both hands and one forearm on some rough ground, bumped my head, and finally flopped to a stop against a tree stump, hard enough to make me wheeze. I lay there, panting, while my poor old car kept up her break for freedom, plunging down the hill in a chorus of snapping branches and shattering glass. I plucked a large splinter out of my palm and wondered if this was Ruiner's fault. It probably was, but I surprised myself by wishing my brother was here anyway. There's something about being abandoned in an enchanted forest that does make you wish for your family a little.

Only a little, though. After all, if he'd been here, I'd've had to listen to him whining about this as well as everything else. I sat up, discovered everything still seemed to be bending in the right places, and got slowly to my feet. I stood there for a moment, thinking about my options, then turned and started to slog my way up the raw path torn through the undergrowth by the car, back toward the road. I wasn't going to risk going cross-country. I did *not* want to be in the enchanted bloody forest come nightfall. That way lay madness. More madness, anyway.

TWENTY-ONE

Definitely cursed

I WAS HALFWAY BACK to town before I saw another vehicle. I'd passed my own lying sadly in a ditch at the bottom of the hill, but not only was there no way I could get it out, I wasn't sure I wanted to. There was no mechanical explanation for what had just happened, and driving an enchanted car seemed a bit silly. I stopped long enough to dig my backpack out from where it had wedged itself under the seats, then kept limping toward Hollowbeck, everything getting steadily more painful with every step.

The car approached me from behind, down out of the hills that encircled the village, and came to a stop next to me. Ben peered out. "Are you alright?" he asked.

"Not really," I replied.

He looked at my torn jeans and said, "Fashion choice, or accident?"

"My car ... I crashed," I said.

"You crashed?" He killed the engine and scrambled out, hurrying around the car to take my bag from me. "You're walking, so that seems good. Anything hurt particularly badly?"

"I don't know," I said. "I crashed."

"Right. Got it." He dropped my bag in the car, rummaged in the boot, and came out with a packet of Jammy Dodgers. "Will these help?"

"Probably," I said and took them from him.

"How did you crash?" he asked. "What happened?"

"Is this what happens when you try to leave town and you're not meant to?" I asked. "Am I trapped here?"

"I've never heard of that," he said.

"Even though Theodore told me not to leave? Has he locked me in somehow?"

He frowned. "I *suppose* it's possible, but I hardly think he'd go so far as to make anyone crash to stop them leaving. Are you sure it wasn't an accident?"

"I'm sure. The car just kept accelerating," I said. "It wasn't ... you shouldn't be able to do that. I was going uphill. Uphill!" I stared from him to the packet of biscuits, then my legs decided they'd had enough and started to fold. He grabbed my arm, keeping me upright, and opened the passenger side door, guiding me into the seat with my feet still on the ground outside.

"Let's get you back into town," he said. "We'll go straight to the doctor's."

"I don't think I'm hurt," I said.

He pointed to the ripped knees of my jeans, and I peered down at them. I had noticed before, of course, just as I'd noticed the grazes on my palms, but they hadn't really hurt. Now, settled safely in a presumably non-possessed car, clutching the packet of Jammy Dodgers, I realised that *everything* hurt, and my left arm was throbbing. I lifted it, and discovered a heavy graze, still clotted with bits of forest debris, running from my elbow all the way to my wrist. "Oh. Maybe I am, a little bit."

He took the biscuits off me, opened them, then went

into the boot again and came back with a can of fizzy orange. "It's warm, but the sugar'll help."

I took the can. "Were you shopping?"

"Yeah. Hollowbeck doesn't do any brands you've ever heard of, so I go junk food shopping once a month."

"Fair enough." I took a sip of soft drink, the sweetness making me wince. But it tasted deeply, reassuringly familiar, too, and I could understand why he'd make the trip every month. You'd need that touchstone of normality in this place.

"Where's your cat?" he asked.

"I don't know," I replied. "I threw him out of the car before the crash."

"Oh. Right." He didn't ask me anything else, just went around to his side of the car and got in, and we sat there in the afternoon sun while I waited for the shaking to stop.

BY THE TIME we were passing the first houses on the edge of Hollowbeck, the fizzy drink and biscuits had worked a very human sort of magic. I'd stopped shaking, and my thoughts were slightly more collected. As much as they ever got with me, anyway.

"We need to go to the Cosy Cauldron," I told Ben.

He glanced at me. "You need to go to the doctor."

"I don't. It's just some scrapes and bruises."

He pointed at my arm. "You've got half the forest floor still in there."

I examined it, and brushed the worst patch tentatively, scattering dirt and leaves and, presumably, dried blood, all over the seat. "Oh. Sorry."

"It's fine," he said, his face screwed up slightly. "But let's get it cleaned up at least, alright?"

"After we go to the Cosy Cauldron."

"Why?"

"Because if it wasn't some sort of trap to stop me leaving Hollowbeck, then someone cursed my car and sent me off the road. And I'm certain it's to do with Norma's missing spell book and the debts and all that."

He looked at me sharply. "How do you know about the debts?"

"My brother."

"Right." We drove in silence for a moment longer, then he said, "You think Starlight cursed your car?"

I wrinkled my nose. "Not directly, maybe. But you can buy curses, right?"

"Right."

"So I want to know if there's a record of someone buying anything that could've done this." And with Starlight presumably still out of action, I could have a good poke around the ledgers with this as an excuse.

"I don't think Starlight would sell a curse like that. Or any curse, really."

"Maybe not," I admitted. "But maybe Norma did. If it was an old one." Like the notes.

"Will you go to the doctor after we've seen Starlight?" Ben asked.

"Yes. I promise."

"I'm weirdly unconvinced, but fine." He indicated to turn toward the main street. "If someone really cursed your car, we should be going straight to Theodore."

"He's sleeping," I pointed out. Plus I still wasn't convinced that he hadn't done something to keep me here. If you're a one-person police department who can't go out in daylight, you're going to need *some* way to keep suspects in place.

"You could wait until tonight."

"I could, but I don't want to. Someone cursed my car, and I barely made it out. I want answers."

He sighed. "I should've bought more Jammy Dodgers."

A few minutes later, we pulled into a parking space just down from the Cosy Cauldron, the street golden with afternoon light and peopled by coffee drinkers and shoppers ambling about in a dreamy sort of happiness. I clambered out of the car and went to march purposefully straight to the shop, but it turned into more of a wobble. Apparently, my spill from the car had been even less graceful than I'd thought.

I checked my arm again, but I certainly didn't seem to be dying from blood loss. The wound was already scabbing up.

I righted myself and then headed for the shop door, pushing it open so hard that it rebounded and flew back, almost catching me in the face. It whacked my knee instead, which really helped matters.

I hobbled toward the counter while Ben followed me without comment. I stopped and he stood there looking slightly uncomfortable. Starlight was halfway through the beaded curtain, looking almost as rough as I felt with her artfully messy bun half-undone and now simply messy, and one side of her long skirt pulled up higher than the other.

"You're awake," I said.

"What in the Goddess' name happened to you?" she asked. "You've got half a bush in your hair."

I patted my head. She was exaggerating, but there were definitely some twigs in it. I pulled them out carefully. "Are you alright?"

She narrowed her eyes slightly. "It *was* you! I thought I heard your voice when I was unconscious. Did you attack me?"

"What?" Ben asked, but neither of us looked at him.

"I *helped* you," I said. "Probably bloody saved you, actually, so don't try and turn this around. Who did you give the curse too?"

"What curse?"

I waved at myself wildly. "This curse! The one that made my car go rogue and almost kill me! I had to jump out in the middle of the forest, and now it's up there stuck in a ditch. You killed my car and almost me!"

Starlight looked at me carefully then said, "I'm terribly sorry about your car, but I don't know anything about it. I don't know anything about any cars. I ride a bike." She pointed at the display windows, her aim wandering a little. "And what d'you mean, *saved* me? I was just about asphyxiated by whatever you did to my pots!"

"I didn't do anything to your pots! I was the one who found you and got help." I pressed my palms flat onto the counter and leaned toward her, more to keep myself upright than for any sort of dramatic effect. "And you don't need to know anything about a car to be able to put a curse on it."

"You might have to," Ben said. "From what you said, the brakes weren't working but the accelerator was. You probably have to have some basic knowledge…" He trailed off as I looked at him. "Then again," he said, "magic."

"Exactly," I said. "Magic." I looked back at Starlight. "I know you're looking for Norma's book."

"Of course I'm looking for Norma's book," she snapped. "Every charm and spell she did was in that book. It'd been passed down for generations. It's absolutely *full* of the most valuable knowledge, as well as lots of the recipes for shop's products. Of course I need it." She frowned at me. "But how do you know I'm looking for it anyway?"

"I've done my research," I replied, crossing my arms, then wincing and uncrossing them again. I went for hands on hips instead. "You're going to take on everyone's debts. *Own* them."

"I'm going to *clear* everyone's debts," Starlight said, folding her own arms rather more elegantly, even if she was swaying a bit. She raised her eyebrows at me. "If I have ownership of the book, I can gift the oaths back. Everyone's released. That's why you tried to kill me and get it, just like you did Norma!"

"I did *not*," I snarled. "I didn't even know Norma!"

"You didn't have to, did you? You said your brother worked with her, and we all know what that means." She glared at me a little wildly. "But then you had to try and kill me too!"

"Yes, by running out and getting you help. Very deadly, that."

We scowled at each other for a moment, then I looked at Ben. "Would what she said even work? About releasing people from their debts?"

He shrugged. "My knowledge on magical spell books isn't that up to speed," he said. "But it sounds reasonable."

I turned back to Starlight. "But you could still take on the debts if you wanted. You know how the book works."

"I could," she said. "But I don't want to. It was the worst thing about working for Norma. I *hated* how she did those deals. It wasn't right. She ruined people, turned them against each other, used them. Sometimes it wasn't even for the money, just the fun of it."

"But I heard you arguing with Ruby," I said. "You were telling her that you'd continue the deal."

"Of course I told her that. She's so invested in it. But if I can get the book, I'll work something else out." She frowned at me. "*If* I can get it, since it went missing when Norma was killed. You know, after you were in the shop."

"I don't have it," I said, but I couldn't quite look at her.

She sniffed. "If the wrong person gets hold of it, they'll control half the town. More than half. And who knows what they'll make people do."

I wiped my mouth, suddenly feeling a little queasy, and touched my head again gingerly. I didn't seem to have any tender spots, but who knew. Mum always said I had a really hard head. I refocused on Starlight. "But you're taking the shop on. Surely you'd want to take *everything* on. You can't tell me Norma made enough from bloody taxidermy and…" I waved vaguely, looking around the cluttered shelves. "And crystal teddy bears to be worthwhile."

Starlight actually rolled her eyes at me. "Your generation. Everything's so transactional. You need a figure on everything."

"Excuse *me*. I'm barely any older than you are." I glared at her, but she just arched her eyebrows at me, and after a moment I raised my hands. "Fine. But money does matter. And what, you were just going to tell everyone they owed you nothing?"

"Of course. I don't want the responsibility. I don't want people owing me things, you know?" She shrugged, playing with one of her necklaces. "What do I need? I've got my bike. I've got a tiny home that I can afford to live in. I'm happy for people to pay me in tomatoes and apples. I'm fine with that. That's why I moved here, to get away from materialism."

I rubbed my forehead. I already knew the answer to the next question, but I'd come this far and offended her this much. May as well go all in. "So you definitely didn't murder Norma in order to take over? Because you had means, motive, and…" I couldn't remember what the third element was. "Access to the cauldron."

Starlight stared at me for a long, stretched moment, then said, "I am completely opposed to violence." She snatched a witchy snow globe off the counter, and hurled it at me.

I yelped and ducked, and Ben gave a rather more pained yell as it caught him in the shoulder. "Bloody hell, Starlight," he complained, but she ignored him completely.

"How *dare* you!" she yelled at me, and apparently fully overcame her non-violent principles. She started throwing everything she could get her hands on: notebooks and pens, insects trapped in lumps of amber, juggling balls, slinkies still in their boxes. They all followed the snow globe over the counter, and I covered my head with both hands, backing away.

"How dare you!" she shouted again. "I am anti-capitalist! I believe in personal responsibility! I do not believe in debt! I believe in helping others! I believe in community! I believe—"

Ben grabbed my arm and dragged me toward the door. "We're leaving," he shouted. "We're going, Starlight."

"I should curse you!" she yelled, hefting a taxidermy ferret at me. "I don't believe in cursing people, but if I did, I would *totally* curse you."

"I'm sorry!" I yelped. "I'm really, really sorry."

"I'll curse you with hiccoughs!" she shouted. "I'll do it! That feels okay with my conscience."

Ben pushed me out the door and pulled it shut behind us.

I stood on the pavement with both hands over my face. "That went really badly," I said.

"Well, she hasn't actually cursed you yet," he said. "Or turned you into a frog. So it could be worse."

"Now I really do need to leave town," I said. "I can never show my face around here again."

He snorted and turned to the car. "Come on," he said.

"Let's get you to the GP before you come down with terminal hiccoughs."

~

AS WITH EVERYTHING IN HOLLOWBECK, the doctor's surgery was almost annoyingly old-fashioned. Rather than a purpose-built office, we walked into the front room of an ivy-clad building, the garden in the front a riot of rose bushes. The front room with equipped with deep, soft sofas and the requisite five-year-old magazines on the coffee table, although they were all titled *Charmed Monthly* and *Tall Tales* rather than the usual celebrity gossip tat. No one else was in there, which I suppose made sense. If you could magic up a fix for everything you needed, the GP probably didn't see a lot of business.

Not that he seemed bothered as he ushered me into a clean, white-painted room with a mug of tea in one hand. He wore ancient, worn-down trainers, and trousers with what appeared to be floury handprints on them under his white coat, and he made sympathetic noises over my arm while twisting it in uncompromising directions and poking my ribs and back hard enough to make me yelp. In the end, he cleaned up my grazes, put dressings on the worst ones on my left arm and hand. After declaring me absolutely fine, he pulled his gloves off and handed me a small, unlabelled tub of cream with a flourish.

I looked at it dubiously. "Is this herbal?"

"A healing salve," he said. "Very effective. A recipe of my own devising."

"You're a doctor," I said.

"Yes," he agreed brightly.

"Shouldn't you be giving me antibiotics or something?"

"It's not infected," he replied. "And if you look after it,

it won't be. Keep it clean, use the cream, and no more running off roads."

I gave up and took the tub, then followed him back out into the waiting room. Ben got up hurriedly, dropping a magazine back onto the table. "Everything alright?"

"Fine," I said, as the doctor waved us off and vanished back into his office. "I just seem to have been seen by a herbalist rather than a GP."

Ben made a slight face. "Yeah, everyone in town seems to be a herbalist of some sort."

"Or an alchemist," I said, remembering Tanya, and he flinched slightly.

"Or that," he agreed. "Come on, let's get you a cup of tea."

"I'd rather have a coffee," I said.

"Not as good for calming down curse-shattered nerves," he said, and I sighed. It might be true, but it didn't mean I had to like it.

TWENTY-TWO

Narrow escapes

I WAITED until we were in the car before I looked at Ben and said, "I think I need to get out of Hollowbeck. I'm running around in circles looking for this bloody book, which isn't even my responsibility, and which my brother keeps *lying* about, and now I've just had a magical car accident. I don't want to be here anymore."

He gave me a careful look, then nodded and said, "I'll drive you."

"Really?"

"Of course. I just have to swing by the library and tell Dee I won't be back today."

"You really don't have to drive me," I said, without much enthusiasm. "I'm sure I can get my car fixed."

"You can come back for your car," he said. "I'll get it sorted for you."

I looked at my hands, scuffed with grazes where they weren't swathed with bandages, and said, "Thanks." It should have felt like more of a relief than it did, and I couldn't quite work out why.

We drove the rest of the way to the library in silence.

Ben parked in the shade of a heavy old oak tree and said, "Do you want that tea while we're here?"

I still wanted a coffee, but tea was a decent fallback option. "Actually, yes," I said. "Maybe that'll make me feel a bit more human."

"It's basically magic," he said and grinned when I scowled at him.

We went through the quiet stacks to the staff room, which was starting to feel as familiar as my old office, and Ben busied himself with mugs and leaves. A few minutes later, he set a flower-studded brew in front of me, before leaving me sitting in one of the wobbly old chairs to find Dee.

I cradled my tea in both hands, the left one cushioned by bandages, and wondered if I was making the right choice. What if leaving wasn't going to be enough? What if Ruiner was going to be stuck as cat forever unless I helped him? What if he really had been trying to protect me?

But how could I *possibly* believe him? He'd stolen that book knowing how important it was, knowing that he could use it to take control of half this town. How did I even know it was really missing? He could have stashed it, knowing I'd find out how important it was. He might be hoarding it for his own use. I wouldn't put it past him.

I took a sip of the tea and made a face. It didn't taste right. I'd never been an herbal tea fan, but the ones Ben had made before had been soothing and smooth and this caught at the back of my throat. I tipped it down the sink a little guiltily, then ambled around the room as I waited for Ben to come back.

My fingers traced the books that were piled on the table in various states of repair, kids' books with cheese smushed into the pages, and paperbacks with the tell-tale swelling that suggested they'd suffered a bathtub incident. More arcane volumes were there too, scorched in places, and one looking a lot like something had been gnawing on the corner of it.

One book lay open on a cluttered desk in the corner. It looked fairly safe, and I closed it carefully to read the cover, using my finger to mark the place where it had been open. *The Alchemist's Dictionary.* A leaf was stuck in it further on like a bookmark. I opened to it and read aloud, "*Moonshade. While the plant is harmless alone, and the leaves can even be chewed to attain a mild euphoria —*" *Ha!* I knew this place had weird stuff. I examined the picture by the text. It was finely drawn in black ink, a delicate flower suspended between fine leaves.

"*In combination with other substances, moonshade can be harmful. It should therefore always be used in isolation, by brewing into a pleasant aniseed-scented tea, or used in oil diffusers to enchant invasive fairies.*" I stopped reading, frowning. "Aniseed," I murmured. That sounded familiar too. The hairs on the back of my neck started to stand up and I glanced at the door to see if Ben had returned, but it was still closed and I didn't hear or see anyone approaching down the hall.

Feeling like my time might be running out, I flipped through the book even faster. W, W, W — Whisperwind. "*A mostly harmless plant with small yellow flowers, whisperwind is often used as a mild sedative or sleep aid. It is not known to be habit-forming but should not be combined with other substances.*" I ran my finger further down the page. "*Warning: Do not use in conjunction with moonshade. Even in small amounts this combination is deadly.*"

I stood there, one finger still on the book, then closed it gently. Small yellow flowers, like Ben's tea. And the taste. It had tasted so different today. I went back to the sink, my legs feeling stiff and unfamiliar, picked up my mug, and sniffed it. I hadn't rinsed it out and there it was. A faint, desperately faint, but clear scent of aniseed.

"He tried to poison me," I said to the empty room. "Ben tried to poison me in the library with the moon-shade." A ragged little laugh escaped me. I mean, anyone else I could have understood, but the *librarian?* Which was about the point that I realised I probably hadn't drunk enough for it to be deadly, but I had evidently drunk enough for my thinking processes to be a teeny bit impaired.

I pulled my phone from my pocket as I staggered back to the book, snapped photos of the two pages, then let myself out of the staff room, moving as quickly and quietly as I could. There was no one in the hallway so I scurried down it and emerged warily into the main library. A group of children were keeping Dee occupied at the counter. I kept my head down, scooted around them, and made for the exit.

A moment later I was back outside in the sun, my head spinning, and suddenly not sure where to go next. If Ben was behind Norma's death, I couldn't go to Isabella, since she and Ben seemed to be besties. Theodore wouldn't be up for another few hours, and so who did that leave me? I turned and hurried toward the centre of town, my back itching as if I thought Ben was going to come lunging out of the bushes at any moment and tackle me.

Ben. It was *Ben.* I wondered what he had owed Norma, what favour. Or maybe it wasn't even a deal. Maybe it was the book. Maybe he wanted it and knew we'd had it right from the start, and the whole car crash had been a set-up to try and get it off me. That still didn't explain where it was now, but I wasn't feeling ready to think that through. Maybe Theodore really did have it.

The town felt fraught, the heat oppressive. Every

window held curtain twitchers, watching my uncertain progress down the pavement, every tree held spying crows, with their sharp beaks and beady eyes, just like Ruiner had said. I pressed a hand to my forehead, finding it too hot and slick with an unpleasant sweat. I needed to clear my head. I needed a coffee, something to wash away the effects of the tea. Then I'd be able to think.

~

I MADE it back to the little main street without anyone pointing at me and screeching like a body snatcher, flying monkeys sweeping down to carry me away, or whatever else my addled brain insisted could happen. I paused on the corner, wondering if there was a rental car place, and how I was going to rent anything in my current state.

I glanced at Bewitching Brews. There was no one outside, and it looked almost empty. A coffee would go a long way to making me feel human again, but I had an uneasy feeling I really had been spending too much time taking tea with possible murderers, just like Ruiner had said. Coffee would have to wait.

I put one hand on a crowded bike rack to support myself, the day still too bright and too fragile, and peered at the Cosy Cauldron. If Ben thought Starlight knew where the book was, then she could be in danger. And now I was onto him, he'd be in a rush to get hold of the book before I could tell Theodore. Assuming Theodore could be trusted, of course, which was questionable. I wondered what sort of moral code vampires lived by. It had to be either fairly loose or fairly convoluted to make slurping on people's necks acceptable.

I stepped cautiously off of the pavement and then paused before venturing any further. It was too hot out here, the air stifling, and everything just felt *too much*. The hanging baskets vomiting flowers on every lamp post, the window boxes full of yet more life, the hodgepodge of European-style bistro tables on the pavement, the canopies and wrought iron rubbing shoulders with wooden porches like some Americana small town postcard, all wedged into the grey stone and slate roof backdrop of the Lakes, like the town had sprouted everyone's ideals with no regard for where we were.

It made me seasick, like jet lag without the travel. All I could think of was how much I wanted to be out of here and away from the constant aroma of cut grass and fresh flowers, the whiff of hot bread and baking cookies. Away from the *niceness*. Right then, I'd have given anything for some second-hand cigarette smoke and exhaust fumes.

I pulled my shoulder back, bracing myself to brave the Cosy Cauldron and hoping Starlight didn't follow through on the hiccough curse. I wasn't even sure she'd listen to my warning, but I felt I needed to at least tell her. And if she was as dedicated to reversing Norma's deals as she seemed to be, then maybe she'd even help me. I started forward, then was halted by a shout behind me. I swayed around, my vision swooping dizzyingly, and saw Edith waving at me from the doorstep of Bewitching Brews.

"Are you alright there, Morgan?" she called. "You look a bit wobbly."

"Um…" Suddenly I wanted a piece of Edith's short-bread more than I'd wanted anything else in my life.

"Morgan?" She hurried down the pavement, taking my arm to pull me off the road. "It's no good standing there, dear. We're a quiet town, not a dead one."

"Right. Sorry." I let her lead me toward the coffeeshop, her hand reassuringly warm in the small of my back.

"Let's get you a coffee and a bite to eat," she said as she

waved me in the door ahead of her. "You look like you could use it."

"I think maybe," I said. I manoeuvred myself onto a stool, not without a moment of thinking I was going to pitch head-first onto the floor. I wasn't sure if it was the moonshade or the accident, or a combination of both, but sitting down seemed wise.

Edith dished a slab of carrot cake, studded with raisins and crowned with a froth of white icing, onto a plate and slid it in front of me. "Is that alright? I can make you a toastie if you'd prefer something a little more substantial."

The cake was rich and heavy and looked like it could sink small ships. I doubted anything toast-based could be more substantial, so I just thanked her and dug in. I wasn't sure Hollowbeck was good for my health. Leaving aside the bit about someone trying to kill me, I mean. I'd eaten more baked goods since arriving than seemed prudent.

Edith busied herself with the coffee machine while I ate, then set a coffee down next to the cake and clasped her hands together on the counter. "Get that down you too. It'll make everything feel so much better."

I mumbled agreement around a mouthful of cake, picking up the mug in my mostly good hand. Edith watched without comment, even though my bandaged arm was resting next to the plate. She was either very discreet or very disinterested. I took a sip of coffee, and the world swung around me, focus tightening and colours brightening almost painfully. I set the mug down, blinking, and rubbed my eyes. It didn't taste right, and I wondered if moonshade or whisperwind or a combination of the two could do even weirder things when combined with caffeine.

"Drink up," she said, smiling encouragingly at me. "Doesn't do much good in the mug."

"No," I agreed, but I didn't pick up the cup again. I pushed the plate away, the cake half-finished but suddenly heavy in my belly, and pressed my hands to my face. "I've made a mistake."

"What's that?"

I shook my head, setting the room swinging. "I need to find my brother."

"Don't you mean your cat?" Edith said mildly. I looked up at her sharply, and she smiled at me. "I knew he wasn't any regular cat, dear. At first I thought he was your familiar, but the connection was all wrong."

I stared at her. "Have you seen that sort of thing before?"

"One sees almost everything if one spends enough time in magical towns."

"Can you help him?"

"That rather depends. Have some more coffee." She pushed the cup toward me and I picked it up automatically.

I started to take a mouthful, then remembered. Charms in the coffee. I set it back down. "Depends on what?"

"Everything has a price," she said, smiling slightly.

I frowned at her, thinking of the infestations and Hollowbeck-style corporate espionage. "You were very busy this morning. Busier than anywhere else."

"I make excellent coffee," she replied, shrugging slightly. "It's all about the beans. I put a lot of research in."

She was right, of course, but if anywhere looked like it should be overrun with tearooms and cake shops, Hollowbeck did. A coffeeshop was a risk, really. Especially one that had its own roaster and scorned whipped cream and caramel syrup. It belonged in a city full of the upwardly mobile, not a little backwater relying on tourists looking for twee charm among the herbs and crystals. And that reminded me of what James had said. About how Edith loved this place, but it had been a change after having a herbalist shop. Which was a weird pivot. "Why do you have a coffee shop?" I asked.

"I like coffee," she said simply.

"I've never seen you drink coffee. James always has a coffee. You don't."

"I can't be drinking all my wares, can I?" she replied. "Go on, eat your cake. You're looking positively peaky. That car accident must have really shaken you."

I picked up my fork, then put it down again. "I didn't say I had a car accident."

"Did you not? Ah, well." She tapped the side of her head. "I'm a little psychic, you know. It's how I can tell just what sort of coffee people need, a pick-me-up or a calm-them-down, or what kind of cake is going to be just right for a sunny day or a rainy one." She smiled at me, calm and relaxed in her *caffeinate* T-shirt. Her greying hair was tied back in a bun, and her eyes were a cool, watchful blue.

"I think I'd better go," I said, trying to stand up. The stool seemed inordinately hard to get up from, as if I were pushing myself out of a tub of quicksand.

"You should finish your cake first."

"I don't want to," I said, more sharply than I'd intended, and her mouth tightened. She started to say something else, but the bell hanging over the door jangled, cutting her off. I twisted in my seat to see who it was and encountered the unsmiling visage of one of the Upstanding Ladies.

"Edith," she said, "Mystic Munchies has put their trolls out in the restaurant area. We can't abide those things. Can you make us some take out coffees?"

"Of course," Edith said, smiling. "Sit yourself down and I'll be right out."

"I'd better be off then, seeing you're busy," I said, trying to stand up again. I couldn't seem to get any purchase on the stool at all.

Edith frowned at me. "I rather think you should stay and get over the shock of your accident, dear. We'll talk to Theodore about it as soon as he's up."

"No, I want to leave," I said, my voice rising slightly.

"Edith, whatever you're doing to this woman, let her go," the Upstanding Lady said, startling us both. I peered around at her and she crossed her arms, a big woman with heavy legs planted wide where she stood in the door. She scowled at Edith.

"I'm not doing anything," she said, and quite abruptly I popped straight out of the stool and sprawled to the floor, catching myself on my poor abused hands and knees. "Do be careful, Morgan." She looked at the Upstanding Lady. "She's not feeling like herself."

The Upstanding Lady sniffed and didn't move as I got up and hurried past her out the door. I stopped on the pavement, breathing too hard, and pressed one hand to my chest. I certainly felt more awake than I had before I went in, so that was something.

"Are you alright?" one of the other ladies asked, from where they'd seated themselves at a table under the canopy. "You seem a little distraught."

For one wild moment I considered throwing myself on their mercy and telling them everything, but considering the two nicest people I'd met since being here had just separately tried to drug me — or charm me, or whatever was going on with Edith's coffee — it didn't seem worth the risk. Instead I just mumbled a thank you to the woman who'd followed me out of the coffeeshop, and she sniffed again.

"That's what you get for dabbling in magic," she told me. "You should go home and learn how to make a good floral centerpiece instead."

"I'll definitely think about it," I said and hurried toward the Cosy Cauldron, managing to limit myself to just a couple of backward glances back sure Edith wasn't following me, wielding carrot cake. Given how she'd helped me earlier with Starlight, I thought she was probably just trying to keep me calm, but I didn't have time for this. I had to stay ahead of Ben.

TWENTY-THREE

Love & other magic

I WENT STRAIGHT in the shop door, setting the bell jangling wildly, stopped at what I hoped was a safe enough distance to avoid hiccoughing curses, and called, "Starlight, I need to borrow your bike."

"What?" she asked, emerging through the beaded curtain. "*Seriously?*"

"Seriously, and I'm still sorry. I need your bike."

She stared at me. "Why?"

"I've lost my cat and my car, and I need at least one back."

She touched her dishevelled hair, frowning, then shrugged. "Fine. There's only two gears, no suspension, and the back brakes don't work, so if you fall off it's totally on you."

"Got it. Thank you." I was already hurrying out again as she called after me, "Wear the helmet!"

I grabbed the helmet out of the bike's handlebar basket, jammed it on without doing it up, then swung on, wobbling halfway across the street and back before I got the hang of it. Then I was off, peddling frantically out of town toward where I'd abandoned Ruiner. I didn't trust him, not exactly, but given how the afternoon had gone, I trusted him more than anyone else here.

It didn't take long to find him once I was out on the stone-walled road. He was stomping back toward Hollow-beck, his ears back, being followed by a murder of crows who swooped and ducked over him, plucking at his tail and ears. He was keeping up a steady stream of curses that sounded as exhausted as they were heartfelt.

I wobbled to a stop in front of him, almost pitching myself over the handlebars when I cranked on the front brake, and he glared up at me.

"About bloody time. What're you doing on a bike? Where's the car? And what's wrong with your face?"

I dropped the bike, picked him up, and hugged him to me, pressing my face into the soft, dust-scented fur of his back. He squawked in alarm, pressing all four paws to my chest and arching away from me.

"Stop it! What're you doing? Morgan! Gross!"

"I'm so glad to see you," I mumbled into his fur.

"Put me *down!*"

I didn't. He was small and warm and *real*, and, despite the fact he was straining against me, deeply comforting after the chaos of the afternoon.

"Morgan?" His voice was quieter, and I felt him relax his resistance a little. "What's happened?"

I eased my grip but didn't put him down. I shifted him to one arm instead, pointed at the crows, and said, "Just bugger off, will you?"

They looked at each other, then broke into a chorus of caws that sounded a lot like the sort of thing you hear around pub closing time on a Friday night.

Ruiner looked up at me, his eyes bright and wide. "What's wrong with you?"

"You're not trying to kill me, are you?" I asked him.

"Well, no. I mean, annoying as you are, I've been trying to *stop* you getting killed, remember?"

I sighed. "Do you know where the book is?"

"No." His reply was flat and tired, and I wondered if I believed him. I thought I did, but believing Ruiner had rarely turned out well in the past. Not that I had a lot of options right now.

"Alright," I said. "So I think I just got drugged by Ben, and almost charmed by Edith, but I think that was her trying to help. Plus Starlight wants to curse me with hiccoughs. Oh, and I crashed the car. But I crashed it going uphill, so I'm pretty sure someone cursed it."

He stared up at me, whiskers twitching, then said, "That's impressive."

"It's this *town.*"

"I don't seem that bad now, do I?"

I snorted. "It's a very poor standard to hold yourself against."

"Still."

I hugged him again, and this time he gave me a rough, reluctant purr. It was good enough for me.

RUINER and I sat there by the side of the road, being abused by crows, with neither of us entirely sure what to say or where to go next.

Finally he said, "You're out of my sight for five minutes and you've upset half the town and almost been poisoned by the other half."

"*Slight* exaggeration," I said. "But yeah. It didn't go super well."

"And we still don't know where the spell book is."

"No," I admitted. "But I think I believe Starlight, at least. She doesn't have it, and she seems really genuine about wanting to let everyone out of their deals, so we should try and get it to her."

"I always find it very convincing when people throw things at me, too," he said, arching his whiskers.

"Well, you've had enough practise."

"*Rude.* What about book boy? You really think he was poisoning you?"

I rubbed my face gingerly with my hands, feeling scabs at my hairline. At least I just had a bit of a headache now, rather than the whole world having wobbly edges. "I don't know. He seemed so *nice*."

"There's your problem. He's too quiet. I bet he irons his underwear."

"I didn't realise being quiet and tidy were the hallmarks of an evil mastermind."

"He tried to *drug* you, Morgs," Ruiner said. "I mean, I have terrible taste in women, but you have spectacularly bad taste in men."

"You don't have terrible taste in women. You're just a terrible person. *You're* the problem, not them."

"That's not always true," he said. "What about … what was her name? Blonde. She keyed my car."

"The fact that you can't remember her name probably has something to do with why she keyed your car."

He huffed. "Well, *maybe*, I suppose." We both fell silent for a bit, then he said, "What do we do now? We can't exactly cycle out of town on your stolen bike."

I looked at the bike. "Borrowed, and no, we can't. We need to find the book still."

"We can—"

"Can *not* break into the town hall."

"Well, what's your idea, then?"

I watched a low pale cloud for a moment, fleeting and ill-defined as a memory, then said, "I think we go and talk to Starlight. She understands the book, at least, and I think she'll help."

"I thought she threatened to curse you?"

"She did, but she also loaned me her bike," I pointed out. "And she didn't *actually* curse me."

"Oh, well. In *that* case."

I sighed. "She seems to be the only one that really isn't after the book for the wrong reasons. Besides, I have to give her bike back, so we've got to go there anyway."

"Alright," he said. "You being such a good judge of human nature and all. Lead on."

We cycled back into town with Ruiner crouched in the basket on the front of the bike, his ears back against the wind while he complained constantly about his fur getting messed up. I ignored him, peddling straight to the Cosy Cauldron and propping the bike up outside.

"If she turns you into a rat, I'm leaving," Ruiner said. "After I say *told you so.*"

"No talking," I reminded him, and he gave me that look I was certain was him trying to roll his eyes. I grinned and headed into the shop.

Starlight was stacking bundles of sage on a shelf, and she squinted at me as I came in. "Oh. It's you."

"I brought your bike back."

"Great. Anything you want to accuse me of while you're here?"

"I'm really sorry about that," I said. "I'd just had a car accident. I was freaking out a bit."

She examined me. "I broke two crystal balls and a fossilised dragonfly," she said.

"I can pay for them," I offered, then remembered my

bank account, which was pretty fossilised itself. "Some of them, anyway."

"I shouldn't have let anger get the better of me."

"I don't know. Sometimes it's healthy, you know?"

"It's a very negative energy." She climbed down from the ladder. "Do you want anything else? My shoes? The shirt off my back?"

"I just wanted to say that I believe you. About the book and the debts."

She raised her eyebrows. "Oh, I'm so pleased. That makes all the difference. Thank you for validating me."

We stared at each other for a moment, then I tried for a grin. "Sorry again. Look, it's been a hell of a day. A few days, to be honest. My brother's all tied up with Norma's deals, and I can't figure out how to fix it. I had a car accident. And it just felt like you were the most obvious suspect."

She folded her arms. "Me? When you found the body and were sneaking around in here when I was attacked?"

"Wrong place, wrong time, both times," I said. "Or actually, right place right time for you, since I think we scared off whoever actually attacked you."

She acknowledged that with a tilt of her head. "You took the book, didn't you?"

"Yes. Well, no, actually." I took a breath and pointed at Ruiner, who was sat on the floor next to me. He glared up at me, ears back. "My brother did."

Starlight stared at Ruiner, her eyes widening. "Your *brother?*"

"Yeah. Ruiner. Well, Rainier. Rainier Winters."

"*Rain,*" she breathed. "Oh *wow.*" She hurried forward and crouched down in front of him, her long hair swinging softly. "Look at you! I think you're better looking as a cat."

He growled, looking at me. "No talking, you said."

"Be nice," I said to him, and he hissed at me, then looked back at Starlight.

"Hi, Starlight."

She looked at me. "Oh, this is *brilliant*."

"It's not," Ruiner and I both said.

"How did it happen?" she asked him. "What did you do?"

"Why does everyone assume it's because of something I did?" he demanded. "That's victim blaming!"

Starlight and I both made doubtful noises, and he glared at us.

"He took the book," I said to her.

"Of course he did," she said, standing up. "You were going to take the deals on, weren't you, Rain?"

"No," he said, "I just wanted to not be a cat anymore. I thought there might be a counter-curse in the book, plus I was trying to look out for my sister, even though she doesn't believe that."

"Did Norma turn you into a cat?" Starlight asked.

"No," he said and didn't offer anything further.

"Yeah, he won't tell me either," I said. "But he sneaked the book out of the shop and I took it. I didn't realise what it was at the time — I was more worried about being stuck with a whinging feline for a brother."

"I do *not* whinge," Ruiner snapped.

Starlight looked from me to him and back again. "But then you were in here accusing *me* of having it … oh, you've *lost* it. You've lost the book!"

"Yes," I admitted. "We've been staying at Petunia's, and someone took it the other night. We must've interrupted them when we found Norma, and they figured we took it."

"How did you find it?" Starlight asked. "Even I didn't know where it was."

She looked at my brother, and he sighed slightly. "Yes, *fine*, I spied a couple of times. I knew where she kept the bloody thing."

"And there we go," she said. "Are you sure Rain—"

"Ruiner," I said.

"Oh. Yeah, that's better," she agreed, ignoring Ruiner's growl. "Are you sure he hasn't just stashed it somewhere?"

"I am here," he said. "Just because I look like a dumb animal doesn't mean I am one."

"Animals are pretty smart," Starlight said. "Smarter than humans, a lot of the time."

"Whatever. I don't have the book. And someone's after Morgan."

"Because of the car accident?" she asked, frowning.

"Not just that. There was a note on the fridge when we found Norma's body, telling her to get out of town."

Starlight looked at me for confirmation, and I nodded. "There was. And when the spell book vanished, they left another one. In my *bed.*"

"And you're still here?" She sounded bewildered, and frankly, I was feeling a bit the same way.

"I figured that if they were that keen, they'd track me down anywhere."

"*Hmm.* Fair point, I suppose. But why you? You haven't even been to Hollowbeck before, have you? Or are you involved in the magic world outside?"

"I didn't even think magic was a thing until a few days ago," I said.

"That makes no sense, then. Why a note for you?"

I shrugged a bit helplessly, and Ruiner said, "We think whoever killed Norma and is after the book, is probably also the one that's after Morgan, for whatever reason. And Ben the Book Boy just tried drugging her, so he's suspect numero uno."

"Ben? Really? But he's not magic," Starlight said.

"Doesn't have to be to drug me," I pointed out. "I think he put moonshade and whisperwind in my tea, just like he did to Norma. And maybe you. I smelled aniseed when I came in."

Starlight nodded, frowning. "Someone put it in the pots. When they boiled, the fumes got me. But Ben wouldn't be able to do anything with the book."

"Maybe he thought he could," Ruiner said, an uneasy edge in his voice.

"He's too smart for that," Starlight said. "He's studied magic a lot since he came here. He's always asking about it."

"Seems like there could be a reason for that," I said. "Maybe he's working with someone else, too."

Starlight examined me, her gaze so direct it made me shift uncomfortably. "Interesting that someone's trying to scare you, though," she said. "No offence, but I'm not getting big magic vibes off you. Your aura's a bit murky, though. Do you drink coffee?"

"Thinking of giving it up."

"You should. It's terrible for magical abilities. And you should probably give up Petunia's cocktails, too."

"I don't need to worry about magical abilities," I said. "The first I knew about magic was a cat jumping in my window and claiming it was my brother."

"Not an it," Ruiner said.

"Whatever. So you don't know anything about the note?"

Starlight shook her head. "It wasn't there the day before, and I was off with a cold the day she died. Which was really weird, actually. It came on very fast, and very strong. I had fever and everything, but then the next day I was fine."

I looked at her thoughtfully. "You eat anywhere different, maybe? Drink anything different?"

She thought about it. "I had a tea."

"Where?"

"I went to Mystic Munchies. With Ben. We take tea together sometimes."

"Told you he was too quiet," Ruiner said.

I shushed him with a wave. "Rudy wanted something the other day. A spell. But you wanted to stop it."

"A spell that Norma was making more expensive," Starlight said quietly.

"What sort of spell? Is it for the restaurant?"

"No, it's a love spell. You know the guy that works with her? The blond one?"

I wasn't about to admit how intimately I'd met Asger, so I just nodded.

"He's a Norwegian backpacker who wound up here about five years ago. He stayed for six months, then was meant to go back to Norway."

"So she put a love spell on him?" I asked.

"And you say *my* relationships are unhealthy," Ruiner said.

"Norma created the spell for her," Starlight said. "But it needs to be renewed every new moon, and she kept putting the price up, and asking for more favours. Ruby's besotted with him, so she just kept agreeing."

"That would seem to be a good motive," I said quietly. "If we think Ben might be working with someone else, maybe he hooked up with Ruby."

"But I like Ruby," Starlight protested. "She has a lovely aura."

I managed not to snort, but Ruiner wasn't so polite, so I looked at him disapprovingly, and he bared his teeth at me. "If she got the spell book, she'd be free of her debt, and could make her own love spells, right?" I asked.

Starlight sighed. "Those ridiculous deals! Norma was just so greedy with it all. I don't think she even needed the money. She just liked the power."

I nodded, looking around for somewhere to sit. There wasn't anywhere, so I sat down in the middle of the floor with my knees up, resting my elbows on them.

Starlight sat down cross-legged in front of me, rather more gracefully. "Are you alright?"

"Not sure. Might be the being slightly drugged, might be the car accident. Just needed a little bit of a sit down."

She nodded as if that was quite reasonable. "I'll get you a tea."

She got up and went through the beaded curtain behind the counter. Ruiner and I looked at each other. "Do you think you should be drinking her tea?" he asked.

"Maybe not," I said. "But it can't hurt at this stage."

All we could be sure of was that someone was still after me, the book was still missing, and Ruiner was still a cat. Everything else was up for debate, although I supposed if Ruiner found himself compelled to start doing favours, that'd give us a hint, at least.

TWENTY-FOUR

Bait in a trap

———————

STARLIGHT CAME BACK with a couple of large bean bags, arranging them on the shop floor so that we had somewhere to sit. It was hardly suitable for the middle of a shop, but it wasn't as though there were customers stampeding through the doors, so I just sat there and watched her pour two cups of tea from a little glass pot full of floating herbs.

She drank from both cups before handing me one, because, as she pointed out, she didn't want to be accused of poisoning me, because then she'd have to throw more things and she couldn't really afford to lose that much inventory. Unless it was the taxidermy animals. She should have chucked those long ago.

"Why *do* you have so many taxidermy animals?" I asked, sipping the tea. It was light and crisp and tasted of spring.

"Oh, it's old George. He lives up in the woods, and it's about the only thing that he's got to trade. So when he comes in for his blood pressure tisane, he brings taxidermy animals."

I looked at her and said, "Shouldn't he be getting something from the GP if he's got blood pressure problems?"

She shrugged. "I always tell him to go there as well, and I make sure that nothing he takes interferes with his actual medication. But sometimes, when you're stressed, ritual can do almost as much good as medicine. Boiling the kettle, heating the pot, steeping the tea. It's got its own magic."

I couldn't really argue with that, since the tea was certainly calming me at the moment. She'd also brought out some horrifyingly healthy-looking biscuits, which seemed to be all hemp seed and large chewy oats. I'd been working on my first bite for so long my jaw was starting to hurt.

Starlight wrapped her fingers around her cup and said, "What are we going to do?"

"What are *we* going to do?" I asked.

"Yes," she said. "I want the book back so I can release everyone from their debts. You want the book back so you can maybe figure out who's after you. And your brother wants the book back so he can stop being a cat."

"I very much want that," Ruiner said.

She regarded him for a moment, then said, "It mightn't be that easy. Some curses have to be lifted by the witch who placed it."

"I know," he said. "But it's worth trying, right?"

She gave a little shrug and took another sip of tea.

"So you're going to help us?" I asked.

"Yes. We can't have this sort of thing happening in Hollowbeck. It's a good place. I knew as soon as I found it that it was where I was meant to be. It's a place that you do everything you can to protect. People look out for their neighbours, and for the interests of the town. It's a *real* place."

"James said something about that, how Edith does everything for the good of the town rather than the good of herself," I said.

Starlight made a noncommittal sound. "Mostly yes," she said. "Everyone has some self-interest, though. It's how humans work."

I smiled. She had a satisfyingly cynical streak for all her rose-tinted hippy, crystals-and-sandalwood inclinations.

"I think we can come up with a plan," she said.

"What sort of plan?"

"I think we can draw out whoever's after the book, whether it's Ben or Ruby or someone else entirely."

"How does that help us?" I asked. "We need the book, not whoever's looking for it."

"Whoever took it doesn't *have* it, as such, because they haven't claimed it."

"Claimed it?"

Starlight nodded. "You don't just pick up a magic book and start using it. You have to claim it, and everything in the shop would've changed if that had happened. I'd feel it. So whoever has it probably thinks you're bonded to it, and they'll want to break that."

"That sounds bad."

"Yes. And we can use it." She grinned at me encouragingly and I tried to think of that as a positive thing. I couldn't.

WHICH IS how I found myself an hour later heading back down the road to Petunia's, my bag chafing uncomfortably on my shoulder, which seemed to be bruised. *Everything*

seemed to be bruised, or grazed, or both. I let myself in, and Petunia popped her head out of the kitchen.

"Hello dear," she said. "I'm glad you're back. I was a bit worried when I went to see if you wanted lunch and there was nothing in your room."

"Yes," I said. "I thought I was leaving, but I decided to stay a little bit longer."

"Excellent," she said, smiling at me, and emerged out of the kitchen. Before I could step back, she embraced me lightly, kissed me on each cheek, then held her hand out in a fist, palm down. I fist-bumped her lightly, confused, and she laughed, grabbed my hand, and turned it palm up. I opened my hand automatically, and she dropped a frog into it. I managed to swallow a squawk and also not to drop him. "Can you take him upstairs?" she asked.

"Um, sure. Is it Clarence?"

"Oh no, that's Douglas. He normally lives in the bathroom."

"Okay," I said and walked upstairs with the frog in my hand. I placed him carefully next to the bathroom door, where he ribbeted at me in what could have been a thanks and vanished behind the toilet. Ruiner and I looked at each other, then continued back up to our attic bedroom. Everything was as we'd left it. Either Petunia hadn't been in, or she'd been careful not to disturb very much.

I went back down to the bathroom for a quick and very cold wash, Douglas goggling at me as I gasped and yelped. Petunia had been quite right about there being no hot water in the day, and I didn't linger over it, just got the worst of the day's dirt off, then ran back upstairs to pull fresh jeans and a T-shirt on.

Ruiner was nowhere to be seen, and I went down to the kitchen alone. Petunia poured me an elderflower cordial, offered me the vodka, then shrugged when I turned it down.

"Far too sensible, you young people," she said, topping up her own glass. "There's no fun in it."

I made an agreeable noise, then said, "Petunia," and stopped. This was the bit I really wasn't looking forward to, because I had no desire to join Douglas up behind the toilet cistern.

"Yes, dear?" she said, looking at me expectantly.

"Do you ever go into guests' rooms?"

"Oh, because I saw you weren't there? No, all I did was knock, then popped my head around the door when you didn't answer. Your room is your room while you're here. So you'll have to clean it yourself, as well," she added with a wink.

I managed a smile in return. "So you wouldn't have taken anything from the room?"

She frowned. "Of course not. Are you missing something?"

"Well, Theodore was in my room the other night. And I've been missing something since."

She raised her eyebrows at me. "Theodore, *hmm?* I wouldn't have thought he was your style, really."

"Oh no," I said hurriedly. "*No.* I mean, he's very nice, but no. Not like that. *Definitely* not in my room like that."

"If you say so," she said, eyeing me over the rim of her glass with a sparkle in her eye. "No judgement here, dear. We all have our preferences."

"Really, no. We — Ruiner and I — came back and he was just there, standing in the middle of the room. He said you let him in."

She sighed, putting her glass down. "Oh, that man does take liberties. Years ago, I invited him into the house, and he seems to think that invite stands for all time now."

"So you didn't let him in?"

"No, I had no idea he was here. And I certainly wouldn't have let him go up to your room without your permission. Not into any of the guests' rooms."

I wondered again about the other guests. I still hadn't even heard any, let alone seen anyone. Aloud, I said, "Well, that's odd, then. You didn't see him at all?"

"I saw you walking with someone when you left," she said. "I assumed you'd arranged to meet them."

"Okay." I scratched my cheek, braced myself for potential frog-based disaster, but I had to know. I blurted, "Did you ever make a deal with Norma?"

Petunia's smile vanished, and the temperature in the kitchen dropped by about five degrees. I shivered. "With that woman?" she said, her voice as cold as the room. "*Never.*"

"Right," I said, hugging my arms around myself. It seemed to be getting colder still, and I'd be able to see my breath if it kept up much longer. "So you wouldn't be interested in her spell book or anything like that?"

"That thing should be destroyed," she said. "Nasty, grimy piece of dirty magic."

"If it was destroyed, would it release everyone?" I asked.

"Yes. All the knowledge would be lost with it, of course, but ... Oh, that Norma. There are many different kinds of magic workers in the world, and she was not one of the better ones."

"I'm getting that impression," I said. "You wouldn't know anyone who might've been in debt to her, who might've wanted the book, or wanted her dead, anything like that?" I tried to make it sound like casual conversation, but it fell as flat as the crickets in the terrarium, which seemed to be going into hibernation from the unexpected chill.

Petunia folded her arms on the table and regarded me thoughtfully. "I think you might be trying to interrogate me, dear, but you're terribly bad at it."

The heat rose in my cheeks so quickly that I was suddenly overheating rather than freezing. I thought I was going to pass out right there at the table and save her the effort of turning me into a frog.

"Sorry," I brandished my battered arms at her. "I'm a bit off. I think someone cursed my car."

She sat bolt upright. "Someone *cursed* your car?"

"I'm pretty sure. I was trying to leave, and it went completely out of control on the hill. The brakes wouldn't work, and it just kept going faster and faster. I managed to make two of the turns, then I just ended up going into the trees. I had to throw myself out because it wouldn't stop." I looked at my elderflower. "I think I may have a small concussion."

"Well, that is *unconscionable*," Petunia said. She got up, brushing her hands off. "Where's your car now?"

"In a ditch at the bottom of the hill."

"I'll deal with it," she said. "This is *utterly* unacceptable. I'll have a look right now and find out who did this."

"You don't need to do that," I protested. "I'll sort it out."

"You'll do no such thing. You'll stay here and rest up, and tomorrow you'll have your car back as good as new." I started to protest again, but she held an imperious hand up, glugging a generous measure of vodka into my glass with the other. "Drink that," she ordered.

I picked the glass up meekly. "Thank you," I said. "Umm ... I might have it in my room, actually."

"Off you go then," she said, accompanying me into the

hall and shooing me up the stairs. I trotted away obediently and left the glass on my bedside table as I sat down to wait.

It didn't take long. A guttural mechanical snarl came from the street outside, and a few moments later Ruiner slipped around the door like a shadow given mass to tell me Petunia had left on a motorbike that she could barely touch the ground from.

"Did you find anything?" I asked him. He'd been snooping while I was talking to Petunia, which I had to admit was probably only slightly less risky than my job had been.

"Nothing," he said. "No book."

"Any guests?"

"Just frogs. Frogs *everywhere*."

"She keeps talking about other guests," I said. "But I've never seen anyone."

"Maybe she means the frogs?"

"You think they *were* guests?"

"That's a lot of missing guests."

We stared at each other dubiously, then I got up. "Come on," I said. "We're not frogs yet, so let's go and tackle a murderer."

"Awesome," he said. "This place just gets better and better."

"You—"

"Brought us here, I know."

We headed out into the oncoming dusk, our shadows long and the scents of the night coming in on the wind.

DARK WAS CRUMPLING the edges of the day when we got back to the Cosy Cauldron. The lights were on in the shop, and I knocked warily, aware that between the light from the windows and that washing off the street, I may as well have had stage lights on me. It made me feel like a target and my shoulders itch.

When I glanced behind me, I spotted Ruby peering through the big window of Mystic Munchies, and further down the road shapes moved outside Bewitching Brews as Hollowbeck's day residents retired and the night ones arrived. I shivered, more violently than expected, and my bag slipped off my shoulder. Ruiner gave me a startled look.

I was just about to knock again when Starlight opened the door.

"It's open," she said.

"Why?" I asked.

"Why not? We always keep odd hours."

"Again, why?" I said, as she stepped back from the door to let me in. "How does anyone know when you're open?"

"They come and find out," she said and locked the door behind me. "Now we're closed, see?"

I decided that some things weren't worth trying to understand and followed her through to the back room. The new cauldron evidently still hadn't arrived, as the hearth gaped open, slightly blackened from the events of earlier in the day. I shivered again as I looked at the bare stone, unable to shake the image of the still, pale body and the feel of the cold skin of the witch underneath my fingertips. It seemed like a year ago.

"Right," I said. "Now what?"

"Now we wait," Starlight replied. "Do you want some tea?"

"Not really," I said, going to check the back door. I was bait in a trap, and knowing I was bait didn't make it any better. But if we were right, someone would've been keeping an eye on me this whole time, by crow or cat or crystal bloody ball, hoping I'd lead them to the missing book. And they would have seen me coming in here with my bag clutched protectively close to me and the outline of a book just visible if anyone looked close enough. So we had every reason to expect that whoever was hunting me would be on the way.

"Did you tell anyone?" I asked Starlight.

She shook her head. "No. I still think we should've at least told Isabella, though."

"We don't know she isn't involved," I said. "Her or Theodore. And you said you can restrain anyone who gets in here, right?"

"Yes, I've laid the charms." She waved a little vaguely, and I hoped both that she had more than hiccoughing curses in mind, and that she was more recovered from the attack than she looked. She'd gathered half her hair back in a clip, and her skirt seemed even more lopsided than earlier, but that could've been a style choice. It was hard to tell with her. "Are you sure about the tea?" she asked.

"Well, go on, then," I said, and she busied herself with the kettle.

Ten minutes later, we were sitting in the deep sofa, playing a pretty poor game of gin rummy because neither of us could remember the rules properly. Plus, I had a sneaking suspicion we needed more players.

The banging on the back door startled all of us. We'd been arguing about how many points a queen counted for, and I'd half-forgotten we were here to lure a murderer out into the open. All three of us yelped, Ruiner included, and we stared at each other. Whoever it was banged again, even harder this time.

"Open it," I whispered.

"Really?" Starlight asked, her eyes wide, and I almost

took it back, almost suggested we just sit here very quietly and hope that whoever was out there went away without cursing us or killing us or turning us into tadpoles.

Then Ruiner hissed, "Do it before they blow the door off or something."

Starlight gave a little hiss of alarm and jumped up, hurrying across the room, and we braced ourselves to come face to face with a murderer.

TWENTY-FIVE

Trapped

STARLIGHT TURNED THE LOCK CAUTIOUSLY, and the door exploded open as Ruby pushed her way in.

"Ruby?" I said, scrambling up. I suddenly wished I'd asked for a spell or a charm or a magic bloody wand, or simply a large stick to defend myself with. Starlight having charms was all very well, but I felt distinctly unprepared.

"*You*," Ruby said, pointing at me. "You've got Norma's book. I saw you come in with it." She shifted her finger to Starlight. "You need to make my spell *now*. It's wearing off. Asger's acting weird."

Starlight gave me an anxious look, and I said, "I don't actually have the book."

Ruby scowled. "Don't play silly beggars. I saw you sneaking in tonight, *and* the other night. You're always bloody well around. And you found the body. You really expect me to think you're not behind the whole thing?" Her gaze darted to my bag, lying on the floor by the hearth, and she lunged forward. I didn't move to stop her, and she snatched it up, ripping it open in the same movement.

"Ha!" she shouted as she pulled out a chunky old recipe book called *Cooking for Frogs*, which I'd discovered to my mortified amusement was actually about French cooking when I'd looked through it earlier. She waved it at us. "I *knew* — Wait." She stared at the cover. "What the hell is this?"

"I told you I don't have it," I said.

She stared at me for a moment, then launched herself forward, laying into me wildly with the book. I yelped, protecting my face with my hands. "*Where is it?*" she screamed. "*Where's the damn book! I need that spell! I need it!*"

"Stop it!" I shouted back. "*Ow! Stop!*"

"Ruby!" Starlight yelled, grabbing for her arm, and Ruby promptly turned on her, wielding the book so furiously that I hoped Petunia didn't use it much. It wasn't going back in one piece. "*Stop!*"

I tackled Ruby from behind, flinging both arms around her and hauling her off Starlight, before wrestling for the book. Ruiner looked on from under the coffee table, where he'd bravely taken cover.

"Give it — *give it!*" I wrenched *Cooking for Frogs* out of her grip and pushed her away. "Stop being ridiculous."

"You don't understand!" she shouted, her face pink. Tears stood out in her eyes. "I *need* that spell! I'll pay whatever you want. *Anything.*"

"I really don't have it," I said. "And even if I did, I wouldn't give it to you. I mean, a love spell? I know nothing about magic, and even I can see that's a seriously bad idea."

"It is," Starlight said. Her soft pale hair had moved from dishevelled to looking like she'd been wrestling with the electrics. "You have to stop."

"I can't," Ruby said, her voice small.

"Of course you can," I said. "If he's going to stay, he's

going to stay, right? And isn't it better that than wondering what happens if the spell stops working one day?"

She wiped her eyes, blinking hard. "You don't understand. Everything I do, it just falls apart. *Everything*. Mystic Munchies wouldn't have even got off the ground if it hadn't been for Norma's spells."

"So you had a little help to get it off the ground," I said. "It looks like you do good business now."

"Maybe. But what do I do if he leaves? What would even be the *point* then?"

"If you love something, set it free," Starlight began.

"Shut up," Ruby and I said together.

She huffed, and Ruiner said, "They've got a point. The whole setting it free thing never worked for me, either."

"That's because you've never set anything free in your life," I told him. "People have to escape from you."

"Says the woman who needed to literally trip over her cheating hubby to finally leave."

"Can we not do this here?"

Ruby looked from me to Ruiner and said, "Your familiar speaks."

"Oops," Ruiner said. "Forgot. Miaow and all that."

"It's her brother," Starlight said.

"Your brother's a cat? Didn't you just say you know nothing about magic?"

"It's been a full immersion week," I said, rubbing my face. "Alright. We don't have the book. And you don't have the book. And you wanted Norma to keep making these charms."

She sat down on the sofa with a sigh. "Of course I did. He's going to go back to bloody Norway, and I'm never going to see him again."

"You don't know that. He might choose to stay, or you could go with him."

She snorted. "Yeah, I somehow don't think there's a Hollowbeck in Norway."

"There's a Hollowbeck everywhere," Starlight said. "Even the most normal places have Hollowbecks. Not as Hollowbeck as this, but they're still there."

I looked at Ruby and she sighed again. "Maybe."

"You could also take up boxing or something rather than hitting people with books," I suggested. "You know, for stress management."

"Sorry," she said, looking at her hands. "Do you have any wine or anything? I think I need one."

That sounded like a fantastic idea, if we weren't still waiting for the killer to walk in the door. Plus, I had another question. "What charm was Asger after?" I'd forgotten to ask earlier. The nudity had thrown me off somewhat.

"Asger?" she asked, looking genuinely puzzled. "I don't know."

"Might he have known about the spell?"

"He can't have. I was really careful. And what d'you mean, he was sneaking around?"

Starlight and I looked at each other. I'd filled her in on our possible suspects and my chat with the Viking earlier, and now she gave me a solemn nod, accompanied by a wink and a tap of the nose. I blinked at her. I still wasn't sure how much of her behaviour was down to the near-asphyxiation earlier, and how much was just Starlight.

"He found Norma before I did. And was in here when Starlight was attacked, too."

She frowned. "Asger wouldn't hurt anyone."

"What if he did know about the spell?" Starlight asked. "Maybe he was trying to get Norma to reverse it."

Ruby stiffened, the colour draining from her face, then got up abruptly. "I have to go."

"Hang about," I said. "You can't rush out there and confront him. What if he *does* know, and … well, you know."

Starlight gave me a horrified look, but Ruby just shook her head. "He *wouldn't*," she said again.

"He might," I insisted. "If he hasn't been able to get the book, and thinks there's only one way out of the spell…" I trailed off, hoping I wasn't going to have to spell it out, then added, "If you wait with us, and he does come after the book, well, safety in numbers, right?"

Ruby looked from me with my bandaged arm and scraped face, to Starlight with her tie-dye and slightly glazed look, then down at Ruiner, and it was quite clear from her expression that she wasn't at all convinced by our numbers. "No," she said. "I'm going."

She had one hand on the door. I was still protesting that we were actually very capable when the whole place was suddenly plunged into darkness. I yelped, grabbing for my phone and cursing as I realised it was in my bag rather than my pocket.

"Ruiner!" I yelled. "What's happening?"

"How the hell should I know?"

"*Cat vision,*" I snarled, just as Starlight shouted something quick and sharp. A row of candles on the windowsill jumped into flame, sparking blue and green. Almost immediately they were blown out by a gust of wind which ran around the room, plucking angrily at my clothes, feeling too much like sharp, hard fingers for comfort.

"What's going on?" I asked, both hands out. I couldn't see anything, and I was sure the curtains hadn't been shut. We should have had *some* light coming in from outside, but all I could see was the afterimage of the candles. There was no difference between having my eyes open or shut. "Ruby? Are you doing this?"

"No," she said, her voice tight. "Someone's here." I could hear her scrabbling at the door. "Let me out. *Please* let me out!"

There was a breath of pressure through the room, then the clunk of the door handle. Ruby ripped the door open. "I'm going," she shouted, whether at us or to the presence in the shop, I wasn't sure. "I'm *going!*" She fled out, silhouetted for a moment against the paler dark before she was gone.

"Us too," I said in the general direction of where I thought Starlight was. The darkness seemed to be hanging about us like ink, the light from outside not daring to venture over the threshold.

"Quick," she said, and I heard the swift pad of her bare feet on the floor, then saw the shape of her silhouetted against the gap of the door.

I started after her, then felt that pressure change again. "*Stop!*" I shouted and stuck my foot out instinctively. Ruiner collided with it, hissing, and the door slammed shut so hard that Starlight gave a little scream. "Starlight? Are you okay?"

"Yes. Ow, though. It got my toe."

I fumbled toward where the door had been, and found the handle, wrenching it as hard as I could. There was no give to it at all. I might as well have been trying to turn a piece of rock. "We're stuck."

"I'm fine," Ruiner said. "If you were wondering."

"Only because I tripped you," I pointed out. "You'd have lost more than your whiskers if I hadn't."

"Can you smell that?" he asked, ignoring me.

"Is it your breath?"

"No, he's right," Starlight said. "Something's burning."

"The candles?" I asked uncertainly. There weren't any alight in here now, but I could smell it too.

"They all blew out," she said, rather unnecessarily, and I could hear her fumbling in the kitchen.

"Were there others?" I asked. "That thing you did, would it have lit some in the shop or something?"

"No," she said, sounding almost certain. "It was very targeted."

I had another tug at the door, but nothing had changed, and suddenly light flooded the room. I looked at Starlight, who was holding a tiny little LED torch. It was blinding after the almost physical dark.

"Souvenir magnet," she said, grinning.

"I like her," Ruiner said.

"I'd rather you didn't," she replied.

"I definitely like you," I said. We ran for the hallway door which had apparently slammed shut along with the back one. I raised my right fist as if I thought I could punch the magic and grabbed the handle with my left hand. Heat shot through the bandage on my hand and I let go of the handle with a squawk. What the—? If it hadn't been for the gauze padding, I'd have scorched myself.

"There's fire out there," I said, trying to keep my voice even. "Is there another way out? Another back door?"

"There's the windows," Starlight said.

I didn't answer, just ran to the windows that looked over the back, suddenly aware that the room was getting hotter and hotter, the air thickening around us and somehow gaining weight. I felt like I was swimming through it as I charged across the room, barely lit by the jumping light of the little torch.

"They won't open!" Starlight called from the kitchen, her voice a little too high over the sound of her scrabbling at the window.

I jiggled the latch furiously on the closest one, then moved to the next, but they were all the same. There was no more give to them than the door, and they were all made of heavy little mullion panes divided by metal framing. There was no way we were smashing one out.

"This sucks," Ruiner announced. "Do you think cats actually have nine lives?"

"Shall we test it?" I snapped at him.

"Who's doing this?" Starlight screamed. "Who is it? Show yourself!"

There was no answer, just that steadily building heat. Sweat ran down my forehead and stuck my T-shirt to my back, and I could hear the crackle and *whoomph* of fire outside the door. "You're going to burn the book!" I yelled. "Don't you want to know where the book is?"

There was a pause, then the pressure in the room plummeted, so fast my ears popped painfully, and a toothy cold came rushing in. My heart was going far too fast, and in the shaky light of Starlight's torch I could see Ruiner with his tail and spine pouffed up like an alarmed porcupine fish. It would've been funny if we hadn't been about to be either burned or frozen. I couldn't tell which anymore, the sweat chilling on my skin violently.

The door to the hall swung open, smooth and silent. I thought smoke would come flooding around it, and I pulled the neck of my T-shirt up hurriedly to cover my nose. But there was nothing. There wasn't even the *scent* of smoke, or any remnant of heat.

"It was an illusion," Starlight whispered.

"It seemed real," I said.

"It's powerful magic." She stepped forward, still clutching the torch and aiming it at the door. "Who's there?"

The book. The words dropped into my consciousness, less like hearing a voice and more like feeling it reverberating in my chest, forming the words without bothering with little things like ears. It was impossible to tell anything about it, if it was feminine or masculine, accented or not. I wanted it to be Asger, but I knew it had to be Ben. He'd hardly drugged me for the fun of it. And that sucked. Librarians are meant to be the good guys.

The book, the intruder said again, and Ruiner hissed, his ears flat. I felt like that voice could shake my flesh right off my bones, and I pressed my hands to my ears, as if that could stop it.

"We don't have it!" I shouted.

The book.

I dropped my hands, looking around wildly for help.

"*We don't have it!*" Starlight almost screamed, and over her, dimly, I heard what sounded like pounding on the back door.

I staggered to it, still with the sense of running in slow motion. Someone shouted outside, barely audible through the pressure and the banging, and I pressed my hands to the door as that voice shook into my bones again, demanding the bloody book.

"I can't open it," I told the door, not sure if I was shouting or whispering.

Someone said something outside, but my ears were so stuffy with pressure I couldn't understand what they were saying. I only realised they were going to try breaking it down when Ruiner grabbed my jeans in his teeth, tugging me away. I tried to tell them it wouldn't work, but the voice in my head was crushing the world.

The book.

I clawed my way along the furniture to Starlight, walking like a sailor in a storm. She had both hands clasped to her ears, the torch in one and pointing at the ceiling. She stared at me wildly, and I pulled one of her hands away to hiss in her ear, "How strong's your magic?"

Not strong enough, the voice said. *The book*.

Blue flames climbed the walls and heat flared again. I raised my bandaged hand to examine it, and I could see scorch marks on the cloth. It wasn't entirely an illusion. Or if it was, it had very strong roots in the world.

"Starlight," I said, and she stared at me with wide eyes. I looked from her to Ruiner, who was turning in circles, yowling and shaking his head as if to get the voice out of his ears. I took a few unsteady steps to the fireplace and picked up the poker. I was going through the hall door, heat or no, even if it was only to stop that bloody *voice*. I felt like the weight of it was going to liquify my brain.

The book.

"Enough about the bloody book!" I shouted, then I put my head down and ran for the door.

TWENTY-SIX

Someone needs to get violent

I CHARGED the doorway in slow motion, Ruiner joining me in a graceful yet oddly stilted sprint. I don't know what he thought he was going to do — chuck a hairball up on someone, maybe. But even as I raised the poker, shouting something completely pointless (Ruiner later told me it was "*Death to Frogs!*" but I think he was lying), someone appeared in the doorway. I staggered to a stop, staring.

As much as I'd been hoping it wasn't Ben, I'd still expected it would be, that he'd walk in demanding the book for his private bibliophile collection or his own nefarious reasons or whatever. But it wasn't. It wasn't even Asger. It was Edith, her hair pinned neatly back, giving us that charming smile, her hands in the back pockets of her jeans.

"The book, dears," she said in her normal voice.

"Edith?" Starlight said, and I looked around to see her just behind me, a saucepan brandished over her shoulder. "But ... you didn't owe her anything."

"No," she said, "I didn't. I made sure of it. But that

book can't be handled by just anyone. It's precious. It needs someone who knows how to deal with it."

I looked at the pale flames running up the wall and said, "Well, why didn't you take it when you killed her, then?"

Edith gave me an amused look. "I couldn't find it."

I shifted my grip on the poker, which suddenly felt leaden. That simple statement of fact chilled me. She didn't even try and deny she'd killed Norma, and that meant she wasn't worried about us knowing. Which, in turn, meant she had every intention of killing us as well. "You really killed her," I said.

"Of course I did," she said with a shrug. "She never locked the back door. It was very easy to drop a little something into her cauldron. Everyone knew about her whisper-wind habit, so it wasn't exactly hard. Then all I had to do was pop in and help myself to the book. But I couldn't find it."

She pointed at Starlight. "I made sure you were out of the way for the day, but it seems I got it wrong on the book. I even checked your house, but you must've hidden it well."

"My house?" Starlight said. "I *thought* the vibrations were off. And you've been coming in here, too, haven't you? You left the door unlocked the other night."

Edith looked puzzled. "Locks don't concern me."

"Yeah, that was me," I said.

Starlight scowled at me. "Really? You broke in? That's very bad karma."

"I was investigating," I said.

"You're not the Famous Five," she replied, shaking the saucepan at me.

"Well, evidently," I said. "I'm four short."

"Three," Ruiner said.

Edith clicked her tongue irritably, and blue flame fled

across the floor, encircling us. All three of us yelped, and I took a couple of swings at the fire with my poker, the reality — or *unreality* — of the situation rushing back in. "That's not going to do anything, dear," Edith said. "Hand over the book."

I shrugged. "I *said* we don't have it."

"You must have," she replied. "I searched the car. Although I was interrupted by that bloody Petunia, which was irritating."

"Petunia? What did you do to Petunia?" I demanded.

"She's fine. She's with her frogs."

"*Where?* Not in the toilet cistern? *Did you put her in the toilet cistern?*"

She stared at me. "There's something wrong with you, you know."

"There is not," I said, brandishing the poker at her.

"Where is the book?" Edith asked, ignoring the poker. "You need to give it to me, or there will be consequences."

I just about took a swing at her out of sheer frustration. "What part of *we don't have the book* are you not getting?" I asked. "Honestly, asking louder doesn't change anything."

She flicked her fingers at me, and flames flared up the leg of my jeans, scorching the skin beneath. I yelped and dropped the poker, using my bandaged arm to beat the flames.

"Stop it!" Starlight shouted, rushing forward with the pot at the ready, the flames leaped hungrily to her long skirt. She screamed, twisting wildly as she attempted to put them out.

"Edith!" I shouted, smothering the flames on my jeans and turning to help Starlight, who was still smouldering. "Burning us isn't going to do anything."

"It'll be very satisfying, though," Edith said.

The banging on the back door had stopped, so all I

could hope was that whoever was out there had gone to get a crowbar or a fire engine, or preferably both.

"I still don't understand how you could kill her," Starlight said, staring at her charred skirt. "You were friends."

"Hardly," Edith said. "We were just two old witches who'd known each other a long time. She always thought she was so much *better* than me, too."

"But why now?" I asked. "What made you do it now if you'd known each other so long?"

Edith sighed. "We had a deal for years. Norma would make sure no competition came in for my herbalism store. But people were spending less and less on that, and more and more on bloody *prescriptions*. Plus she was selling her own tinctures and so on, and as she was the 'town witch'" — she made air quotes with a grimace —"everyone was going to her. So I decided I needed to do something different anyway. I set up a coffeeshop. But instead of supporting me, when coffee got so bloody popular she started trading deals all over the place, and said she'd only help me if I *paid* her. Me! I *made* her."

"What does that mean?" I asked.

"You don't just become a witch. You have to be a witch's apprentice. Like this thing here, who thinks she's so special." She nodded at Starlight, who frowned.

"I do not. No more than every person is special in their own divine way."

Edith made a vomiting sound, which I would have agreed with under normal circumstances, but I wasn't about to agree with her, now or ever. "Look," she said to me. "It's very simple. You hand over the book, or this entire shop burns down with you two in it, due to an accident caused by inexperienced little apprentices making mistakes."

"I don't have it," I said.

You might want to rethink that." She didn't move, didn't raise her hands, or whip out a magic wand, but suddenly the heat in the room was unbearable. I could actually smell my hair singeing.

I cried out, covered my head with both arms, and stumbled toward the hearth, as if I thought it could somehow protect me. Starlight screamed behind me, battling with her skirts as they re-ignited, and I half-turned to pull her with me.

As I did so, a new shriek went up. It wasn't from Starlight.

The heat faltered enough that I could drop my arms and I saw Edith struggling to tear my brother off her face. He dug his claws into her, screeching at the top of his tiny lungs in the sort of language that would've given our mother conniptions.

I lurched toward them as she got a grip on Ruiner and tore him off, but Starlight was closer. Skirts forgotten, she swung the saucepan in a short, furious arc, and kneecapped the old witch with the sort of enthusiasm I'm sure even karma would've approved of.

The crunch was hideously audible, and Edith went down with a scream. The last of the flames fading out and the room filling with shadow and light from outside. Starlight clicked her fingers, and the candles came back on. I rushed toward Edith and Ruiner.

"*I will tear him to pieces if you don't stop!*" Edith shouted.

I crashed to a halt barely a stride from her, the poker raised over my shoulder, and Starlight and I looked at each other.

Edith sprawled on the floor with Ruiner's teeth and claws buried in her forearm, blood trickling down it, one hand clenched around his belly, deep in his fur, and the other on his neck. "I'll tear his head off," she said. "You see if I don't."

"You monster," Starlight said. "That poor little cat."

"He's no more a poor little cat than I am," she said, giving him a shake. To Ruiner's credit, he just bit down harder, a rumbling growl shaking him and his tail whipping. Edith tightened her hands, looking at me.

"Alright," I said, and put the poker down. "Let him go."

"Put that saucepan down," she said, nodding at Starlight.

Reluctantly, Starlight did, and we both took a step back. Edith levered herself awkwardly up to sitting, still with Ruiner in both hands, and looked at her knee. It was already swelling.

"Let him go," I said.

She looked up at me. "You silly girl," she said. "He *bit* me." Her hand twisted on my brother's neck, cruel and sure and deadly.

For one moment I was frozen as Ruiner's eyes flicked toward me. He didn't release his grip on Edith, and she didn't waver. I couldn't look away from her hands. This woman was going to kill my brother right in front of me, and there was absolutely nothing I could do about it. I lurched forward anyway, knowing I couldn't reach her in time, but before I could take more than a step, my feet were frozen to the floor, ten times worse than in the stool at the cafe. I tugged desperately, trying to move, and saw Starlight doing the same, but we were both mired. The horror of it sunk in a cold, sick weight to the pit of my belly, and I let out a little sob.

"Please stop," I managed, finding my voice somewhere. "Please, please don't."

"I don't see why not," she said. "He's annoying. And

you're all going to perish in this little shop fire anyway, so you may as well have the fun of seeing him go first." Her voice had the same almost indifferent tones as earlier, but the heat hadn't started building again yet. Her arms trembled as she clutched Ruiner, and I thought of Starlight saying *powerful magic.* That had to take it out of someone, all the pyrotechnics and vocal theatrics, and now she was holding us both in place as well. So maybe there was a chance, however small.

Something knocked into my foot, and I risked a glance down. It was a taxidermy squirrel, and I blinked at it. There was no time to wonder where it came from. I dropped to my knees as if I was begging, my hands clutched in front of me. It didn't take much acting, to be honest, and the shake in my voice took me by surprise. "Please," I said. "*Please* don't hurt him. He's my family."

"You should have thought of that before you got into this mess, shouldn't you?" Edith said.

Starlight abruptly broke into a sobbing, impassioned plea which was barely comprehensible, although I caught something about all small creatures being blessed by the goddess. Edith looked like she wasn't paying much attention either, but it didn't matter, because it had distracted her for just long enough.

I snatched the squirrel up in both hands and hurled it as hard as I could, not bothering to straighten up or get a decent angle, just putting everything I could into the throw and feeling my injured shoulder twinge violently.

Edith glimpsed the movement, jerking toward me, and it would've been too little, too late, except that right as I threw the squirrel, a rat dropped out of the ceiling and buried its teeth in her neck.

She screamed and dropped Ruiner just as the taxidermy squirrel hit her square in the face, and her scream went up an octave. The rat gave me a horrified look, as if it thought I'd been aiming at it rather than the witch, and vanished.

"Sorry, rat!" I shouted, scrambling to my feet as the quicksand grip vanished. "That wasn't for you."

Starlight charged forward and I was only a step behind her. We hit Edith like we were trying out for the Hollowbeck rugby team, and we took her to the floor with a crash that shook the old wooden boards. I trapped her legs, kneeling on them, and Starlight pinned her arms above her head, but our moment of triumph was short-lived.

Edith didn't bother to fight or even to rage at us. She just closed her eyes and muttered furiously to herself, which was a lot more frightening than any screaming and shouting.

The heat started to build, so fast it made me gasp, as if it were stealing the air from around us.

"How do we stop her?" I demanded. "Can we gag her or something?"

Starlight shook her head. "That won't stop her. She doesn't have to say the words. Do you think that's a spell she's saying?"

I listened for a moment. What she was saying was quite graphic, and also anatomically impossible. "Yeah, fair enough. That doesn't sound like a spell."

Ruiner had been sprawled on the floor since Edith let him go, panting wildly, and now he staggered to all fours. "Just hit her, then! Bloody well knock her out!"

"I'm not going to hit her," Starlight said, shifting her grip on Edith's arms. "I'm ethically nonviolent."

"This is about to get very violent if you don't do something," Ruiner pointed out.

I had to agree with my brother on this one. My jeans

were already starting to smoulder again. "Can't you do a spell?" I asked Starlight. "Some sort of charm?"

"I'm not strong enough," she said, her voice wobbling. "I can't stop this. I *can't.*"

A fresh flood of heat accompanied her words, and when I looked at Edith, she'd opened her eyes, glittering with heat and triumph. We'd never make it out of the doors even if we ran, and she was going to burn us alive without thinking twice about it. We were *done* unless someone did something distinctly violent, and very quickly.

I lurched forward over Edith, shoving Starlight out of the way, and pulled a fist back to punch the very nice older woman who had welcomed me to town and made me such lovely coffee, wondering wildly how you actually hit someone hard enough to knock them out, and if there was a technique, or if you just sort of chucked a fist in and hoped for the best, and how you could ever be sure you weren't going to do one of those terrible one-punch kill things, and how many knuckles I was going to break, and just how bad my karma was going to be after this, and as all of that was still roaring through my head and my fist hovered in mid-air, someone burst out of the hall and dropped to their knees beside us.

Ben, his shirt still neatly buttoned even though one sleeve was burnt off, grabbed Edith's face, forced her jaw open, and tipped an entire jar of something straight down her throat. He clamped her mouth shut with one hand and pinched her nose with the other, and Starlight and I clung to grimly as she thrashed about. The heat roared around us, so hot that Ruiner scrambled onto my shoulders to get off the floor. I had to squint my eyes closed. It felt like my eyeballs were roasting in their sockets.

Then it eased, at first only slightly, then dropping steadily, and I felt some of the tension go out of Edith's legs. I still didn't let go, not even after Ben released her face and rocked back on his heels, letting out a shaky breath. Edith coughed and spluttered a couple of times before muttering some very slurred and questionable claims about his parentage. We just watched, and finally she hiccoughed and subsided into sleep with a little snore.

I released her legs cautiously, looking at Ben. "What the hell was that?" I asked.

"Camomile," he offered with a small smile.

TWENTY-SEVEN

A witchy transition

I SCRAMBLED TO MY FEET, backing away from Ben, my heart still too fast and my face too hot. "You tried to drug me," I said, pointing at him with a wobbly hand.

"It was whisperwind," he said. "I was just trying to calm you a little. You'd had a car accident, you were panicking about your cat — it's like giving someone brandy, but better for you."

I jabbed my finger at him urgently, looking at Starlight. "I smelled aniseed in the tea. Like moonshade. *With* the whisperwind flowers."

Starlight gave a gratifying gasp of horror. "You tried to murder her!"

"It was liquorice tea!" Ben said, looking almost as horrified as Starlight. "Yes, with whisperwind, but it was *just tea!*"

"He *drugged* me," I said to Starlight. "He did!"

"That's so off," she said, getting up as well. "Sneaking stuff into people's tea? Trying to *calm* someone with drugs? Honestly, Ben. There's a name for that."

"Okay, I get your point," he said. "But—"

"It might be him," I said to Starlight. "He might have the book. He was here when Ruiner took it."

"Do you have the book?" Starlight demanded, hands on her hips.

"What?"

"Well, you're going around drugging women. Are you a thief too?"

"I'm not *drugging women*," he protested, and we all looked at Edith. "I was helping!"

"Just like you were helping me?" I demanded, Starlight nodding furiously.

"Dude, even I've never stooped that low," Ruiner said. "And my sister will tell you I've stooped pretty low."

"He has," I agreed.

Ben stared at Ruiner. "*That's* your brother?"

"Again, oops," Ruiner said. "It's really hard remembering not to talk."

"Stop avoiding the question," I said to Ben. "Do you have the book?"

"What book? What book are we talking about? I mean, I have all the books. I'm the bloody librarian."

"You're still not answering the question!" Starlight yelled, grabbing the squirrel and brandishing it at him.

"What is *wrong* with you two?" he shouted back. "I just went through a bloody burning shop to help you!"

"Unless you were working with her!" Ruiner yelled, and Starlight and I both gasped.

"I just knocked her out!" Ben waved at Edith wildly. "How can I be working with her?"

"It's a ruse," Starlight said.

"Told you it was the quiet ones you had to watch," Ruiner said with some satisfaction, then Ben said something about skinning cats that was drowned out by Starlight, Ruiner, and I all yelling at him at once about animal cruelty, picking on someone his own size, and the book, respectively, while he shouted back with increasing frustration. At least I was still on message.

We were all still shouting at each other when I suddenly became aware that there was a cool draught coming from the back door. I turned to see Theodore standing on the threshold, watching. He leaned against the doorframe, looking particularly elegant in a dark grey suit with a pale blue shirt that set off his orange skin nicely. Asger, Ruby, and Isabella peered over his shoulders.

"What exactly has been happening here?" Theodore asked.

We fell silent and I looked around. The wind Edith had sent through had swept every surface clear, and the whole place was covered in debris. Vases were shattered, tubs of creams and jars of tinctures crushed and oozing, wine bottles bleeding across the wooden boards, and bunches of herbs and dried flowers were scattered like confetti. The kitchen table had fetched up against the fridge, the chairs were overturned, and a coffee table was wedged into the hearth. Edith was snoring in the centre of the floor while we argued over her prone form.

"Hi," I said. "We were going to call you."

"We were just trying to find out who had the book," Starlight put in.

Isabella frowned. "What book?"

"Norma's spell book," I said.

She pointed into the hallway, and we all turned to look at the rat, which had crept into view again. It sat back on its haunches, little front paws fiddling with each other. "Why don't you ask the rat?"

"The rat?" I asked.

"Her familiar."

I looked at the rat, then at Starlight. "That's not your familiar?"

"That's Jacqueline," she said. "Hello, Jackie. I haven't seen you for a while. Are you alright?"

The rat looked at her, then back at me. Then it dropped to all fours, pattered into the room, climbed onto my trainer, and perched there, eyeing Ruiner suspiciously.

I stared down at it. "What's happening?"

"I believe you have just inherited a familiar," Isabella said.

"I've already got a cat," I replied.

"That is not a cat," Asger said. "Or a familiar."

"Quite. Most cats don't swear at the town librarian," Theodore said, then looked thoughtful. "Certainly not in English, anyway."

There was silence for a long time while the rat and I looked at each other and everyone else looked at me.

"Do you know where the book is?" I asked her finally. "One squeak for yes, two for no."

She squeaked, just once.

"Right. Um … can you show us?"

Two squeaks.

"Helpful," I said.

"Perhaps you can show just Morgan?" Isabella asked.

The rat scrutinised me, then gave one small squeak.

"*Ohhh,*" Starlight said. "You've inherited the book *and* the familiar."

"All hail the new witch," Theodore said, and I stared at him. He smiled at me, looking far too amused and showing just a few too many teeth.

"Excuse me, *no,*" I said.

The rat tugged on my jeans, and I looked down at her. She gave me her one irritating squeak again.

"I'm not sure you have a choice," Isabella said.

I said some things that would've impressed even Edith, and I was still saying them when they herded me out of the shop, Jacqueline balancing easily on my shoulder, and up the street to the Witching Hour, leaving Theodore to arrest Edith and compose himself. I was showing a few too many grazes, apparently.

And if that didn't really just top the bloody day, I don't know what would have.

THEODORE DIDN'T REAPPEAR for a good couple of hours, by which point Starlight and Asger were singing Abba, Ben and Ruby were arguing about the merits of truffle oil, and Ruiner and Jacqueline had almost stopped hissing at each other. I was working my way steadily through some very comforting cocktails, and Isabella sat next to me, every now and then sniffing everyone's drinks and making appreciative noises.

I leaned back and pressed both hands over my eyes, my bandages smelling of smoke and sweat. My head hurt, even with the cocktails in me, and the sight of my brother and Jacqueline sitting one to either side of me was giving me the same weird seesawing feeling I'd had when Ruiner had first turned up.

"Are you alright, Morgan?" Isabella asked, her voice gentle.

"Not really," I said.

"Is it Jacqueline that's worrying you?"

"Among other things." I uncovered my eyes and looked at her, still in her low-cut blouse and full skirts, smiling at me with her skin faintly flushed in the low light of the beer garden. "What did Theodore mean, *all hail the new witch?*"

"The book has chosen you as its new keeper."

"*How?* I haven't even seen it since ... well, whatever happened."

"I imagine Petunia's frogs claimed the book until Jacqueline could get it. She's the link between book keepers. Familiars protect their books, and those who persist after the death of a witch have the power to pass the book on if the witch hasn't done so already."

"*Book keeper,*" Ruiner said, twitching his ears at me. "I mean, it's on-brand, right?"

"Hardly the same thing," I said, and looked back at Isabella. "I'm not a witch, though."

"Aren't you? You found Hollowbeck. You navigated a magical world without panicking or fleeing. You saw it for what it was and never tried to explain it away. And you stood up to the most powerful witch in town."

I shivered. "That was a joint effort."

"Is that any less magic? The ability to draw others together?"

I wrinkled my nose and didn't answer. I'd spotted Theodore slipping across the beer garden, shadowy and graceful, and sucking furiously on what was almost certainly not a Bloody Mary. Petunia followed him, wearing a spectacularly fluffy, multi-coloured jumper in deference to the evening air. I jumped up, limping over to her so I could throw my arms around her. She smelled of wood smoke and tannins.

"I'm so sorry," I said. "Are you alright?"

Petunia hugged me back, her grip surprisingly fierce. "Quite alright," she said, then *ribbeted* and made a face. She took a sip from a tall, curved glass filled with something frozen and bright blue. "That damn Edith took me entirely by surprise, and there was a frog incident."

"A what?"

"Petunia is rather good at creating weather events," Isabella said. "But there are occasionally side effects."

Petunia coughed once, spat a small, startled-looking frog into her hand, and said, "They do get everywhere. Edith froze me for a little and left me in a ditch, but she was in a bit of a hurry. Seemed to forget ditches are hardly an issue when one has friends." She winked at the frog and put it in her pocket, then had a hearty swig of her drink.

"I'm really sorry," I said again. "I didn't realise it'd be so dangerous." I was startled to find I was close to tears, and I swallowed hard, then sat down abruptly, trying to concentrate on my breathing.

Theodore had been watching us all while working on his drink, and now he took another couple of gulps, then sat down next to Asger, who almost climbed into Ruby's lap.

"Dangerous?" Petunia asked. "Hardly. Edith was nothing but a jealous old witch with an over-inflated ego. Thought everything in town should go her way. Not that Norma was any better. It'll be good to have new blood in." She nodded at Starlight and me approvingly. Starlight looked delighted, but I just shook my head and looked at Theodore.

"What happened with Edith, then?"

"She will not be working magic anymore or remaining in Hollowbeck. She has been dispatched."

"*Excuse me?*"

He gave me a puzzled look. "She has left."

"Oh." I relaxed a little and had another sip of my drink. "I thought she'd been *dispatched*, you know."

"She has," he said, looking to Isabella for help. "I dispatched her out of town."

She gave us both an enormous smile and said, "It's most distressing. But dear James has chosen to remain and run the coffee shop, at least for now, so you will still have your beverages."

I wondered how that worked. If he'd had suspicions about his aunt, or if he'd somehow been charmed into staying by someone. The latter seemed entirely possible. It was starting to feel like you couldn't move without tripping over a charm around here, and I had no intentions of adding to them, even if I'd known how to.

Theodore and Isabella were both still looking at me, so I pointed at Ruby and Asger. "What were you after, then, Asger? Why were you so cagey?"

He flushed, his face luminous even in the low light, and took a large gulp from a dainty martini glass full of something translucent and pink. "I had an ongoing deal with Norma." He shot Ruby and embarrassed glance. "A love spell."

Starlight and I looked at each other and burst out laughing.

"Shut up," Ruby said. "It's not funny! We were both on the hook to that old witch, and we didn't even realise that the other was doing the same thing."

"And that they would've cancelled each other out," Starlight said. "So you're just quite normally in love with each other." She heaved a dramatic sigh, one hand pressed to her chest, and smiled brilliantly. "So sweet!"

Ruiner and I made matching gagging noises, and she gave us an offended look.

THINGS GOT a little blurry after that. It had been a long day, and half a piece of enchanted carrot cake and some Jammy Dodgers hadn't exactly equipped me for three of Tanya's deceptively smooth cocktails. I do know that I told

Ben I loved all librarians, declared that Asger had a very nice bum, and that Starlight and I declared eternal friendship for each other at least three times. But eventually Petunia and I tottered off down the road and back to the B&B, where Ruiner, Jacqueline, and I struggled back up the stairs to the attic room.

Or I struggled. Ruiner loped ahead of me, complaining that he couldn't have alcohol, although I had a clear memory of Tanya giving him a catnip cocktail that had had him rolling happily across the table with his tongue hanging out. Jackie rode silently on my shoulder, sighing now and then. I wondered if she missed Norma. I supposed she must, having been her familiar, so when I collapsed on the bed and she curled herself into the crook of my neck, I didn't complain. She'd been pretty handy with a taxidermy squirrel, after all. Besides, I was asleep about two minutes later. I didn't have the energy to worry about rat co-sleeping too much.

I woke with a less sticky mouth than might've been expected, and to the sensation of small teeth nibbling my ear. I sat straight up with a shriek, sending Ruiner catapulting off the bed and fleeing for the far end of the room while Jackie chittered at me irritably. I grabbed my ear, checking for bleeding.

"What are you *doing?* Are you hungry? Is this some familiar thing?"

Jackie raised herself on her haunches and gave me an unmistakably disapproving glare. I looked around the room. We hadn't been that late last night, but the light was already strong in the room. I'd slept in more than long enough.

I groaned and got up, pattering downstairs to see if the bathroom was free. It wasn't. I could hear the odd muted splash in the bath when I pressed my ear to the door, so I returned to our room with a sigh and pulled some clothes on. A generous application of deodorant was going to have to suffice.

Five minutes later, in fresh clothes but still without being able to find my hairbrush, I ventured out into a slightly cooler morning. Jacqueline was back on my shoulder, and the few people we passed barely glanced at me, even with Ruiner ambling next to me.

We went straight to the Cosy Cauldron, even though I wanted to stop for coffee, because the damn rat screamed in my ear and tried to pull one of my earrings out when I veered toward Bewitching Brews. So I went straight to the back door of the shop instead and let myself into the clutter and chaos of the night's battle. It looked cold and stark in the morning light, everything a little tattered and run down.

I stood there for a moment, then started collecting broken jars and dumping them in the bin. That was a start, anyway.

I was still sifting through the debris when a squeak drew my attention. I looked around and saw Jacqueline standing in the door to the pantry, one paw on the spell book.

"Hello," I said. "There you are."

Jacqueline chittered again, and I walked over to crouch down next to her. She watched me put one hand out and poke the book lightly, as if it might bite, then grabbed my finger in both her paws and pulled it back to the book. I resisted, my stomach tight and sick-feeling.

"Don't," Ruiner said, and I looked around at him. He was standing in the middle of the devastated room, his pupils wide in his blue eyes.

"Don't touch it? Why not?"

"I don't know," he admitted. "But if touching it means you claim it, there's no going back."

"What did you do?" I asked. "What did you touch?"

He sighed. "I wasn't invited, Morgan. I talked myself into the right circles, and pretended I knew more than I did, because I knew there was money to be made. Everything I've done has been by trading and buying other people's magic. Which means I don't have any power. But it also means I can walk away."

"So you could never have done the counter-curse if you have no magic," I said.

"No," he admitted.

I looked at Jacqueline, who had stopped tugging my finger and just held it, waiting. There was a soft dusting of grey on her brown muzzle, and it made me inexplicably sad.

"Did you think I could, Ruiner?" I asked him.

"I knew you'd find a way to make it work. Someone who could do the spell for us. For me. But not like this. You can't go back to the normal world if you do this."

I thought of the shoddy little apartment and the screaming sirens, the mould-infested bookshop and its leering proprietor, thought of Jason and boredom and book-keeping of the numerical sort, and said to my brother, "Are we really going to find someone else to take this curse off?"

"I don't know," he admitted. "Norma was the strongest witch I knew."

"Right, then," I said, and reached for the book.

"*Morgan!*" my brother shouted, and I squeezed my eyes shut, bracing myself for an electric shock, or for the book to turn into a trap and latch itself around my wrist, or to swallow me whole and spit me out again as a newly minted witch.

Instead, I felt a sharp but very small pain in one finger, and I yelped. When I looked down, Jacqueline was still clinging to my hand, and a single drop of blood welled from a neat bite mark on my index finger and splodged onto the book's cover.

"*Ow!*" I said, jerking my finger away from her. She let me go, looking down at the book with a satisfied air, and I stared at the bite. I could hardly suck it clean. Jacqueline was a very nice rat, but she was still a rat.

I got up to find a cloth, leaving the book on the floor.

"Is that it?" Ruiner asked.

"No idea," I said.

He examined me. "You look just the same."

"I feel just the same."

"I thought it'd have fixed your hair, at least."

I threw the cloth at him and had to go and find another.

IT TOOK Starlight and I all morning to clean up the back of the Cosy Cauldron, but by lunchtime it looked cleaner than it had before the Edith-storm. We took the beanbags out to the front of the shop and sat in the sun on the pavement to eat a salad that was full of grains I couldn't pronounce, but, I had to admit, looked healthier than my original lunch plan of cake from Bewitching Brews. Hollowbeck was quietly busy, people greeting each other on the street, and the heat of the previous days had eased.

"We're almost due rain," Starlight said.

"It comes on a schedule, does it?"

"When Petunia remembers. Sometimes she gets distracted and we get snowstorms in July, or a scorcher in January, or just a week of drizzle."

"A week of drizzle sounds pretty normal."

"Not for here," she said, smiling, then immediately added, "So, are you staying?"

I looked at Ruiner, his eyes half-closed in the sunlight, and down the street at the jumbled architecture and a woman walking a giant pig into the juice bar, and a small girl pushing a badger in a wheelbarrow, and three boys with towels tied around their necks cycling wildly down the middle of the street, almost bowling over a man carrying an onion fully as big as his head.

"For now," I said, and felt something within me loosen, a constriction I hadn't known I was clinging to releasing, melting in the warmth and the easiness of the company, the rat and the cat and the star-girl. I tipped my face up to the sun, closing my eyes, and thought, *yes. For now.* Until Ruiner was sorted, at least. Until *I* was sorted, whatever that looked like.

I opened my eyes to one of the boys on bikes tearing past.

"Delivery!" he bellowed and hurled something at us. I yelped and ducked, but Starlight caught it.

It was an envelope, white and textured, and she stared at it, then held it out to me. I knew what it was going to be before I took it. My name on the front, in looping, curving script. And inside: *You were warned.*

Ruiner and I stared at each other, then I said, "This is all your fault."

"*Mine?* Who decided to be town bloody witch?"

"Who *brought* me here?"

"Who *stayed?*"

"What're we going to do?" I demanded, at the same time as he said, "So what now?"

We held each other's gazes furiously, then I crossed my arms and leaned back in the beanbag.

"Are you alright?" Starlight asked, almost timidly.

"Yeah," I said.

"Fine," Ruiner said, and yawned. "Best get practising ways to zap your enemies or something, Morgs."

"I'll just throw you at them," I said, closing my eyes again. "That'd put anyone off."

He growled, and sat down next to me, where he could lean against my leg without seeming to. Me and my useless brother, no one's ideas of heroes. But just this once, Ruiner hadn't sabotaged himself and everyone else. Just this once, I hadn't made myself small and hidden behind pretending to be a grownup.

And just this once, we weren't going anywhere. For whatever that was worth.

The End

What To Read Next

When the carnival comes to town, mayhem follows.

When Masters of Mayhem, a traveling carnival, comes to Hollowbeck, it seems like the perfect opportunity to consult a wizard. Morgan's brother, Ruiner, has been trapped in the shape of a cat, and she can't change him back. She's no witch, after all. They need outside help.

Get One Smart Witch Today!

About the Authors

Amelia Ash likes the quiet life. During the week, she works at the tea shop inside a friend's quirky bookstore, and on the weekends, she combs the countryside for estate sales, collecting trinkets, old furniture, and, in one memorable case, a clawfoot tub. In the evenings, she likes to binge-watch HGTV with her life companion: a barely domesticated cat named Lizard, who she suspects might possibly kill her if he could double his size and operate a can opener.

~

Kim M. Watt: Originally from New Zealand, Kim (she/her) now inhabits a slightly different world, crafting funny fantasies and off-beat cosy (or cozy) mysteries in which tea-drinking dragons collude with resourceful ladies of a certain age, baking-obsessed reapers run petting cafes for baby ghouls, and cats always bring the snark.

Kim's stories blend myth and reality in small and spectacular ways, where the Apocalypse comes on a Vespa, and the healing magic of tea and a really good lemon drizzle cake is unquestioned. But most of all, her tales are about friendship, loyalty, and people of all species looking out for one another. Because these, above all things, are magic.

Also By Amelia Ash and Kim M. Watts

The Hollowbeck Paranormal Cozy Mysteries

Witch Slap

One Smart Witch